CRY OUT IN SILENCE

CRY OUT IN SILENCE

Carol Rozzoli

BROADCAST

This is a work of fiction. Names, places and incidents are products of the author's imagination or are used fictitiously. Any resemblance to actual events, locales or persons, living or dead, is entirely coincidental.

First published in Australia in 2024 by Kevin Rozzoli
Written by Carol Rozzoli. Copyright © Kevin Rozzoli, 2024

A catalogue record for this book is available from the National Library of Australia

ISBN: 978 0 6458440 6 1 (Paperback)
ISBN: 978 0 6458440 7 8 (Ebook)

Produced by Broadcast Books, www.broadcastbooks.com.au
Edited by Bernadette Foley and Sophie Bellotti
Proofread by Puddingburn Publishing Services
Cover and text design by Liz Seymour, Seymour Design, seymourdesign.net
Typeset in Adobe Garamond Pro 12.5/17pt by Seymour Design
Cover images by Omid Armin/Unsplash
Printed by IngramSpark

PROLOGUE

Echo Point, 6 May 1973

Rain spattered again, heavy drops disrupting the late afternoon silence. From the depths of the Jamison Valley, with its canopy of eucalypts, the famous rock formations known as the Three Sisters peered through the wispy mist at two isolated figures on the narrow track: a man and a boy.

The man reached out a blotched hand to touch the boy. 'What are you doing here, Sean? Are you in some sort of trouble?'

The boy looked up at him with a tense, white face. Catching the sour smell on the man's breath, he turned away. His thin body was racked with a sudden spasm of coughing.

The man straightened. 'Does anyone know you're here?'

Sean wiped a hand across his mouth and shook his head, heard the man laugh softly. He stared at the man for a moment, before forcing his cracked, bleeding lips into a smile.

'You know, Sean, nothing is ever as bad as we think,' the man said.

'This is.' The words had come out as a whisper as pain stabbed again in his chest.

'Is it … Peter?'

Sean blinked.

The man seemed to look right through him. A reddish-purple flush spread over his ageing, fleshy face; a tiny vein pulsed in and out near one eye as he glanced along the deserted track, then down towards the spectacular Giant Stairway walking trail.

Sean slowly backed away, feeling the safety fence press cold against his legs. Shivers tightened over his skin; tears slid down his icy cheeks.

'Please …'

Silence wrapped around them.

The man reached his hands towards the boy. Sean heard himself cry out as he desperately scrambled to put the barrier between them, the wire fence scraping his skin.

He clutched at the wire, pushed his freezing fingers through its mesh and held on tight, not daring to look into the void below. He edged along the fence, his feet teetering near the frayed, narrow ledge.

The man moved closer, their faces almost touching now. Sean choked on the man's warm, stale breath, his lungs struggling for fresh air.

He cried out in terror. But the blotched hands reached out again, fumbling with his jacket.

'No, noooooo …'

Unbearable lightness embraced Sean, his small arms flailing like impotent wings, faster and faster, scraping against rocks, grabbing at branches, bushes.

His long scream went on, a lone cry whipped away into the drifting mist long before he became one with the valley floor.

1

She caught the sound of footsteps before she heard the voice: 'Mrs Preece, Mrs Preece.'

Turning, Caitlin saw from under her umbrella the tall, black figure of Brother Loudé running across the quadrangle. At Saint Anthony's Catholic Orphanage, and among the serried ranks of Enmore's parish, she always thought of him as the spymaster. The bleak Thursday morning suddenly seemed bleaker.

The brother stopped in front of her.

'Mrs Preece,' his reedy voice scratched through heavy breaths, 'didn't you get the principal's message?'

She was taken aback by his terse tone.

'Message? No.' She frowned, looked quickly at her watch. 'I'll go and see him before my first class.'

He held up a thin hand, purple with cold. 'He has the bishop with him. And I don't think he's worrying just now about your art classes – or any classes.'

'But the boys were looking –'

'Didn't your husband tell you?'

'Tell me what, Brother?' she said, watching the rain from his umbrella form puddles around his shoes.

'You don't know about Sean Tessler?'

She stared into his gaunt face, fear creeping through her. 'Has something happened to him?'

'May God have mercy on his soul,' he murmured, and crossed himself with the piety of a pigeon pecking for food. 'Bushwalkers found him two days ago. He fell from a track near the Giant Stairway.'

His words seemed to come from a faraway place. Her mind went back to the café at Echo Point two weekends ago: Sean coughing, shivering, his feet stamping a stiff dance on the café floor; wrapping her woollen scarf around his neck, tucking the ends into his light jacket.

'I saw him on the last day of the excursion … in the afternoon.'

'Where?' he said.

'At Echo Point. I could see he was ill. I took him into the café, wanted to call a taxi, get him back to the hostel, but a group of tourists came in. He disappeared in the confusion. I searched but couldn't find him. When I went back to the hostel the people there said you had left for Sydney half an hour earlier. I thought he was with you.'

'We couldn't delay our departure any longer, so we left the matter with the police and the hostel. We presumed he'd just lost track of the time and would turn up later. You were probably the last person to see him alive.'

She tried to steady her heart, staring at the brother's closed face, wondering whether the loss of his rosary beads would elicit more emotion. Around her, the grey, silent buildings dominated the deserted quadrangle. She pushed back her hair.

'He was a child, a sick and frightened twelve-year-old child. In the state he was in, he shouldn't even have been on that excursion. How could you let this happen?'

His only reaction was a dismissive shrug.

She turned away and left the school.

■

Caitlin peered out across the swimming pool to the row of pine trees on the boundary of her property. The peace she usually felt here in her beloved home eluded her.

She heard the front door close. The moment her husband walked into the kitchen she turned on him, grief fuelling her anger.

'You kept it from me, Martin. Why?'

'What are you talking about?'

'Sean Tessler's death.'

'I knew how upset you would be. I was trying to find a suitable time.'

'Do you know who had to tell me? That acidic Brother Loudé.' Her eyes blurred with tears.

He walked over to her, tried to take her in his arms, but she shook him off.

'Caitlin, I know I should have told you, but how do you think I felt when Brother Finbar rang me? Don't forget, I do pro bono work for those boys – and given the police are involved there's the matter of client confidentiality.'

'Yes, of course. As you never stop telling me.'

He glanced around the kitchen. 'When will dinner be ready?'

'When it's ready.'

He turned away abruptly and walked out of the room.

'You're lucky to get anything,' Caitlin muttered, grateful Maria, her housekeeper, wasn't there to see her serving leftovers.

■

Later when she joined him in the billiard room, Martin was in a more conciliatory mood.

'I am sorry. Have you calmed down?' he said.

She shrugged and crossed the room to sit next to him on the leather sofa in front of the fire. 'I don't suppose you've heard anything from Brother Finbar about the funeral arrangements?'

He stood up, stretched his tall frame and got up to poke at the fire. 'There'll be the autopsy report, and then a coronial enquiry. They won't know anything for a few weeks.'

'But you must know something. Surely you have discussed it with them, you're their legal advisor.' Her voice rose as she scrutinised his passive face.

A smile returned the softness to his mouth. 'The operative word is "legal". The Church doesn't consult me on other matters. Anyway, you have enough to think about with your exhibition and our political commitments. I'd forget the funeral.'

She rubbed at her tired eyes. 'I can't.'

He frowned. 'You really want to go?'

'I have to, for Sean, and for Peter, especially for Peter.'

Martin sat down on the sofa beside her. 'So, he was still the extraordinary boy?'

She reached for his hand a fleeting smile on her lips. 'You remembered.'

He lent down and kissed her fingertips. 'You wouldn't let me forget your discovery of a prodigy.'

'He really was extraordinary. I've known artists in their fifties who would give ten years of their life to draw like him. Twelve years old. Incredible.' She shivered and moved closer to him. 'I can still see him on my first day at Saint Anthony's, six months ago, staring through me as if I were glass, with those unusual, navy-coloured eyes. And that strange, clever drawing lying half hidden under another on his desk. It took all my first month's teaching before he let me see any of his work.'

'Trust is hard for those boys. People come and go in their lives. He probably thought you were no different.'

'It was like that at first, but as time rolled on, things changed. Gradually, that sullenness eased and a more affectionate nature emerged. He became more like his little brother, Peter. From his work over the last months, I could see he realised how important my teaching was if he wanted to reach his potential.'

She gazed into the fire for a few seconds, then looked up at him. 'I have to be there at his funeral, to honour a well-liked boy and give Peter any help I can. After all, the little fellow's only six.'

He sighed. 'I doubt Finbar will be pleased.'

'Why should he object?'

'Caitlin, just leave the brothers to their private grief.'

'It's my grief too.'

■

When she got up the next morning, Caitlin knew she had to make the call to Brother Finbar. Martin mightn't like it, but the thought of doing any work was impossible if she didn't.

She dialled Saint Anthony's from her study. When the principal's familiar voice answered, she rushed out the words: 'Good morning,

Brother Finbar. It's Caitlin Preece speaking.'

'How can I help you?'

His coldness took her breath away.

'I wanted to say how deeply sorry I am about Sean's accident. I want to help. In some ways, I got to know him quite well through my art class. He was my most talented pupil after all. And he and his brother were so close; Peter must be feeling very lonely. I'm sure I could provide some support.'

'Thank you, Mrs Preece, but there is nothing you can do to help. Now, if you will excuse me, I have someone waiting for me.'

'Brother –'

The dead silence denied even the chance of a ritualistic 'God bless you.' She had never heard Brother Finbar so brusque, so dismissive.

If that's his attitude, her next call could be worse. She dialled the number. A woman answered after a few rings.

'Father MacManus isn't here,' his housekeeper said tersely. 'He's doing a school visit. He should be back at … No, here he is.'

A pause.

'Father MacManus speaking.'

'Father, it's Mrs Preece, the art teacher at Saint Anthony's. I'd like to talk to you about the arrangements for Sean Tessler's funeral.'

The priest was silent.

'Father? Hello, are you there, Father?'

'What is it you would like to know, Mrs Preece?'

She hesitated, frowning as she fiddled with the phone cord. 'I'd like to help in some way. Perhaps I could decorate the church for the Requiem Mass, ask the boys from my art class to help. I'm sure they would want to do it, for Sean.'

'There will be no Requiem Mass, Mrs Preece.'

'But I thought –'

'Surely you know the Church's attitude on suicide.'

Caitlin froze. 'Sean didn't commit suicide, Father.'

'I'm sorry, but we feel there can be no other explanation.'

'Father, a boy like Sean was a survivor. He would never have committed suicide.'

'Are you in any position to make that judgement?'

'Are you, Father?'

'I don't think we have anything more to say. Good morning, Mrs Preece.'

'Father MacManus … Father?'

Caitlin slammed the receiver down.

Sean had opened up under her tuition, gained confidence, taken pride in his work and responded with enthusiasm to her suggestion that he could one day study at her old art school. Christian charity would at least suggest an accident.

'Good morning to you too, Father, the devil's breath on your soul.'

2

Martin pushed his chair back from the patio table and stood to gaze out into the autumn garden. 'Saturday morning in chambers,' he said, grimacing. 'I won't be home for lunch, Caitlin. I'm off to the rugby. Oh, and I've arranged a dinner here on Friday.'

'What!'

'Greasing palms for my preselection in a fortnight.'

'Martin, you can't.'

'Darling, I'll need all the time I can get. The election could be as early as August or as late as November. After the redistribution, Hunters Hill is no longer Liberal heartland.' He kissed her and started to walk inside.

'Wait!' She threw her serviette on the table, her chair screeching back over the ceramic tiles as she rose. 'It's impossible.'

He sighed, turned back. 'Of course it isn't. That's why you have Maria.'

'Put it off or take them to your club. But don't count on me.'

He glanced down at her. 'But I do count on you. Here. Friday. And you'll be the sparkling hostess, just for me.'

'How can I "sparkle" with people I don't even like while Sean's lying in a mortuary fridge?'

'He's dead, Caitlin. Nothing will change that. It might not be an easy night, but this dinner could be just what you need to take your mind off him.'

'They say he committed suicide.'

'What?'

'At least that's what Father MacManus thinks,' she said, glaring up at his surprised face.

'No one's mentioned suicide.'

'The priest blurted it out yesterday, though Brother Loudé seemed to think it was an accident.'

'Suicide or accident; the difference has a considerable bearing on the Church's burden of responsibility. If it were an accident, it could imply negligence on the part of the brothers. Suicide would be an act beyond their control.' Walking down to the hall cupboard, he took out the Sydney University scarf he always wore to the rugby. 'Perhaps it was suicide, perhaps an accident. I don't know. Neither do you. That's why they'll hold a coronial inquiry.'

'I do know.' Her voice cracked. 'Sean would never have suicided. He hated heights. He was too timid. I couldn't even get him to stand on a desk to close a high window. He would never have gone near the edge of that cliff by choice. And he would never have deserted Peter. Those two were like that,' she said, crossing two fingers. 'If you could have seen the drawings Sean did of him, the wonderful, funny comics he created for him and the other boys …'

'I must go. I promise we'll talk about it tonight.' Martin opened the front door and started down the steps. 'I'll be back about six,' he called over his shoulder.

'Six, why so late?'

He raised one eyebrow. 'The chaps like a post-mortem after the match.'

She glared down at him then slammed the front door. Seconds later, the Porsche's engine split the morning's quiet air. Caitlin stared out into the empty portico. Something felt wrong. She sensed this idea of a dinner party hadn't come from Martin.

█

She doubted her smile was warm enough to reach her eyes. Pushing her seafood entree around her plate, she asked, 'How was the rugby?'

'Great. The Galloping Greens were in front, then a couple of late tries and our chaps ruined their day.'

Despite the excitement in his voice, she couldn't have cared less about those Greens or his Sydney University team. What she wanted from her husband was to talk about Sean, keep him to his promise.

He glanced at her. 'I got that call I'd been expecting.'

'Brother Finbar?'

'Finbar? No, Rodney Rushton.'

Her knife scraped the edge of her plate. 'Rodney Rushton?'

Martin's smile was wider now, bringing a boyish look to his face. Yet she sensed a hint of anxiety. 'He's coming on Friday.'

She tugged at her serviette to stop her hands from shaking. 'I won't have him here, Martin. Not in this house.'

'For God's sake, Caitlin, you hardly know the man.'

'Have you forgotten how he ruined my parents' business – a business that took decades to build?'

His eyebrows arched above his deep set, almond eyes. 'As you know, we took Rodney to court over that and won. Your parents got a hefty settlement, sufficient to set them up so they no longer needed to work. Of course, it's a great pity they didn't live long enough to enjoy it, but if it's any consolation, that money is what enables us keep living here and for you to devote yourself to your art.'

'The strain and worry of the court case killed them! But at least the court did find Rushton guilty of fraud.'

'That's not strictly correct. The court found against him on the grounds of fraudulent misrepresentation and damages were awarded, with all losses recoverable.'

'Which makes Rushton guilty of fraud.'

'No, the officers of the company included statements in the contract that, under cross-examination, showed reckless disregard as to their truth. Rodney knew nothing about that until it came out in court. But, as the owner of the company, he had to bear the consequences. He paid up, sacked the employees concerned. The hearing showcased my talents and so he retained me to check all his future contracts.'

'I just don't know how you can work for a man like that.'

'A barrister is a hired gun. Over the years, we've all benefitted.'

Caitlin looked at him in astonishment. 'How am I supposed to have benefitted? It can't bring my parents back.'

'Let's not quibble over who was right or wrong. That's all in the past. For the moment, his support is vital. If you must, think of him as a stepping stone to something bigger and better – for me, for us.'

'You may see it like that. I don't.' She picked at the fine Portuguese embroidery on her serviette with her fingernail. 'Martin, you're not that naive. If you win Hunters Hill owing favours to people like Rushton, you'll never shake off the obligation. Why not win on your merits?'

For a moment, she saw his gaze become more concentrated; perhaps she'd won him over.

He shook his head. 'Merit alone has few rewards in politics. You have to work the system.'

The tightness in her throat made it difficult for her to speak. 'I don't want him here! Whenever we've met him at Liberal functions, he's always reminded me of a predator, assessing the market value of everyone he meets.'

'He's a businessman, it's intuitive.'

She stared at him. Was he so obsessed with ambition he believed what he said? 'Men like him never let go. He'll become a part of our lives if you're elected.'

'Is that so bad?'

'Martin, you know the world is increasingly driven by economics. The quest for money puts a price tag on everything. We need people who contribute to making a better world without asking how much they'll be paid for their contribution.'

'That's rot. You can't develop major projects without a cost. Sydney would not be the city it is without entrepreneurs like Rodney.'

'That doesn't mean I have to invite them into my home.'

'Our home, Caitlin. Our home,' he said softly, though she didn't miss the sharp edge to his words. 'Anyway, I can't offend him by rescinding the invitation. Hunters Hill may no longer be blue ribbon, but it's winnable. Rodney's a power broker. I need his guarantees for the preselection.'

Caitlin knew she would have to be careful if she wanted to keep Martin as an ally in her dealings with Brother Finbar. She glanced over at him, hoping a radiant smile would hide her feelings.

'If it's a question of political power brokers, why not ask Richard Brinsmead?'

'Richard Brinsmead?'

'Why not? The Leader of the Opposition would have more influence on your dinner guests than Rushton. Richard's likeable and probably more popular with what you call the rank and file, and there'd be no strings attached. Of course, it's up to you, but if I could get him here …' She fingered her glass of Chardonnay in the sudden silence.

Martin looked at her as if she'd announced a desire to do cartwheels along the corridors of his chambers in Phillip Street. 'How do you think you're going to get him here at such short notice?'

'I've told you he collects my work.' She forced a false smile. Her thoughts went out to Richard: *Forgive me, I'm doing this so Rushton won't be at this wretched dinner.*

A slight frown creased his forehead. 'Tell me, what other secrets are you hiding behind those lovely eyes?'

'You don't listen. He opened my first exhibition six years ago at Lexy's gallery. We meet from time to time at the gallery.'

'You think he'll reorganise his diary just to please you and your best friend?'

Her heart beat harder, as if her whole body was struggling for oxygen. Richard was so charismatic she had, in a sense, loved him at first sight. But he and Lexy had been together then.

'He would, for Lexy. If he has some engagement he can't juggle, you could change the night. After all, Richard is the leader of the parliamentary party.'

Martin was silent a moment, then nodded. 'Fine. And in the

meantime, just for you, I'll talk to Finbar.'

She tensed. Her small, grey poodle, Simeon Peppercorn, cautiously stuck his head around the door, button nose twitching. Martin hated the dog being in the room when they were eating. Maria must have given Sim a tit-bit of the chocolate torte she was now placing on the table. The taste had made him adventurous enough to slip her guard and now he was hot on the scent for more.

'Not puppy food,' said Caitlin, rising to chase him out of the room. 'And you must learn to mark your safety zones, little fellow.'

Martin laughed and took a tiny piece of the dessert, offering it to the pup.

'You know he shouldn't eat chocolate. It's no good for him,' she snapped.

Martin wiped his hands on his serviette. 'Making the most of our opportunities, eh, Sim?'

Richard came up the front steps accompanied by his staffer, Esther Fiske. Heat spread to Caitlin's face when he said her name, smiling in that way she always remembered, his eyes lingering on her a moment before she exchanged a quick hug with Esther.

'Lexy's inside,' she said, then turned back to Richard. 'I hope you don't mind about tonight.'

'I don't. But this dinner, did you really want it?'

Surprised by his perspicacity, she looked away. A feeling, long suppressed, stirred inside her before shrinking back into its cocoon.

'Do you need to ask?' she murmured.

'You look tired. You're not working too hard?'

Caitlin shrugged. 'These last couple of weeks have been difficult. Lexy's pressuring me for work for my exhibition.'

'And you don't need tonight. Why was Martin in such a rush to organise it?'

'Rodney Rushton's off to Europe on Tuesday, so we had to get the unholy trinity together.'

Richard raised his eyebrows.

She gave him a wintery smile. 'Rushton, Marjorie Wainwright and Neal McCabe. Martin insisted it was important in the lead-up to the preselection. But you're right, I was reluctant. Very reluctant.'

'But there's something else.'

She hesitated, but she could see he was really listening, not just being polite.

'Three weeks ago, I was in the Blue Mountains on a school excursion with some of the boys from Saint Anthony's. We were taking in the landscape, trying to inspire their interest in art. On the last day … there was an accident.' She thrust her trembling hands into the deep pockets of her culottes, the sadness of those words catching in her throat.

A burst of loud laughter filtered out from the living room. His eyes remained fixed on her despite the distraction, and she knew what she was saying was important to him. An invisible thread of understanding seemed to link them, unlike anything she'd ever felt with Martin. 'One of the boys …' She turned away, trying to control again that choking feeling in her throat. 'One of the boys, Sean Tessler, fell from a track near the Giant Stairway.'

'Oh God, Caitlin, I'm sorry.' He took a step closer, the tenderness, the sympathy in those few words, made her shiver. 'Do they know how it happened?'

'No. I … I was probably the last person to see him. If I'd only stopped him going off by himself, he'd still be alive.'

'You can't blame yourself. You know what boys are like – mischievous, high spirited.'

She shook her head slowly. 'It wasn't that. There was something strange in his behaviour that day. And now the brothers –'

'The brothers?'

'Sean's death must have been a great shock for them, but their reaction has been odd. A wall of silence, almost antagonism, as if Sean has somehow maliciously inconvenienced them, or he never existed. I know there can't be a funeral until the coroner releases his … him, but they won't even talk to me about the funeral arrangements. Martin's on their management board as a legal advisor, he does pro bono work on behalf of the boys, but he knows nothing.'

'That is strange.'

She stared past him. Her husband was standing near the fluted oak columns at the entrance to the living room.

Her eyes flicked back to Richard.

Richard swung around, walked towards him. 'Oh, Martin, it's good to see you. Thank you for the invitation.'

'That was a deep and earnest conversation,' Martin said, glancing from one to the other, a slightly crooked smile on his face.

Richard grasped his immaculately manicured hand. 'We were discussing your political career.'

'My political career.' Martin gazed at his wife for a moment. 'Well, it's always important to have the woman's point of view, isn't it, Caitlin?'

She was almost relieved to see the tall, ebullient Rushton stride through the open front door, his raucous voice filling every corner of the small entrance hall.

'Martin, Richard and our gracious hostess.' He stamped over to her, arms outstretched. He grabbed at her hands, pulling her close as if he was going to kiss her.

Smile, she told herself, trying to lean back from the nearness of his bloated, red-veined face, sensing Richard watching. Not knowing what to say, she managed to evade him and turned to greet his wife, Helen.

Martin gave them an engaging smile. 'Come in and meet everyone. Champagne?'

Rushton laughed. 'As long as it's French.'

'Dom Pérignon?'

'Excellent, excellent.'

■

Caitlin glanced around the table, watching the faces of their guests as gleaming glass and silver cutlery passed from hand to mouth. What an odd collection of people she and Martin had gathered for this dinner.

They'd hardly begun their entree when Caitlin's closest ally, the feisty red-headed Alexia Lipchitz, Lexy to all her friends, raised her glass.

'A toast attributed to Francis Bacon,' Lexy said. Her large topaz eyes were wicked with humour. 'Champagne for my real friends, real pain for my sham friends.'

Caitlin looked across at Lexy's latest boyfriend, sitting opposite. He seemed enchanted by any word that came out of her sensuous mouth.

Next to them sat Marjorie Wainwright – an imposing woman in her sixties, with tightly coiffured blue hair and a shelf-like bosom that rose and fell dramatically with every breath. She was a powerful cog in the local electoral machine. As secretary of the Hunters Hill State Electoral Conference, politics was everything to her. Now her attention was firmly centred on Martin's end of the table.

Opposite her, Marjorie's husband Alfred showed no interest in politics. Slurping Maria's cream and walnut soup, he smirked through nicotine-stained teeth whenever Lexy favoured him with a smile.

Sitting to Alfred's right, Esther looked as if she would prefer not to be sharing such close company with him. She turned towards Richard in response to a question, her long, curly blond hair falling forward to obscure her attractive profile from her vulgar dinner partner and his obsession with golf. Her gaze remained fixed in Richard's direction.

Having rescued Esther from Alfred, Richard now turned to talk with Helen Rushton. Her remote expression and monosyllabic comments conveyed the impression the evening was, for her too, martyrdom; the emeralds, diamonds and Givenchy dress came at a price. After several attempts that fell short of even moderate success, he seemed to give up.

For the last fifteen minutes, Rushton had ignored the woman beside him. Married to The Honourable Neal McCabe, an Upper House member and factional power broker, Frances, habitually quiet, even withdrawn, had valiantly tried to make small talk, only to be totally ignored.

Listening to their voices, each word blurring into the next, Caitlin wondered how many occasions like this would be her fate if Martin were elected.

Marjorie's booming voice cut through her reverie. 'But we disputed those figures.'

Rushton tried to override her. 'We can't afford to waste time going over trivialities.'

'Hardly trivial,' Richard said.

A moment's awkward silence.

Then Richard raised his glass. 'Martin, this wine is excellent. I think we should acknowledge our discerning hosts.'

'Charming,' Frances murmured.

Caitlin looked at Richard. It happened in a second, but she

caught the faintest suggestion of a wink. She noticed that Esther had seen it too.

They all raised their glasses. 'Our hosts' reverberated around the table in differing degrees of sobriety.

'Thank you for the toast and thank you for coming,' Martin said, 'but much of the credit goes to Caitlin, who, by the way, has a birthday tomorrow, her thirtieth.'

The ripple of 'Happy birthday, Caitlin' had barely subsided before Rushton pursed his lips. 'Changing the subject, I read the other day the government is about to release a White Paper on the incidence of child abuse in the community. As Chairman of Saint Anthony's board of management, I will undoubtedly read it, but' – his voice took on a ridiculing note – 'child abuse in our civilized society? That's nonsense. I hope they're not intending to bring in legislation. Well, at least we know you wouldn't do such a damn fool thing, Richard. It's not government's role to interfere in family matters –'

'Why not?' Caitlin broke in. 'With so much pressure on many families, child abuse might become one of the hidden problems of this generation. We need politicians who care about these issues.'

'We can be grateful your wife is not standing for parliament,' Rushton said, looking at Martin.

He shrugged. 'Caitlin's her own person.'

Richard's moderating tone cut across the brittle exchange. 'Research shows child abuse is widespread. It goes beyond families, penetrating every section of the community.'

'You must agree with that, Martin?' Esther said. 'From the pro bono cases you handle for Saint Anthony's, you must see many distressing instances of neglect and abuse.'

He stared at her, then nodded. 'Neglect is often the forerunner of abuse. Usually, I'm involved in the aftermath, the legal consequences of separating the child from their abusive circumstances. The law does what it can. I often think more should be done, probably by the welfare services.'

Esther looked at him thoughtfully. 'Do the boys talk to you about their lives?'

'The barest details. It's difficult for them; they mostly choose to be silent. I deal with custodial matters, not criminal proceedings.'

Esther gazed at him for a few seconds before glancing at Richard. She raised her eyebrows and turned back to Martin. 'Richard has recently established a Children's Custodial Care Committee. Do you think you could arrange for us to speak with the brothers?'

'It would have to be cleared with the diocesan authorities.'

Frances looked pensively around the table, her eyes finally focusing on Caitlin. 'Didn't the boy who was killed a few weeks ago somewhere in the Blue Mountains come from Saint Anthony's?'

Caitlin leant forward, resting her arms on the table. 'Yes, Sean Tessler. One of the nicest boys I've ever met, and he had an amazing talent. I'm sure he'd experienced abuse sometime.'

Martin darted a sharp glance at her. 'I think –'

But she wasn't listening. 'And now the Church, which supposedly gave Sean and his brother, Peter, their "Christian" protection, wants to insult his memory.'

Martin attempted a wry smile, but his eyes betrayed him. 'That's a terrible exaggeration.'

'Is it?' Richard said.

Martin shot him a look. Caitlin didn't care. She was beginning to feel lost in herself as grief and frustration gave power to her words. She fixed her eyes on Richard.

'Well, what else can I think?' she said. 'Before the coronial inquiry has even begun, the parish priest is claiming Sean committed suicide, and you know how the Church and the law treat suicides – as criminals. Sean was a fighter. He would never have committed suicide, no matter how tough life was at Saint Anthony's. He loved his brother; he was very protective towards him. He wouldn't have abandoned Peter.'

'That's so, so utterly sad,' Frances said, taking a deep gulp of wine. She seemed on the brink of tears.

'You'll have Frances drowning in her glass if we don't talk about something more cheerful,' Rushton muttered.

'That's my point,' Caitlin said. 'A promising life snuffed out, and no one cares, no one wants to know. A young life reduced to a conversation around a dinner table.' She paused. 'It's like Sean was nobody's child.'

'Richard,' Martin said brusquely. 'How are the preselections going? Getting good candidates?'

Richard ignored him. 'What you were just saying about nobody's child, it really is a good description of the emotional desert many of these children live in.'

Caitlin nodded. 'And that's why I want to go to Sean's funeral whenever it's held. It may be a poor offering, but I might be able to give some comfort to Peter and the other boys.'

'It could be a healing process for you, too.'

She shrugged. 'Perhaps, but with this ridiculous theory of suicide and the brothers' silence, God knows what sort of funeral it will be; a pauper's, I imagine.'

Esther turned to Martin. 'You'd think they would have been in contact with you or Caitlin by now.'

Martin hesitated, then, leaning forward, said, 'More wine, Frances?'

She nodded. 'With all this distressing talk of suicide and funerals, I need it.'

Caitlin watched Martin move along the table to fill Frances' glass, heard Neal say, 'I'll have a top up too, thanks.'

While Martin circled the table, topping up the glasses, Caitlin's thoughts stayed with memories of Sean and the horror that must have enveloped him. It wasn't until an exchange between Martin and Rushton claimed her attention that she asked, 'What was that, Rodney?' She tried to keep her tone casual.

'I said, it is strange Brother Finbar hasn't mentioned anything about the funeral.'

Frances took another mouthful of wine and put the glass down to give Rushton a slap on the arm. 'Oh, you are a comic, Rodney. You said Finbar told you it's over a week and Martin still hasn't returned his call.' She wagged an accusing finger at Martin. 'That's not like you.'

Caitlin felt the colour drain from her face. So, Martin had lied this morning when he told her the brothers said they would give him the details of the funeral when they were arranged.

Richard turned to Martin. 'Is that true?'

'I don't know, Richard, I really don't know what he was thinking to say that. I've heard nothing from Finbar.'

■

Caitlin eased herself into the comfort of the billiard room's leather sofa, a sea of words rushing through her head. Painful words.

Lexy had taken her hint to show the other guests the garden. If Frances fell into the swimming pool, so much the better. At least the evening would end with a splash.

And poor Maria. She must be tired of these guests too, summoned like a servant to the dining room so the philistine Rushton could praise her cooking, when he probably knew nothing of cordon bleu.

She closed her eyes.

Suddenly, she felt someone near her. She opened her eyes, sat up. Richard was behind the sofa, staring at her large triptych, titled *Chinamans Beach*, above the flickering fire.

'I love the way you've captured the light shining on the water,' he said, looking down at her. 'It's like the light of your eyes, brightening the grey of a rainy day.'

'A poetic bid, but still no sale,' she said, laughing.

'I can only try.' Laughing too. 'May I join you?'

She nodded. 'What do you think of that performance in the dining room?'

'Which one?'

She turned back to gaze into the fire. 'Martin not returning Brother Finbar's call.' She looked at him then let out a rasping laugh from somewhere deep in her throat. 'He told me only this morning he'd not heard anything. Why would he lie?'

Richard stared at her. 'Caitlin, you have to keep things in perspective. Martin is juggling a legal practice while trying to win preselection. Not easy. Maybe he hasn't had time. Or perhaps …'

She waited for him to finish, but he remained silent. He sighed, as if caught up in matters he was now regretting. Like being here tonight, perhaps.

Finally, he continued. 'Martin may be reluctant to intrude into something he sees as pastoral business. Brother Finbar answers to the bishop. He might have thought it better not to interfere. More politic.'

'So why obfuscate?'

A different voice began hammering in her head, the painful words of that priest MacManus.

'Surely the bishop and Finbar wouldn't believe that ridiculous idea of Sean's suicide? It must have been an accident.' She paused. 'On the other hand, could he have felt so troubled he was driven to something desperate? And if he was, am I partly to blame because I let him leave the café?'

'No and no.'

For a moment, she thought he was going to say something more, but he seemed to change his mind, his eyes fixed on the Turkish carpet at their feet. Caitlin watched the restless shift of one of his burgundy shoes tracing its intricate pattern.

'Richard?' She leant towards him. 'What is it?'

He raised his eyes again to the triptych. 'There is such wild, mysterious beauty in that painting. I've always loved it.'

Suddenly he turned to her, twisting to look into her face with an intensity she couldn't remember ever seeing in him before. She edged a little away from him, towards the end of the sofa.

'Caitlin, you need to be careful how far you allow this young boy's death to intrude into your life. Don't feel responsible. And you must remember, this is also an important time for Martin. For someone like him …' He shrugged. 'Of course, I could be wrong. I don't know him that well. But he will need your full support. Juggling Martin's needs and your work will be difficult.'

He glanced again at the triptych. 'How many more paintings like that will you do if you allow anything else to distract you? Tell me, how often in the last couple of weeks have you picked up a pencil or a brush?'

Caitlin gazed at the painting, as his words reverberated in her head. She waited for him to say something more, something that would confirm the thoughts stirring in the inner recesses of her mind.

A gust of laughter accompanied the other guests as they came into the billiard room. Caitlin jerked her head towards their voices, anger rising within her at the intrusion.

Richard stood and touched her arm. Speaking in a voice only she could hear, he said, 'You don't get the support of powerful party people like Rodney, Neal and Marjorie with half measures.'

'So, what's important to me must be sacrificed?' Her voice was almost a whisper.

She grimaced, ran her hands through her hair and leant back, craning her neck to catch a glimpse of Martin. He was preoccupied, in animated conversation with the unholy trinity. Already the lie, if that was what it had been, was history and he, more than anyone, would be surprised if she were to raise it again.

4

Caitlin answered the doorbell to see two men in uniform, and a warrant card of the New South Wales Police Force pressed against the glass pane of the front door.

She opened the door to the full extent of the security chain.

'How can I help you?' she said to the closest man, her skin prickling as she took in his metallic grey eyes.

'Detective Sergeant Hurd. This is Detective Constable Cline.' He flicked the warrant card towards his younger colleague. Tall, with sandy blond hair, brown eyes and dark eyelashes, he could probably coerce some women to say anything. But the Detective Sergeant, short and heavy set, was a man she would paint almost entirely in shades of grey: crew cut, greyish skin, crumpled suit; only colourful stripes in his tie to break the monotone.

'Are you Mrs Preece?' the Detective Sergeant said.

She nodded.

'We're investigating the death of a boy at Echo Point.'

'Sean Tessler. Have you found some new information about how he died?'

'Can we talk inside, Mrs Preece?'

'Just a moment,' she said, slipping off the chain to open the door. They followed her through to the living room.

'Won't you sit down?' she said, indicating the sofa while choosing one of the wingback chairs for herself.

She watched as Detective Cline pulled a notebook and pen from his jacket, then flicked it with an officious click.

'We appreciate your time, Mrs Preece. This won't take long,' Detective Hurd said. 'We need to clear up one or two matters with you about the day Sean Tessler died. We're trying to trace his movements just before he disappeared.' The detective looked at her intently. 'I understand you were one of the adults who accompanied the boys on the excursion to the Blue Mountains.'

'Yes, that's right.'

'In what capacity?'

'I teach art at Saint Anthony's.'

'I see. Did you stay at the Travellers Rest Hostel with the boys and the brothers?'

'No, I stayed with an artist friend, Henry Gibbons, he lives a few blocks from Echo Point.'

The detective raised his eyebrows, and she noticed what could have been a slight sneer settle over his features.

'Do you have the address of this artist friend?'

Caitlin tried not to smile as the young detective dutifully awaited her response. In her mind's eye, she could see the detectives salivating over Henry and her having a naughty weekend, jokes all round at the station. She wished she could send their thoughts winging to eighty-one-year-old Henry. He would enjoy a good laugh when the sour looking Hurd fronted up at his door. For him, those days were long gone – if they were ever there, Henry would say.

'I'm sorry, Detective, what did you say?' Her moment's reverie was broken by Hurd's grating voice.

'I said, so you had no role in looking after the boys, except when you were involved in their art activities?'

'That is correct.'

'Did you at any time see Sean Tessler on his own?'

'Yes, several times. He is ... was an exceptionally talented boy and I gave him some extra time after the rest of the boys had left for other activities.'

'When did you last see him?'

'Sunday afternoon in the café at Echo Point.'

Hurd leant towards her. 'Another art lesson?'

Her eyes narrowed. 'No.'

'Did you arrange to meet him there?'

'Why would I do that?'

'I'm asking the questions, Mrs Preece. Did you arrange to meet him there?'

She looked across at the younger detective, but he was busy with his pen. She turned back to Hurd. 'No, of course I didn't. I went to collect my things from Henry's place. When I turned out of his street, I came across Sean. I thought he might be walking towards the café, not far away, or perhaps the lookout. I really didn't know.'

'What time was that?'

'I'm not sure – three, maybe a little after.'

'Was he alone?'

'Yes.'

'What did he say?'

'He was going for a walk.'

'Meeting someone, perhaps? A friend, a relative?'

'I don't think Sean has ... had any relatives, apart from his brother, Peter. And the brothers are always very strict about the boys wandering off by themselves.'

'I want you to think carefully, Mrs Preece. How did he react when he saw you?'

Caitlin frowned, gazed out into the garden, tried to find the truth in her memories. Finally, she said, 'It was odd. He seemed anxious.'

'Anxious?' Hurd repeated, exchanging a glance with his colleague.

She saw the exchange, blinked, tried to even out her breathing.

'Shouldn't you have taken him back to the hostel? The brothers being so strict about the boys' whereabouts.'

'I tried, but he wouldn't go. So, I suggested he have a hot drink and a piece of cake in the café. I hoped that would give me time to talk to him, try to find out what was worrying him, before bringing him back to the hostel.'

'And did you get him to talk?'

'No. A busload of tourists came into the café. Sean said he wanted to go to the toilet. He never came back.'

'Did you try to find him?'

'Of course I did. In the café, down to the Echo Point lookout, back to the café.'

'Did you go back to the hostel, check if he was there?'

'Yes, but by the time I got there they said the group had just left. There was no mention of a missing boy, so I thought everything was all right.'

She caught him smiling at Detective Cline. 'Refresh Mrs Preece's memory.'

The young man flipped back a page in his notebook. 'I tried to but he wouldn't go,' he said, repeating her words.

The smirk on Detective Hurd's thin mouth was full of disdain. 'The moment he disappeared from the café, he was a young Houdini, vanishing from the street. A boy who you said was anxious, out by himself in a strange place, a storm brewing. Yet, you weren't too worried?'

A moment's silence.

She stared from one policeman to the other, then stood up. 'I was worried, I did try to find him, I searched the area for about twenty minutes, but by then he could have been anywhere. There are lots of side streets. As I said, when I went back to the hostel the people there told me the group had left. I assumed he was with them. I thought they would hardly leave without him. If you want answers, you should be talking to the brothers. I wasn't there, they were.'

She rose to her feet, assuming the interview was at an end.

'Please sit down, Mrs Preece, I haven't finished. According to the principal of Saint Anthony's, Brother Finbar, the three-day excursion to the Blue Mountains was your suggestion. What was its purpose?'

She glared at him. 'Have you any idea what it must be like to live in an orphanage? I thought a break from that dreary place, a different environment, would boost morale and maybe I could get them more interested in their art. Why? Is that important?'

'Is it, Mrs Preece?'

Caitlin studied his blank expression, a face that seemed to have mastered every way to hide emotion.

'I thought I was helping your enquiries, Detective Hurd. I do want to help. But I don't like being made to feel responsible.'

Hurd glanced up at her. 'Aren't you?'

'What exactly do you mean?'

'From what you have just told us, you were the last person to see the boy alive. That makes you very significant in our enquiries.'

'That's ridiculous! Sean could have met anyone after I saw him.'

'Anyone? Another Houdini?'

She felt anger vivid on her face. 'I resent you suggesting I'm not telling the truth. I want you to leave.'

'Mrs Preece,' the young detective said gently, 'we do need your help.'

She saw his sympathetic expression and sat down.

'Unfortunately, the storm that afternoon destroyed any evidence that might have been in the area and, well, Sean not being found sooner has made our investigation even more difficult,' he said.

'So, you don't think it was an accident?'

'We don't know the circumstances of his fall. From where we think he may have fallen, and considering the weather conditions, it could well have been an accident. All Detective Hurd was trying to say is that you're an important witness. Being an artist, you would probably observe what others might miss.' A sudden smile softened the sharp angles of his face. 'Your help is invaluable in trying to piece together what happened that day, particularly at the café. So, please, think carefully, Mrs Preece. Imagine yourself back there, the people at the tables, coming in, going out. At Echo Point, the hostel. Did you see any anyone at all vaguely familiar, but out of context?'

Could she have forgotten a voice, a face? She shook her head. 'I've told you everything I remember.'

'Do you think it's at all possible he could have been meeting someone?'

'It's possible. I can't think of any other reason why he was there. Sean was too sensible to be out in that weather for no reason. That's why I wanted to talk to him, it was all so strange.' She tried not to look at Hurd, instead focusing on the younger policeman tapping his pen on the edge of his spiral notebook, his eyes fixed on her.

'Can you remember anything at all different about Sean earlier that afternoon? Something that might have triggered his decision to be out on his own?'

'No, nothing. Except, when I think about it, that toilet ruse ...' She rubbed at her forehead, shook her head. 'He wasn't a devious boy. Maybe I was wrong. Perhaps there was something or someone I missed. I don't know.'

The older man eased himself up from the sofa. 'Thanks for your time, Mrs Preece. We'll want a statement. Detective Cline will ring you. Oh, and we need the shoes you were wearing that day.'

'My shoes? What for?'

'Soil testing,' Hurd said, his face expressionless.

·

She waited for the squeak of the front gate before closing the front door.

Soil testing?

Caitlin walked slowly back into the living room, feeling the relief of its emptiness. She read the card the young detective had given her. His words reeled through her mind. Could Sean have been meeting someone? She was sure he didn't know anyone in the Mountains. Her mind circled back to Saint Anthony's and the hostel. It seemed the only possibility.

A tiny spark ignited in her brain and, in its light, she could see Sean drawing in the playground. She shuddered.

Should she tell the police her suspicions? They were so wild and improbable. Irresponsible without more tangible evidence.

'Just stay calm,' she muttered.

Somehow, she must try to get hold of his drawings; they were his language. Intuitively, she knew there would be others like the one she'd seen. But if Brother Loudé found them first, they'd be in the school incinerator. Maybe they were already.

5

Gloomy afternoon shadows played on the walls of the school's art room. Caitlin closed the door and turned on the lights. The eyes of Vincent van Gogh's self-portrait, pinned on the back wall, followed her across the room.

Beside the poster was a wall of thirty-five pigeonholes filled with the boys' recent work, but she doubted Sean would have left his frightening drawing in such a conspicuous place. She scanned past the long, narrow cupboard under the pigeonholes, where art materials were stored. Against the adjacent wall was a large, old-fashioned cupboard that was rarely opened; it stored bulk materials.

She glanced at her watch. One hour before her afternoon class. Plenty of time to search and get out.

She pulled a box of watercolours, a few drawings and a couple of sketch books out from Sean's pigeonhole. As expected, no trace of the drawing or anything like it. The only plausible explanations were that he'd hidden it somewhere else in the school or someone had destroyed it.

Maybe she was being obsessive, indulging a crazy, illogical

compulsion to keep looking. Perhaps the drawing had not been as frightening as she'd imagined. On that day, weeks ago in the playground, when she'd come up behind him, Sean had quickly closed his sketchbook on the black figures, giving her mind little chance to probe their meaning. But she could not forget the fear on Sean's face, nor the sense of foreboding those images had evoked in her.

Sounds from the corridor made her look up. Boys' voices, Brother Loudé's thundering over the top.

'Which of you has been in the art room?'

A chorus of strident, protesting voices erupted, no guilt in any of them. Though Caitlin had every right to be in the room to retrieve her property, her reason for being there made her feel guilty.

She grabbed two craft trays from the cupboard and dumped them on a desk. Rolls of paper and balls of wool jumped before her eyes in coloured confusion.

The door rattled open. 'Whoever left these lights on will be running around the quadrangle tonight in the dark. Oh, it's you, Mrs Preece.'

'Good morning, Brother Loudé. I'm just putting out materials for the boys' collages.'

A glacial smile crept across his mouth. 'I'm glad you're early. The principal would like to see you. Now.'

■

Before Caitlin could raise a hand to knock on Brother Finbar's office, the door flew open. His assistant sidled past Caitlin, balancing an armful of books and papers.

'Morning, Mrs Preece.' Under her breath, she added, 'I should warn you, he's not himself this morning. I think it's to do with the bishop's visit.'

Caitlin nodded. Through the open door, she saw the principal writing at his desk.

At that moment, he looked up. In a soft voice, he murmured, 'Come in, Mrs Preece, and please close the door.'

A cold draught wafted over her. His gentle mien had gone; his long white hands formed a pyramid as he pressed the tips of his index fingers against his thin lips and silently regarded her. She looked away. On the wall beside her, the garish features of a crucified Christ offered no consolation.

She turned back to him. His fine fingers were now rolling a pen over and over on a pile of papers in front of him. Perhaps this interview was as hard for him as it was for her.

'Mrs Preece.' He coughed. 'Now, I know I supported your art class's excursion to the Mountains, but I could not have anticipated such dire consequences.'

His words ground at her emotions like a millstone. 'I don't think any of us could have, Brother Finbar. This tragedy should never have happened.'

She tried to find the familiar patience in his face, in his melodious voice, but all that was left was a shell, whitewashed with melancholy. Evidently, his grief was an emotion to be hidden.

'The excursion was a thoughtful gesture of yours. And the boys certainly enjoyed their first few days. However, I must remind you they were content with the wonderful artwork they were doing with Brother Loudé, without venturing further than the front gates of this school.'

'But Brother Loudé hasn't the experience I –'

A hand shot up, a stop sign.

'The brother has been a teacher for twenty-five years. He's very experienced. Perhaps what happened to Sean is the Lord's way of punishing us for the vanity of thinking someone should give us more than we needed.'

Her eyes widened but she remained silent.

'These boys' lives aren't blank canvases for you to paint on,' he said.

'Brother, I never thought –'

Another stop sign from his trembling hand. 'Please, I would like to finish. These boys' minds have been warped by families broken by poverty and terrible abuse. Here, at least, we have been able to give them security. Until now.'

'Are you sure?'

'Why would you question that? The Church has always offered sanctuary.'

'But there was no sanctuary for Sean. The brothers should have kept a more watchful eye on him.'

'And you, Mrs Preece? I remind you again that the trip was your idea. If we are guilty, don't you share our guilt?'

'That's true. When I saw him near that café alone, no overcoat, the cold wind almost blowing through him, I should have forced him back to the hostel.'

'Children are great dissemblers.'

She grimaced. 'Well, Sean certainly was that. He seemed fine, excited like the rest of them on Saturday. But something must have happened to make him leave the other boys on Sunday. Perhaps he met someone.'

The principal started to play with his pen again. 'I've talked to Brother Loudé and Brother Purcell. They were not aware of anything or anyone.'

'And they were sure that Sean was in the hostel and not wandering the streets by himself? Why did they leave on schedule? Why no proper search to locate him? Why was Brother Loudé so eager to go back to Sydney after lunch?'

Brother Finbar pressed his hands together again. Was he praying silently for patience?

'We try, Mrs Preece, to do all we can for our boys, but for some the damage is deeply rooted. Something probably pushed Sean too hard at the wrong moment. I believe his family spent some time in Katoomba. Perhaps the memories were too much for him.'

Caitlin gazed down at the chipped edge of the desk. 'You think he committed suicide?'

'Can there be any other explanation? Sean wasn't a boy who attracted trouble. Why else would he climb that safety fence?'

She looked up. 'Not to kill himself. It's possible someone else was there, someone who played a role in his death.'

He shook his head. 'All the boys were at the hostel. I don't think he knew anyone else, except you, of course. The police have told me you were the last person to see him. If you hadn't let him go, he could have been saved. It is terrible not knowing why he would risk his immortal soul.'

His eyes turned towards the crucifix. In those seconds, his face became surprisingly calm, as if he and his Christ were in direct communication.

Caitlin glared at him. 'You're wrong, Brother Finbar. People who have a sense of their own value don't commit suicide. And Sean knew his brother needed him. They had such a close bond, it made life bearable, even this one. His funeral should be a celebration of that life.' She hesitated. 'It is important to acknowledge the life of a boy who was extraordinary.'

'There will be no Requiem Mass for Sean. We thought it easier for the boys, for Peter.'

'So, Sean suddenly disappears from all their lives. Wiped from memory as if his death were something shameful.'

'You think suicide isn't shameful, selfish, a rejection of God's love, His guidance?' His voice had taken on more vibrancy, as if he were speaking from the pulpit.

'Do you know, Brother, that the police are doubtful as to whether it was suicide or an accident?'

He was silent. As she gazed at him, she began to feel uncomfortable.

Just when the silence between them was becoming almost unbearable, he broke it: 'I think these semantics are taking us nowhere. I have given careful consideration to your work here, Mrs Preece, and I am aware your husband is seeking preselection for parliament; I am sure he will be successful. I feel your commitment to his career must come first. I have asked Brother Loudé to take over your classes, as of today.'

She stared at him, anger rising within her. So, this is to be my punishment. Not Loudé's, not Purcell's, but mine, she thought.

'Don't you feel the boys would be happier if their classes weren't disrupted just now?'

The principal raised his eyebrows. 'I wouldn't call a change of teacher for an art class disruptive. They have more important subjects in the curriculum to worry about.'

'You mean Latin, so they can rattle off responses at Mass in a dead language, instead of fostering an appreciation for the eternal spirit of Michelangelo's *Pieta*, carved from solid blocks of Carrara marble? Or his magnificent tribute to the glory of God embodied in the architecture of Saint Peter's?'

A smile hovered at the corners of the brother's mouth. 'My mind is made up, Mrs Preece. I would appreciate it, for the boys' sake, if you could make your farewells as short as possible.'

Caitlin stood up.

He rose and extended his hand. 'Thank you for all you have done.'

Their fingers brushed together like two feathers. His steady gaze tore through her.

■

Ten minutes until Brother Loudé would arrive to take over her class. She raced through the halls. *Faster, faster,* she kept telling herself. Along those interminable, rabbit warren corridors from Brother Finbar's office, up and down the stairs, her heart jumping out of her chest, lungs forcing out ragged breaths. *I must find that drawing before Loudé starts his class.*

She wrenched open the door of the art room, closed it none too gently, hesitated, then switched on the light. On the large clockface she could see the seconds flicking by. She flung her bag on the floor and went straight to the pigeonholes.

Her fingers shook as she went through the other boys' work. No luck. What had he done with it?

She glanced at the clock: eight minutes left.

She turned her attention to the cupboards underneath and quickly went through them. Another blank.

Finally, she crossed to the old-fashioned cupboard. Inside, something caught her eye: a roll of special grey drawing paper she'd given Sean, pushed to the back, hidden behind other art materials. She pulled out the roll and took it to the nearest desk.

She glanced at the door. No movement. Her senses were on high alert. Running to the door, she opened it carefully and checked up and down the corridor. It was empty, but she could hear Loudé's voice from somewhere out of sight.

Damn it.

She closed the door, ran back to the desk and tugged off the elastic band that secured the roll. A dozen or so sheets unfurled. She glanced quickly again to the door, then back to the drawings.

Words flashed in her mind, a silent plea to Saint Anthony: 'Help me in my present need.'

The language of Sean's art had always reflected his pleasure in nature, his sense of quiet fun, shared with the other boys through his cartoons and caricatures, never the darker side of life. Was there some connection between the unusual drawing she had seen and Sean's death? What had generated the grim image?

Caitlin took in the top drawing then flicked to the next, the next, the next. She closed her eyes tight for a second. They were all similar, just work he'd done in class.

Hoping she had missed the drawing, she searched through the sheaf again, her perspiring fingers hardly able to pull the papers apart. Nothing. She rubbed at her temples, trying to ease the pounding in her head.

'You all right, Miss?'

Caitlin jerked her head out of her hands and whirled around. She saw a tall boy, somewhat older than the boys in her class. Out in the corridor, she could hear the tramping of boys' feet, voices coming towards the room. Some of her class were already milling around the open doorway.

The boy peered down at Sean's drawings. 'He wasn't half

good was he, Miss? There's more if you want them, on top of the cupboard.'

She looked up, then back at the boy. The expression in his eyes was of someone older than his years.

'I'll get them for you, Miss,' he said. 'I'm sure he'd want you to have them.'

'Thank you, I'd really appreciate that.'

6

Caitlin saw the priest go into the Sacred Heart Church opposite the school. She knew she must speak to him.

Minutes before, sitting in her car, she'd opened the folder of Sean's work, riffled through twelve drawings of the Apostles, their names written on each.

'Christ!'

She was amazed at the quality of the drawings, work of a calibre she'd never seen from Sean. On the surface, nothing seemed significant about the drawings apart from their being faithfully reproduced images. But she remembered the older boy's words in the art room, and those eyes that hinted at secrets. What had Sean shown him that eluded her?

She went back to the first drawing and looked carefully at each one until she came to the last: Judas Iscariot, betrayer of Jesus Christ.

A bleak drawing blackened with crayon in the style of Caravaggio's last religious works, the white, brutish face of Judas in stark relief. It was extraordinary, suggesting the maturity of someone beyond Sean's years. Nor did this image draw its strength from any leaning towards theology; like so many of Caravaggio's works, it curiously blended the sacred and the profane. By contrast, the drawing of the Apostle Peter, who had also betrayed Christ, exhibited only love for the master.

She stared hard at the drawing until, growing frustrated, she placed it back in the folder. She laboured to resolve the confusion of images, trying to make sense of them. Surely she had missed something in the drawing's frightening intensity, but what?

She gazed through the windscreen to the rain-cleansed street. Seconds lengthened into minutes. Her temples throbbed as she tried to unlock the message she was certain lay within the folder.

She took out the twelfth drawing, tried again to distil some meaning. Still nothing. Idly, she turned it over. Sean had lightly pencilled something on the back. Peering more closely, she could make out a drawing of a half-naked child, jointed like a puppet and surrounded by three men. Their predatory faces seared into her consciousness. With horror, Caitlin felt a hint of recognition at one of the men.

Putting the drawing back in the folder, she got out of the car, locked it and walked determinedly across the road.

■

Her footsteps on the cold stone floor echoed around the otherwise silent church. Beyond the empty wooden pews, a light was burning at the altar beside the tabernacle. Father MacManus was nowhere to be seen.

She walked around to one of the side aisles. Watery sun struggled to gleam through stained-glass windows, dust motes dancing in its rays. The fourteen Stations of the Cross, tribulations of Christ's trial and death, marked a pattern from one plaster wall to the opposite one.

Nearing the altar, she caught the stale smell of incense, could see tiers of burnt-down candles grouped on a large, brass candelabrum, wax forming small stalagmites at its base. A few candles still burned.

She walked slowly to the altar, crossing herself before continuing to the candelabrum, where she took twelve candles from the box. She lit one for each year of Sean's short life.

As she stood in contemplation she saw, from the corner of her eye, the priest's portly figure enter from the sacristy. Shrinking into the shadow beside the candelabra and the wall, she watched him shuffle to the altar and genuflect before the tabernacle, kneeling in prayer for a few brief minutes before rising from his knees with what seemed a weary reverence.

She almost felt sorry for him. But remembering their conversation on the telephone, her pity didn't last long. He couldn't fob her off again when she told him what she knew.

She walked slowly towards him.

'Father MacManus.'

His startled look was almost comical.

'I'm Mrs Preece.'

The priest stared at her without a flicker of recognition.

'The art teacher from Saint Anthony's. I spoke to you recently about Sean Tessler's funeral.'

He frowned, stray hairs from his grey, straggling eyebrows nearly reaching his pallid blue eyes.

'Ah, yes. Sean,' he said, quickly crossing himself as if already closing off his memory of the boy.

She glanced up, meeting the glassy stare of the Virgin Mary behind him. *I know, I know, it's been a long time. Believe me, you can't be more surprised than I am.*

The priest half turned, nodding to the statue. 'She will comfort you. Don't forget the death of Her child bewildered Her too. For many of us, God's mysterious ways often twin Him with the Devil.'

Caitlin raised her eyebrows. That was something unexpected from an elderly priest. She followed his gaze to Christ's crucifixion above the altar.

'Acceptance, Mrs Preece.'

'Acceptance of what?'

'It was a miracle he reached his twelfth year.'

'What do you mean?'

'Just what I said. It was a miracle.'

'Why do you say that, Father? Sean was one of your altar boys. You would have known him well. Why was he so troubled?'

She saw his glance slide around to the sacristy, as if seeking an avenue of escape.

'Father?'

'When Sean arrived at Saint Anthony's, for about the first two years, he wouldn't speak. Not a word.'

Cold shivers ran over her skin. 'I never knew,' she half whispered.

'Sean was almost seven then, long before your husband started his pro bono work at the orphanage. When his brother Peter arrived, Sean became his protector. He had to talk.'

She waited for the next words to emerge from those purple, saliva-moistened lips.

'The brothers knew Sean had been damaged from the years of his stepfather's abuse; that life meant the boy could never be free of fear. He'd have days when he'd hide himself in a broom cupboard or a toilet and not come out for hours.'

'But Father, don't you see? Even though Sean had problems, he would never have deserted Peter.'

'That's what Brother Finbar hoped. And of course, Sean had that wonderful gift. In those early years when he wouldn't talk, the brothers told me he would only draw, nothing else.'

She stared past him to the golden light of a stained-glass window on a far wall, then returned her gaze to the priest. 'The morning of the day he disappeared he seemed fine. But later, in the afternoon, at the café, he was a different boy. Something had happened to him. And yet, I can't believe he was planning suicide. Even if he was, Father, he would have chosen an easier way. Sean was terrified of heights. He couldn't have thrown himself from one of those narrow pathways.'

'Sometimes, Mrs Preece, our burdens are too heavy to bear. God lightens them in His own way.'

Anger dried her throat, but she stayed silent, contemplating whether she still wanted to tell him what she knew.

He sighed. 'If it wasn't suicide, it is possible it was an accident.'

Or foul play, she thought. She should have done or said something to keep Sean with her. She stared blankly again at the Virgin Mary. Not much help there.

She could feel the priest watching her. 'I should have tried to stop him leaving the café.'

'Whatever happened that day, I believe it was God's will.'

She scrutinised the tired old face that revealed nothing of the man's inner feelings. But the Devil tiptoeing through the peaceful House of God conjured up the image she'd seen on the back of Sean's drawing of Judas.

'If it helps, Mrs Preece' – his voice was softer – 'Sean was always talking about you, your work, how you were going to help him get into the art school where you studied. He said you were often kind, like when you gave him your scarf.'

7

Drizzling rain misted through the trees that lined the drive into Rookwood Cemetery. Caitlin peered out at the grey afternoon from the window of Richard Brinsmead's Statesman limousine, struggling to put her thoughts into some form that made sense.

It had been her insistence that brought them here. Four weeks ago, in her billiard room, Richard had said, 'When the time's right, if you want to visit his grave, I could try to find out where he's buried.'

Passion leapt from Sean's skilful drawings of the disciples, but it was their possible relation to his death that haunted her. She didn't know why, but she felt that seeing his grave might give her some understanding. Except now that she was here, the urge to come had given way to a strong impulse to put distance between her and this city of the dead. It was playing weird games with her head.

She reached out to touch Richard's arm. 'I'm sorry to have put you to all this trouble, but it's just too difficult.'

From the corner of her eye, she saw him watching her. It made her feel worse. She had the insane wish to be a child again; to cover her ears so she couldn't hear words of reproach. But Richard was not so easily frustrated.

'There's no hurry,' he said. 'I know how hard it can be. One day our lives are comfortable, familiar, then everything changes; no warning, nothing to help us understand the emotions we can't explain.'

She turned her head. He was looking out the window now. She could see only part of his face. A relaxed, tanned hand reached out to push the gearstick into park. He seemed at ease with the idea of sitting, waiting patiently; she knew his work must be waiting too. Perhaps, like some said, he was the consummate politician, well-versed in managing many conflicting demands, coping with the flaws in people's natures.

'Do you cosset your constituents too?' she said.

'My secretary tells me I do,' he said dryly.

Caitlin turned away to look out her window again, toward the trees, the neatly trimmed shrubbery. The rain had stopped, a ray of sunlight brightened the sky beyond the low clouds.

'I know how stupid this is, Richard. I can't explain it, but I just have this feeling we should leave.'

He shifted in his seat, turned and, for the first time since they'd arrived, looked directly at her. 'Caitlin, our minds use all sorts of tricks to punish us for what we think are our failures. You wanted to go to the funeral, wanted to pay your respects to someone you were fond of. Now you have the opportunity, you feel it's not right.'

'No, it's not that. I really can't explain it. It's like there's something invisible stopping me.'

'Come for a walk,' he said. 'We'll go a little way down the road and see how you feel.'

Caitlin glanced at him. He had that concerned look on his face she had seen before, as if he really cared. She nodded, opened her door.

They'd only walked a short distance when she saw the small mound of a fresh grave not far in from the road. She walked over to it.

Richard consulted the map he'd been given. 'Sean's is further along.'

But she stayed, looking down at the grave. 'It's so tiny. Nothing to mark a child's existence except a heap of dirt. No loving floral messages, nothing to cover the stark reality of this earth to earth, dust to dust.'

'Nice day for it,' a gravelly voice rumbled behind them.

They turned around. A man was sitting on the marble edging of a grave nearby, leaning back against its headstone, his work boots propped on a dirt-clogged shovel.

'You need any help looking for someone?' He slid his tongue along the edge of a rolling paper and pressed it into a cigarette with filthy fingers. 'Or you just looking?' He squinted up at them then spat into the grass.

Richard glanced at Caitlin. 'We're just looking.'

The gravedigger stood up and ambled towards them, nodding his head, lips moving silently. Caitlin wondered whether he was still tasting bits of his tobacco or having a conversation with himself.

When he reached them, he squinted again into the sun before pushing a damp, brown hat down onto his stringy grey hair. 'Lots of folks come looking. Young'uns too, like yourselves.' He shook his head. 'Can't see why, but folks do strange things.'

He stuck the cigarette to the corner of his bottom lip. From a sagging pocket of his soiled overalls, he pulled out a box of matches. Caitlin caught a flash of the Redhead branding, the only colour about him. 'Leave funny things, they do.' He jerked his head along the path. 'New grave over yonder. Strangest thing I ever seen.'

Caitlin looked to where the man was pointing.

'Near that large camellia bush?'

'That's the one. Weird, it were. Yesterday arvo it were barer than a monkey's backside,' he said, pushing his hat further back on his head. 'And bugger me, there they were this morning.'

Caitlin felt Richard take her hand. She pulled away, began to walk in the direction the man was pointing.

Richard caught up to her and grabbed her hand again, trying to slow her down.

'I think you should wait till I have a look,' he said.

The gravedigger was beside Richard. 'Just waiting for the order to tidy it up. Thems in the office want to take photos.'

Caitlin turned back, caught a glimpse of yellow and black rotting teeth as he smiled at her.

'I says if they's such mates with 'im' – he jabbed a thumb at the sky – 'why'd they never see that young'un off to 'im proper like, eh?'

Caitlin stopped, stared at him. 'Are you saying no one was at the burial?'

The man shook his head. 'Just a fella in a long black frock, cross hanging on 'im. Some sort of religious humbug, if you ask me. Had a young'un with 'im. Reel quickie, it were, like the thunder and lightning that day.' He flicked a thumb past Caitlin's face, pointing up to the grey clouds again. 'Perhaps 'im up there was wanting to play round a bit with their high falutin ideas of their selves.'

'No one else?' she muttered, turning away, stumbling on the stones hidden in the coarse grass.

'Wait, Caitlin, it might be easier –'

'He's dead, Richard. What could be worse?' she said in a flat voice, without looking at him.

She kept walking and heard Richard hurrying after her, the gravedigger following.

Caitlin saw the edge of the small grave behind the neatly clipped branches of the camellia. A cool breeze ruffled leaves over her feet as her steps slowed. Her brain refused to accept what her eyes were seeing. Was it just as Richard had said before, all trickery?

She began to shake in spasms of small shivers, stumbling again. She wanted to move closer to Richard, but the warmth of his kindness might make her spirit weaker. Each step became a heavier task.

There was no mistaking Sean's grave. It was a dark place for a child, an innocent soul who couldn't find peace even in this tiny earthen pit. A child who in life would have feared losing each day of sunlight. And here there were darker things.

Caitlin fell to her knees beside the grave, heard Richard's exclamation of disgust.

'Who would do this?' she choked, her husky voice rising.

In the centre of the grave stood a robot toy and Batman and Robin dolls, staring into space. Behind Robin's mask, where eyes should have been, were charred holes in a face stark white against the moist, dark soil. Dying flowers circled the dolls in an odd pattern. At the head of the grave was a skull crowned with thorns, burnt down stubs of black candles either side. Crushed against the skull, a fractured red crucifix had been pushed upside down into the grave.

8

A distant rumble of thunder signalled the storm that had lashed Sydney for the last hour was abating. In their darkened bedroom, Caitlin felt the bed lurch under Martin's weight.

She moved closer to him. The faint tang of cologne and red wine drifted into her face.

'I worry when you're so late.'

The light touch of his fingers down her arm was soothing.

'Can't sleep?' he murmured.

'No.'

'The Attorney General's speech went on forever. You'd think with an election coming up he'd say something relevant. Christ! Why do I bother with these Bar Association dinners?'

His hand slid off her arm. She sensed his frustration, felt him turn away. For a long moment, she listened to the quiet, even rhythm of his breathing, before twisting onto her back to watch the shifting light play over the ceiling.

She could leave telling Martin about her meeting with Brother Finbar for a day or two, but the words of the priest couldn't wait.

'Martin.'

'Hmm.'

She rolled over onto her side, nestling into his back, an arm around his waist. The warmth of his body enclosed her like a cocoon. 'That priest, Father MacManus, I spoke to him today at his church. What do you know about him?'

'Not much. I've no reason to be involved with him.'

'There was something strange in his manner. I need to talk to you about it.'

'Do it tomorrow.'

She stroked his back gently. 'I think it's important, darling. I need your incisive mind.'

'Not tonight.'

She shook his shoulder. 'Talk to me, Martin.'

'About what?'

'The priest and what he said about Sean.'

'Caitlin, I've a complicated matter in the commercial division tomorrow. I need to get some sleep.'

She curled closer, his silky hair tickling her face. 'Martin, please …'

'Leave it to the police. It's their job to work it out. Then we'll all know.'

'But will they?' she said. 'That Hurd fellow seems like he's marking the days till he gets his retirement pension. And that priest –'

'For God's sake, Caitlin, go to sleep.'

The mohair blanket brushed her face as Martin pulled it higher over his shoulder. His warmth and body smells were suddenly smothering, pushing her back to her side of the bed. The heavy silence pressed down on her, punctuated only by his quiet breathing.

She needed sleep, too. Lexy was chasing her for the last canvases for her exhibition; time was running out. She flopped onto her back, stared again at the ceiling. Perhaps Martin was right. Leave it to the police.

She closed her eyes to try an old trick that nearly always worked: a sheet of drawing paper appeared in the dark space of her mind. She began to form lines, one merging into another, quicker with every movement of her hand. Her body grew lighter, until she seemed to float towards the ceiling, becoming one with the lines, fusing into an affinity of form and space.

As she touches the ceiling, the plaster cracks; she bursts into a field of radiant colours.

In the distance is a lake, surely filled with mysteries that lurk within its depths.

Feeling her body jerk with fear, she approaches it slowly, only to be startled by a bolt of lightning, followed by a clap of thunder. A fierce wind tugs at her clothing. Something clings to her face for a second like a blindfold – a piece of bunting carried on the wind? It drops in front of her, just out of reach.

She cries out in surprise, 'My scarf, my scarf!'

Yet every time she reaches for it, the wind blows it further away.

One painful step after another, she follows it to a plain white cross on a simple grave. Flowers strewn around it have shrunk to a withered wreath.

Dark earth spills from the grave and slowly a coffin surfaces.

She peers closer to read the words written on its lid, eyes straining: 'Sean Tessler.' A gust of wind scatters the letters; new words take their place. They remain just long enough for her to read: 'Miss ... Help.'

She hears herself scream, 'What do you want?'

Rain and mist close around her.

The harsh voice of Brother Loudé booms behind her. 'Leave this place. Go, go.'

She woke, shivering, heart thumping, and tried to orientate herself. Martin lay beside her. The warm bedclothes embraced her, and slowly seduced her back into the nightmare.

She holds a child; she watches its head break from its small body. She tries to bind it back on with her scarf, but her hands are slimy, wet with blood. The head slips from her fingers, falls to the ground. Frantically, she scrabbles for it in the long grass.

∎

She awoke with a start and sat up quickly, gulping in air.

Leaning back on the bedhead, she began to massage her breast with a hand, not slippery with blood but cold with sweat. With clumsy, clutching strokes, she gradually managed to slow the racing rhythm of her heart and close off the vomit rising in her throat. Her breathing steadied.

With a corner of the sheet, she wiped the sweat from her face, her breasts. She looked across at Martin, wanting to wake him. She listened for a moment to his soft, even breathing and decided not to, instead scrambling from the twisted bedclothes.

The carpet was soft underfoot as she felt her way along the walls with her hands. She struggled to retain those nightmare images.

'Need paper, pencil, charcoal, anything,' she mumbled, stumbling along the hallway to the glassed-in veranda she used sometimes as a studio.

Plush carpet gave way to cold Florentine tiles. She switched on the overhead light, blinking in its harsh glare. Reflected in the row of windows facing the darkened garden, she saw herself as a creature from her demented nightmare: hair standing on end as if someone had touched it with a wand of electricity, her eyes two round black pools staring out from a white face.

She grabbed a sheet of paper, pinned it to the board she'd propped on an easel. The images of her discordant dream were fading fast; she had to capture them before they disappeared.

She urgently scratched the charcoal across the heavy, grained paper, mirroring her thoughts in the night's silence. Lines appeared, then shapes, until the images petered out.

She pulled back from the easel to study what she'd drawn, trying to find some thread that would trigger a glimmer of understanding. She contemplated the rough images covering the paper, the jagged holes where the charcoal had torn through.

'For God's sake, is that all?' she asked herself.

She needed to elucidate her dream, but it was as if the nightmare was continuing. She threw the charcoal back into its box.

Gently, she massaged the back of her neck; the ache behind her eyes hammered away, relentless. She crossed to the row of windows, sliding one open. The rain had stopped, but moisture still hung heavy on the winter air. It didn't help her mood. More than anything she needed sleep. But another part of her mind railed against it, demanding she find the hidden meaning in those images.

Unpinning the drawing, she replaced it with another sheet and picked up the charcoal again. She closed her eyes. Imagining Sean's frail body as the marionette of her nightmare, she slowly evoked the features of the path at Echo Point.

She blinked away stinging tears. Soon lines covered the paper and the track at Echo Point materialised, the wire fence, Sean clinging desperately to its rusted mesh.

She pulled the drawing off the board. The detritus of discarded ideas lay around her feet; still, she sought the truth. A compulsion to go on.

Pinning up a fresh sheet of paper, she reformed her idea. Then, casting it aside, she grabbed another. Charcoal was smeared everywhere, blotting out more and more lines of her drawings.

Finally, she stood back. Through a weariness that threatened to overwhelm her, she studied her latest composition. Like an image emerging from a slab of marble, she saw a face. Nerve ends vibrated throughout her body. She grabbed a pencil and began to draw in harsher details of the face near the wire fence. A man emerged. An older man. On the other side of the fence, opposite him, was the figure she had drawn of Sean.

She squinted her eyes half shut and focused on the old man again. Was he the reason for the nightmare? She shook her head slowly, ran trembling fingers over its aching heaviness. Too many blank moments.

Through the windows, the wash of daylight crept over the garden. She went to pull the drawing off the easel, but the image of Sean and the man made her hesitate. What was it? She tried to conjure up a picture in her mind of her last moments with Sean at the café: a boy shivering from cold in jeans, a light grey jacket and … Bloody hell, the scarf!

She sketched it in. Then, once again, she focused her attention on the old man.

Grasping the pencil harder, she continued to sketch the likeness that was materialising from her memory. Some tangled meaning began to form from the patterns.

No one else was interested in Sean's death; he was only a poor twelve-year-old boy, unimportant in the wider social scheme. But she needed to find the truth.

9

She had not come to satisfy macabre curiosity or to assuage her guilt for Sean's death, but to solve the puzzle of Father MacManus. She hoped Detective Hurd might be able to provide some logical explanation.

She was escorted to one of Central Police Station's interview rooms, No. 3. It was sparsely furnished, with just a wooden table and four wooden chairs. Its grubby, public service green walls seemed to exude the scent of fear, anger and anguish from the guilty and the innocent. The only source of natural light was a high, grime-crusted window. It was a world away from the comfort of Caitlin's home or her airy studio in The Rocks.

She paced the floor.

The door opened; a uniformed constable peered around it with an apologetic smile. 'DS Hurd won't be long. Can I get you a cup of tea?'

Caffeine laced with too much milk was a queasy prospect for a stomach already rippling with nerves.

'No, thank you,' she said.

She sat down. How to confront the detective? She knew she must rein in her dislike of him. What did her mother sometimes say? 'You catch more flies with honey than vinegar.'

How long did 'won't be too long' mean? Was he really that busy or was he deliberately keeping her waiting? She glanced at her watch, surprised that it had only been five minutes since the constable's appearance.

Quick footsteps in the corridor, muttering voices, and the door handle turned. Hurd's grey aura appeared, Detective Constable Cline in lockstep behind.

Hurd dropped into one of the battered chairs opposite Caitlin. Cline settled next to his superior. When the younger man took a notebook and pen from his jacket and placed them on the table, a slight frown puckered Hurd's eyebrow. She would need to be wary of this watchful man.

Caitlin decided she would leave it to the detective to speak first, hoping whatever he said would give her a lead. But he seemed to have the same idea.

The silence in the small room became oppressive.

She was about to capitulate, when he said, 'Sorry to keep you waiting, Mrs Preece. What can we do for you?'

Her mouth felt dry; she ran her tongue round it. She shifted in the chair, linked her fingers together in her lap.

'I'm sorry to trouble you. I know you're busy men.'

'We're here to help.' He was looking at her as if she were an alien from another planet. She would have to take the initiative.

'Sean Tessler's death. Are there any new developments?'

Hurd's expression turned stony. 'The case is barely seven weeks old, Mrs Preece. Good detective work takes time: tedious forensic examinations, interviews, elimination, confirmation – nothing like your flashy television heroes. There are three things that constitute a good investigation: facts, facts and facts. Facts, Mrs Preece, are what interest me. We present the brief of evidence to the coroner. The coroner returns a finding. If he thinks there's foul play, it comes back to us.'

'What do you think will be the coroner's finding?'

'Suicide.' His heavy face seemed to relax; he was ready to stand up and move on.

Did he believe that was enough to satisfy her? She glanced at Cline. He had closed his notebook and was fiddling with his pen.

She wanted to shout, 'I'm not finished with you yet,' but if she needed their help, she would have to proceed carefully. She leant against the hard edge of the table, hoping a speculative expression was spreading over her face.

'An autopsy, all your interviews, the brief to the coroner; do you think that will be the finding?'

'It doesn't really matter what I think. But if you're interested in my opinion, then I believe that will be the coroner's finding. The boy had a tough life, was an intelligent, highly strung lad who spent lots of time on his own and had been sexually abused. He wouldn't be the first young person to take their life in such circumstances. He leaves the group, goes to Echo Point and jumps.' Hurd frowned. 'If you have any reason to doubt the finding, perhaps you want to add to your statement.'

Attentive, Cline opened his notebook.

'Because if you haven't, Detective Cline will show you out.'

Hurd pushed back his chair, grating it along the floor as he stood up. His short, bulky figure seemed to cut off the light, choke the air from the room. He strode towards the door.

Caitlin gripped the seat of her chair, tried to suck saliva into her mouth. The smell of sweat – perhaps her own – permeated the stuffy room.

'Detective … Wait.'

Hurd turned.

'You've interviewed everyone?' she said.

The frown returned, cutting deeper into the lines between his sparse, brown eyebrows.

'All the clergy who were at Katoomba the weekend Sean died?'

'All of them, Mrs Preece. Nobody saw him after lunch on Sunday. Except you.'

It was like a tiny speck of gold in a panner's dish.

'No one?'

Hurd gazed up at the window. 'Constable, get someone to clean this damn window.'

A flush spread over Cline's handsome features. 'Yes, sir,' he said, making a quick note on his pad.

Hurd looked to be studying the window intently, as if searching for enlightenment in its grimy pattern.

She struggled to keep her voice casual. 'Have you talked to Father MacManus?"

Hurd swung around. 'Why? How well do you know him?'

She turned back to face Cline, easing the ache in her neck. 'Our paths rarely cross.'

'You only know him from the school?' Hurd said.

'Yes. Just glimpses of him walking across the quadrangle. He provides pastoral care to the boys.'

'Pastoral care. Yes, of course.'

She tried to read Cline's reaction to his colleague's new line of questioning. In their interview at her home, she'd felt an element of sympathy from him, but now his face was impassive.

'He told me he was an altar boy.'

'Hmm.' Hurd walked back to the table and sat down, his gaze straying for a moment to Cline, who was juggling his pen between his fingers. 'We're interested in anyone who may have had any connection with the young fellow.'

Caitlin's attention switched from one policeman's face to the other. In the silence that followed, she saw the opportunity she'd been hoping for, to unburden a truth that might bring the stalled investigation back to life.

'I believe Father MacManus may have been the last person to talk to Sean.'

If she was expecting a reaction, she was disappointed.

'Why would you think that?' Hurd said.

'When I spoke to him in the church three weeks ago, he let something slip without either of us realising its significance.'

'Why did you wait so long to give us this information?

"I have only just realised the significance myself.'

'Well, what was it?'

'I can't remember his exact words.'

She saw his lips tighten.

'Try, Mrs Preece. If you want me to treat this as significant, I must know exactly what he said.'

She stared for a second or two at his reddening face. 'It's difficult to recall, exactly.'

'I can be patient, but with four unsolved cases sitting on my desk and a Detective Chief Inspector looking over my shoulder even in the Men's, I have no time to waste.'

Caitlin glared at him before turning to stare at the blank wall behind them. She willed her mind back to the church.

'Father MacManus mentioned Sean talking about me, about my

work, how I'd offered to help get him into art school. He said how kind I'd been to Sean. "Like when you gave him your scarf." That's what he said, exactly.'

The policemen looked at each other, clearly puzzled.

Hurd grimaced. 'What scarf?'

'The scarf. Did you find it on Sean's body?'

Hurd was watching her, an unpleasant, sceptical smile on his face. 'If there was a scarf, how would it prove Father MacManus was the last to have seen the boy?'

Caitlin shot him a venomous look. 'You're twisting my words. Don't you realise the significance? I said he *might* have been the last person to see Sean. It might not prove he was, but it does mean he talked to Sean after I gave him my scarf in the café.'

'I have a problem with that, Mrs Preece. You're the only person who knows about this scarf and Father MacManus told us he didn't see Sean on the day he died. Either you're lying or the priest is.'

She opened her mouth to speak, then quickly closed it. She looked at Cline. His expression was surlier than Hurd's. She felt the ground slipping from under her.

'Are you saying it's the priest's word against mine?'

'We deal with evidence, Mrs Preece. We're not judgemental, but if the Father keeps to his story, then yes, it is his word against yours.'

'Is that so?' She stared at him intently. 'I think, then, that's a problem for the Father. He needs help with the ninth commandment.'

Cline looked blank. 'The ninth commandment?'

Hurd glanced at him with contempt. 'Thou shalt not give false testimony.'

He was full of surprises.

'Go on,' Hurd said, shifting his attention back to Caitlin.

Did she have to spell it out for him?

'Sean told MacManus I'd given him the scarf. But I only gave it to Sean that afternoon. I put it on him myself at the café.' She jumped up, sending her chair clattering to the floor. She leant so close to Hurd that she smelt his sour breath. 'Now, you tell me, Detective, how the hell could he know that if he didn't see Sean, after I had given him the scarf? Is it still his word against mine?'

She spun on her boot heels and strode off down the corridor without another glance at the startled policemen.

10

Confronting Father MacManus on his own territory was a very different proposition to talking to the police this morning. She didn't know whether it would be harder or easier, but she knew she would have to be calm, objective. Truth was her only ally. Would it be enough?

She parked in the street behind the Sacred Heart Church. She could just glimpse the dull red brick walls of Saint Anthony's Orphanage and the school beyond. It felt strange being so near, now an outsider. The boys had become a treasured part of her life; the loss of them was a dark emptiness. Perhaps a psychologist might diagnose a yearning for a child of her own, she thought.

Yells of laughter caught her attention. She squinted through the late morning glare of the sun on her windscreen. A group of six or seven boys was crossing the street with one of the brothers from the school, Brother Purcell. Although he was some distance away, she recognised his shock of hay-coloured hair and that distinctive limp. She waited until they disappeared into the church, then followed.

The wooden front door creaked as she slipped inside. She waited for her eyes to adjust to the dimly lit interior.

Brother Purcell and Father MacManus stood silhouetted against the chancel's bright, reflected light. The boys were clustered at the end of the front pew. From Brother Purcell's agitated hand movements, it seemed an argument was brewing.

She tiptoed to a side aisle, careful to soften her boot steps on the stone floor, slowly moving towards the altar until she was as close to them as she dared. From the shelter of a pillar, her forehead against the cold stone, she strained to hear their words. The softness of their voices and the background chatter of the boys prevented her from catching anything more than the odd fragment.

Whatever the argument, she could see the tension mottling Father MacManus' face. A few of the older boys had stopped talking to watch the exchange.

With a sudden gesture that betrayed pent-up frustration, Brother Purcell gathered the boys together and limped towards the front door.

'Brother Purcell, Brother Purcell, I have to tell you, the festival …' But the priest's last words drifted to an echo in the small church. The brother with his gaggle of boys had gone.

Caitlin walked along the front pew towards Father MacManus. At the sound of her footsteps, he turned, a wry smile twitching the corners of his mouth. 'Come to light more candles, Mrs Preece?'

'Can we talk, Father?'

'Confession is good for the soul, but surely you'd be more comfortable discussing a problem with your own parish priest?'

'But it concerns you, Father.'

'Me?'

'Remember the day I came here after Sean Tessler's death?'

'Yes.'

'You told me Sean often confided in you. Now I need your help. Two days after Sean's funeral, I found a broken crucifix half buried in his grave.'

Watery blue eyes stared wide from his pulpy grey flesh. One trembling hand made the sign of the cross. He sighed. 'Dear Lord. Such mindless acts are hard to understand.'

'There were other things on the grave, Father: Batman and Robin dolls, a tin robot. Mindless acts, too?'

A slight pause. 'Possibly drunken vandals amusing themselves, or objects stolen from another child's grave.'

She studied him for a moment. Was there something behind his words?

He turned away. 'Now, if you'll excuse me …'

She stepped nearer to him. 'But, Father, they were all left on Sean's grave. I searched other children's graves. Nothing on any of them. Curious, wouldn't you say?'

He shrugged. 'In my years of ministry, Mrs Preece, I've learnt to expect the unexpected. Perhaps a relative of the boy's left them.'

'I don't think he has any except his brother, Peter. I never saw either boy take a special interest in toys. And the inverted cross, a child's toy? Isn't that sometimes used as a symbol of unworthiness?'

'Yes, the Petrine Cross.'

'Could someone have put it there because they believed Sean suicided?'

'Possibly, but I doubt it. I cannot think of anyone who knew him who would do such a thing.'

An image of Sean's drawing, the child figure with the three leering men, crept from the edges of her mind.

'Or by an apostate?'

'An apostate?'

'A perverted person, Father. I read recently that the inverted cross features in Black Masses performed by paedophiles.'

Silence filled the empty space between them. The priest crossed himself again.

'What a terrible thing to say. I really have to go. I'm already late for an appointment. I've helped you all I can.'

He sidled away from her and began to walk towards the front door.

Quickly, she overtook him, spun around to face him.

'Have you, Father? I know Sean was holding secrets and I think they're connected to those objects on his grave. You were his parish priest. Did he ever say anything to you?'

'No, nothing. Now …' He tried to push past her.

Time was slipping away. Caitlin backstepped, staying in front of him. 'On the afternoon he died, I'd never seen him so distressed. What did he say when you spoke to him?'

'I didn't speak to him.'

'But you told me about the scarf.'

He looked bewildered. 'What about it?'

'I gave him the scarf that afternoon.'

He shook his head. 'You're confusing me, Mrs Preece. I don't remember any scarf.'

The softly spoken, mild personality had vanished. She caught the tremor in his voice. Silvery beads of sweat glistened above his flabby lips.

'What is it, Father? Are you trying to protect someone?'

He ignored her, already walking away.

She gritted her teeth. Though she had been trying to keep her mind focused on her line of questioning, all she could imagine was Sean's body in the silence of that valley; all she could hear were more lies from the priest.

'If you are, your loyalty and compassion is misplaced,' she called after him.

She saw the priest look up to the choir stall above, caught a blur of movement. She tried to turn, run, but was flung sideways, her body crumpling into the foetal position, plaster shattering, pieces bouncing across the stone floor. White mist clouded the air, slowly drifting down to cover her.

■

Something was dragging at her skin, pressing, pulling so hard she wanted to scream out, 'Let go.' She tried to open her eyes, but they felt as if they were glued together. Even her mouth felt different, tasted gritty.

Soft sounds became a voice: the priest, MacManus. 'Mrs Preece? Dear God! Mrs Preece, can you hear me?'

She felt his hands lightly touch her shoulder and then her head. She almost laughed. Not the last rites, surely?

She lifted her right hand, her drawing, painting, working hand, clenched and unclenched it, then rubbed it over her eyes. The scratchy sensation on her eyelids made her cry out. But now she could see a glimmer of light.

'Please, stay still. I'll get help.' Father MacManus' voice had a distant, ethereal quality.

She eased herself up with her weight on one arm.

'I'm all right,' she managed to say.

Pieces of plaster fell from her. She blinked rapidly, tried to open her eyes wider. When she looked down at herself, she saw everything was white, as if she'd been in a powder storm. Then blood seeping through the whiteness.

'You must not move, Mrs Preece. You're hurt.'

Caitlin shook her head. White dust floated in the air.

'It's just scratches,' she said, staring up at the priest. 'What happened?'

The priest straightened and flexed his shoulders, biting his lip as if in pain.

'The statue of Saint Therese fell from the choir stall.'

She looked up at the empty plinth, then glanced at the priest. 'We were lucky.'

She eased her legs sideways, leaning forward a little to roll onto her knees.

'Thank God you've come,' she heard the priest mutter.

She caught sight of shiny leather shoes and the hem of a black cassock.

Brother Loudé's intent eyes were inches from her face. 'Are you all right, Mrs Preece?'

It was like facing a snake's unblinking stare. Caitlin turned away, grabbing the edge of a pew for support to drag herself up.

The brother moved closer. 'Let me help you.'

'I can manage.'

Edging away from them, she groped her way along the pew until she could sit down.

'You're hurt, Mrs Preece. I'll get the school nurse,' the brother said.

'It's not necessary.'

More than anything, she wanted to quit this House of God. Loudé's suit, she noticed, was not covered in the chalky dust.

11

Driving through the winding streets of Paddington, Caitlin felt a sense of déjà vu. She was heading to the Hungry Palette for lunch – one of her parents' favourites and the haunt of many famous Sydney artists.

She squeezed into a convenient parking spot not far from the restaurant. Like much of Paddington, the location exuded old-world charm, a great contrast to the notorious days when Tilly Devine ruled the razor gangs with a rod of iron and ran the sly grog rackets, illegal narcotics trade and prostitution that characterised the area from the twenties through to the sixties. Just a little over a decade later, the lines of terraces with their wrought-iron lace balconies, interspersed with quaint cottages painted all colours of the rainbow, were the picture of quiet respectability.

Stepping inside, she was greeted by a tall, elegantly dressed woman. 'Welcome to the Hungry Palette. A table for one?'

'There's a booking in the name of Lipchitz,' Caitlin said.

'Oh, Lexy. You must be the friend she mentioned. Yes, a table for three.'

'Three?'

She glanced at her diary. 'That's what it says here. Come this way. I've kept her favourite table.'

Caitlin smiled to herself. Lexy had the knack of spreading goodwill wherever she went. A great asset for a gallery owner.

Seated at a table set for three, Caitlin stared out the window, down the tree-lined streetscape, and contemplated how she would tell her friend of her close brush with death. And who was the mysterious third person?

She looked at her watch. She had arrived a few minutes early, but no sooner had those minutes ticked by than Lexy appeared, walking jauntily beneath the huge trees that touched one another to form a leafy canopy. The two friends had met at art school. Lexy had wanted to be a great artist, but by the time she was twenty, she'd realised that would never happen. Without a second thought, her ambition turned to owning and running a prestigious art gallery that would challenge both her aestheticism and intellect.

For months, she'd argued with her father, who'd wanted Lexy to join him in his highly successful carpet business. She'd tried to explain how and what she felt when she saw great art, even mediocre work, how it filled her with hope for humanity; the contact she had with artists and clients, stimulating and so satisfying to her unique humour. What comparison could there be between that and selling carpets?

When he finally relented, she went to work for a highly regarded gallery in Sydney. Now, she owned it.

Lexy breezed in, breaking through Caitlin's reverie. She waved to the older woman.

'Hi, Ruth,' Lexy said.

Ruth, with plates in both hands nodded towards Caitlin, who

rose to meet her. They kissed one another on both cheeks and within seconds were deep in conversation.

'How are the nudes going?' Lexy said, then starting at the scratches on Caitlin's face, 'Or have you been doing things you shouldn't be doing?'

'Lexy!'

'Don't Lexy me! What is it?'

'It's nothing, just a stupid accident. I went to talk to the priest, Father MacManus, who provides pastoral care to the boys from the orphanage …'

'And?'

'And as I was leaving the church, a statue fell from the choir stall near where I was standing. Please, Lexy, don't stare at me like that and don't worry. I'll finish my work for your exhibition.'

'Caitlin. You could have been killed.'

'As could the priest.' Caitlin gazed at her friend, seeing in those beautiful topaz eyes the light of battle, not daring to tell her she thought she'd been the target. If Lexy knew that, she'd demand they go straight to the police.

'Does this have something to do with the death of the boy we talked about at your dinner?'

'Sean. Yes,' Caitlin murmured.

Lexy looked at her with a penetrating stare. 'Nobody's child.'

Caitlin returned the stare. Although she had known her feisty friend since her late teens, she was still surprised by her perception, the way Lexy could burrow into her mind.

'You remembered,' she said, grasping Lexy's hand. 'I'm certain his death was not suicide or an accident. I feel I owe it to him, and to his brother, to find out what happened.'

'What are the police saying?'

'The police? They think I'm a nuisance. They expect the coroner to bring in a verdict of suicide.'

'But you would not agree with such a verdict?'

'No. I think Father MacManus knows more than he's told the police.'

'Why?'

'I know he saw Sean after I left the café. I'm not saying he knows anything about his death, but he must know something about Sean's later movements. But when I confronted him, he went all vague and denied having seen him at all.'

Caitlin heard the door open behind her and saw Lexy's face light up.

'Good. Richard's here.'

Lexy crossed to meet him and gave him a big hug. 'How's my favourite politician?'

'Frazzled, glad to get out of the rat race for a while.'

Caitlin rose to greet him.

'Lexy didn't tell me you were coming.'

'Half an hour ago I thought I wouldn't make it, but things took a turn for the better. So, here I am.'

■

While they ate, Lexy and Caitlin filled Richard in on their earlier discussion. He listened in silence, breaking it only to comment on how excellent the fish was.

Lexy carefully laid her knife and fork side by side on her plate. 'So, what are your thoughts, Richard?'

'I've been thinking about it since the dinner at your place, wondering if there was something I could do to help. It's a complex area, and one you probably need to understand, Caitlin. You could join my Children's Custodial Care Committee. Not only would you learn a lot from the professional people you meet, but they would benefit from interaction with someone from the community.'

Caitlin, who had been studying the remains of her fish, looked up to see Richard staring intently at her with his blue eyes. She was so overcome by the understanding and sincerity that suffused his face, she almost forgot what he had just said. And for a few precious seconds, she forgot they were in a restaurant, and Lexy was there with them.

The spell was broken by Ruth topping up their glasses, draining the bottle. 'Would you like another?'

They all shook their heads.

Lexy reached out and took Caitlin's hand. 'Well, my darling, what do you think?'

'About what?'

'About joining Richard's committee.'

'I think it's a wonderful idea.'

Richard smiled. 'Well, that's settled then. I'll get Esther to send you the details.'

'Thank you. But I feel I must do more.'

His eyes became troubled. 'There is something else that concerns me. The statue falling may have been an accident, but statues don't usually fall of their own accord. I can't see why anyone would want to attack a priest, so … I think you need a little help. A sort of guardian angel.'

'A guardian angel?'

'A man called Quinn.'

'How does "a man called Quinn" help?'

'He's someone I met through Lexy. A private investigator. A rather special one.'

'Dad has used him with great success and, as you know, my father is not easily pleased. Quinn's enigmatic and a challenge to those who hold their cards too close,' Lexy said. 'As honest as they come. The sort who, if his shoes picked up gold dust from your carpet, he would return it. And he likes nut cases. They stimulate his creative juices.'

'He seems to have a private income,' Richard added, 'because he can pick and choose the work he takes on. Lives in Glebe in a rather unusual house and has an office somewhere in the city, although no one's ever discovered where.'

'I'm not convinced,' Caitlin said. 'But since you both want me to, I'll contact him. Then I'll make up my mind.'

12

The lunch left Caitlin in reflective mood. Though she appreciated the support and concern of her friends, she was still finding it difficult to make sense of it all: her trauma around the falling statue; Richard's committee; a guardian angel called Quinn.

Gazing out through the tall, deep-set windows of her studio in The Rocks, she breathed in the smell of the harbour wafting in on a light breeze. She turned to take in her spacious studio with its two easels, work benches cluttered with palettes, tubes of paint, rags, jars of brushes; a desk in one corner, next to it a couch, and at the far end a small kitchenette. Its welcoming embrace raised her spirits.

Caitlin swung around as her landlady, Mrs Mazzioni, who also ran the restaurant downstairs, came in. For a moment, she paused to glare at a huge canvas on one of the easels. She squinted her brown eyes at the black lines, looped in complex patterns, delicate threads linking tones of greys and whites.

'Why you paint mourning colours? It's not like you.'

'Just playing with lines and tones, Mrs Mazz. I'm trying to work through some ideas I have for a new work. It's not coming very quickly, but if I persevere, something will eventually come.'

'No, it's time for you to have lunch. You need to eat,' she said, lifting the peaked, white napkin from the plate in her hands.

Caitlin limped slowly to one of the windows, swinging herself onto its wide sill to sit with her knees drawn up, her boot-heels pressed against the other side. She gently massaged her temples.

Mrs Mazz handed her the plate and eased her bulky behind onto a hard wooden chair. Caitlin heard the soft, disapproving clicks of her tongue as she looked up and down the long rows of wooden racks stacked with work.

'Too much,' she said, sweeping her pudgy hands through the air in an extravagant gesture. 'You do too much, *bella mia.*'

Caitlin pressed her fingertips harder into her skin. A seagull screeched past the window. Mrs Mazz's sharp eyes caught Caitlin's involuntary jump.

'Why you work yourself so hard?' The old lady leant over, stilled Caitlin's shaking hands with her own and turned back to the canvas she'd been working on. 'It's making you like that' – pointing to the tangled black lines on their sombre background.

'I'm all right, Mrs Mazz, just a little tired. I have an exhibition coming up and I have lots of work to finish.'

'You need the money?'

Caitlin laughed, but not the exuberant kind she knew her landlady would have liked to hear. 'No, it's just that I've given Lexy a firm commitment.'

'Is it Mr Preece and his politics?' Mrs Mazz said, throwing her hands into the air again. 'Ah, these husbands! They run you round and round everywhere to do what they want.' Large breasts strained the polka dots of her voluminous dress as she breathed a heavy sigh. 'I go back down. *La ragazza,* she not put enough on the plates when I don't see.'

She hauled herself to her feet, lifted Caitlin's chin with both hands and gazed for a moment into her eyes. Caitlin knew they must be hollows in dark circles.

'God give you a great gift, but not to be a merchant. Now, you eat and stay off that foot.'

Mrs Mazz picked a stepping stone pattern around the tins of paint covering the tallowwood floor and closed the door behind her. Caitlin stared out the window at a landscape filled with life. It was a landscape of ordinary people: the leisurely progress of ferries arriving at and departing Circular Quay; beyond them, the outline of the Sydney Opera House which, after many delays and much controversy, would soon be open to the public. Somewhere in the distance, a seagull screeched; others flew down to feed on the rich pickings of lunchtime scraps in the park below.

Minutes passed before she could force herself away from the vibrant sounds and sights of normality. Limping on her strapped ankle, she returned to another easel, to a nude sprawled in splendid voluptuousness across a long canvas. She picked up a brush, then hesitated. Were they footsteps from the hallway below? Mrs Mazz returning with more food? She strained to hear, but the noise of the traffic muffled any further sound.

She opened the door and peeked into the landing: empty. She shook her head. Memories of the shattered fragments of Saint Therese's statue were haunting her. Had it been meant for her or the priest?

She shut the door and turned back to the canvas, agonising over what was wrong with the juxtaposition of the nude against the posy of flowers clutched between her breasts, when she heard a tentative knock. Heat spread across her chest.

She opened the door a couple of inches, keeping a foot firmly planted against it. A man in his early twenties peered through the crack.

'Yes? What do you want?'

'You're the woman, the artist, that gives them art lessons at Saint Anthony's school?'

'Yes, but –'

'This is for you.' He thrust a thin, flat, brown paper package through the door opening.

'What is it?'

'Something Sean did.'

'Sean Tessler? How did you know him?'

'I'm his half-brother, Brian.'

She took the package and opened the door.

The young man in dirty work clothes took a few steps into the room. He skimmed his eyes over her gaily patterned couch, the cluttered worktables, easels, ochre-coloured walls covered with paintings, but seemed to find little of interest. He sniffed as if even the air, permeated with oil paint and turpentine, served no purpose to him.

But now, those dark eyes settled on her with a much more particular intensity.

'What do you want?' Caitlin said, inching back towards the worktable.

'I have a message from Sean. It goes with the parcel.'

Among the clutter of paint tubes, jars, brushes, palettes, tangled bits of rags and paper was a Stanley knife. She leant against the solid worktable, fingers lightly reaching for the smooth metal of its handle.

His eyes must have caught the glint of steel and he immediately turned to leave. She loosened her grip on the knife.

'Wait. I thought Peter was his only family.'

He shrugged. 'Just me and them.'

In the bright light of the studio, her initial impression had been that he bore no resemblance to Sean. Yet memory, she knew, could be quicksilver. With a furtive glance at her drawing of his half-brother pinned above the couch, she could now see the same distinctive high forehead hidden under his mop of brown hair, the well-shaped, shell-like ears close to the head.

She limped towards the couch, sat down and glanced at the package, and noticed it wasn't addressed.

She looked at it for a few moments. 'But why would Sean give it to you? Why not give it to me at the school?'

'I was in Sydney a couple of months back. I went to see him. He was in the infirmary. Felt sorry for the little blighter, so when he asked me to give it to you next time I came to Sydney, I said I would.'

She gazed at him. 'What a strange thing to do. But Sean could be secretive.'

'Yeah, a weird kid. Never talked a lot but didn't miss much. Eyes everywhere.'

Not saying a lot seemed to be a family trait.

He turned towards the door. 'I'd better be off.'

'No, stay a moment, Brian, while I open it.'

She pushed a hand under the tape and ripped away the paper. Tentatively, she fingered an exercise book, greasy to the touch, creased and curled at the edges. She opened it, riffled through its pages. Coloured illustrations of the Phantom filled each one, a disarmingly different aesthetic from the drawings of the Apostles she had seen three weeks ago.

'It's a comic book. But why give it to me? You're sure there wasn't a message?'

'Only that it was important to give it to you soon as possible. Now you've got it.'

She raised her eyebrows. 'But two months?'

'Been working in Newcastle – just got back.'

Turning the pages more slowly, she said, 'He must have liked the Phantom. All this detail.' She peered closer. 'Have you read it?'

He laughed, nervously edging towards the door. 'Never one for comics. I'm on me lunch break. Gotta go.'

'Two months. Weren't you curious?'

She saw his hazel eyes lose their gold streaks of light, become two pools of shadowed darkness above the high cheek bones of his tanned, set face. His intent gaze seemed to penetrate her, to invade her secret self, passing judgement.

'I don't get too much time to be curious. That's for people like you and that other woman, Enid.'

'Enid?'

He looked away. 'She fostered the boys before they went to the Christian Brothers. A pity they couldn't stay with her.'

'Why couldn't they?'

He shrugged again. 'Dunno exactly. She was such a lovely lady, real motherly type. I hated going to the Christian Brothers. It was creepy and grey, dreary, like a prison. All them men in long black dresses, watching me all the time, like I shouldn't be there.'

She stared at him for some seconds before she said, 'How do you mean, watching you?'

'Just a feeling, that's all. And Sean, he weren't too happy there.'

'Brian, feelings can do different things to different people. I know what you mean. I remember the first time I walked into the orphanage, I felt –'

'Look', Brian butted in, 'all I know is Sean wanted you to have them comics.'

She flipped over the pages, frowning. 'But how do I know whatever it is I'm supposed to see?'

That intent gaze of his bored into her again, making her face burn.

He turned towards the door. 'Sean said you were one smart lady. I promised I'd give it to you – I've done it. At least that's something I could do for the little bugger.'

'Brian, don't go.' Caitlin stood and hobbled after him. 'Don't go. I didn't mean to upset you.'

Without turning his head, he said, 'Your sort never do.'

'Brian!'

By the time she reached the door, he was halfway down the staircase. She limped to the iron banister and, between heavy breaths, called out to him as he started to disappear from sight. 'This Enid, how can I contact her?'

His voice floated up the stairwell: 'Check the phonebook. Featherstone, Summer Hill.'

■

Enid Featherstone's single-storey home stood well back from the street, a rambling, late Victorian house hidden from its neighbours by a mass of trees, hedges and shrubs. Caitlin shifted an uneasy gaze from their shadows to the black eyes of the narrow windows.

What am I doing here? she wondered.

Enid had sounded friendly enough on the phone this morning, but how long would that last? She pushed open the rustic gate.

The front door stood wide open. She pressed her nose against the wire screen, peering into the dim interior. The house was still, silent.

She knocked.

Then she knocked louder, her knuckles rattling the wooden frame.

A small child shot out from a doorway halfway down the long hall, bobbing towards her before stopping a few feet from the door. The girl regarded her with solemn brown eyes set within a painted face.

'Hello, I'm Caitlin. What a pretty daisy on your cheek.'

The child giggled. 'Silly. It's a weed.'

'Could you ask Enid to do one for me?'

'No. She's trying to get Rushy out from under the table.'

'Can I help? Dogs like me.'

A pudgy hand flew up to the green mouth to smother another giggle. 'You're funny.'

'Funny' seemed to be the password. The latch clicked open and the little one skipped off down the hall, singing, 'Dear, dear, lady here.' She stopped near an open doorway, pointed, then disappeared.

In the dim light, the room seemed empty.

Feeling rather foolish, Caitlin called out, 'Enid?'

The folds of a heavy tapestry cloth covering a round table in the centre of the room started to bulge, and in a moment a clown face was smiling up at her.

A plump woman struggled to her feet, pulled the mask off her flushed face.

'Whew! It's hot under there.' Fingering her loose, grey-streaked bun, she puffed between heavy breaths. 'You must be Caitlin.'

Caitlin nodded at the mask. 'A novel form of hide-and-seek?'

Enid's face crinkled into a laugh. 'The only way to get him out. It's like offering him a sweet.'

'Your dog must be a character. Mine likes soft toys.'

The woman looked puzzled.

'Rushy?' Caitlin said.

'Oh, Rushy is Yasmin's name for him.' She laughed again. 'Though he does follow her around like a dog. But today' – she sighed, twirling the string of the mask on two fingers – 'is one of Tim's bad days. He's only been with me a few weeks and he's still somewhat disorientated. It doesn't help that he is partially deaf as well.'

Colour flushed into Caitlin's face, embarrassed by her misunderstanding, but Enid reached out to grip her hand. 'Don't worry, dear. Sometimes I think this house is like Lucy's wardrobe.'

'Pardon?'

'Lucy who unlocks the magic world in *The Lion, the Witch and the Wardrobe*. The children love that story,' Enid said, walking off down the hallway.

Caitlin started to follow but then turned back. A boy had crawled out from under the table, his mask off, one hand flapping at her.

'Hello, Tim,' she said with a wave. But in an instant the mask was back on and he vanished under the table again. Enid shook her head.

'He's a sad case,' she said. 'I'm to have him for a couple of months to assess him. But there's something strange about it all. I haven't been given much information about his background, they said it might cloud my judgement.' She shrugged. 'It doesn't make sense.

I suppose I shouldn't say this, but I think he has been abused. At least, the signs are there.'

Caitlin was about to ask what she meant, but Enid had already walked on.

In the light, spacious kitchen, she said, 'Sit, sit. Tea all right, dear, or coffee?'

'Tea's fine, milk and two sugars, please.'

While Enid fussed with the tea-making, Caitlin sat down at the long table and took in her surrounds. The kitchen had an air of warm, comfortable chaos.

There was an awkward moment of silence until she ventured, 'Anything I can do to help?'

'No, dear, won't be a tick.'

A tray with two cups and saucers, a steaming teapot and a plate with two slices of fruit cake were soon on the table.

Enid poured the tea and fixed Caitlin with an inscrutable gaze. 'Now, how can I help you?'

Caitlin pulled Sean's comic out of her bag, leant across the table and pushed it towards Enid.

Enid raised her eyebrows, her smile fading. 'Sean's work.'

Caitlin nodded.

'I'd know it anywhere. So, that's it. I wondered what you really wanted to talk about.'

'I could hardly explain on the phone, to a stranger; I'd have seemed completely eccentric. But it's your sixth sense I need. Sean made this comic and sent it to me through his half-brother, Brian. It's supposed to hold an important message for me. But I'm baffled.' She turned over the pages. 'Sean's certainly put a lot into the drawings: those balloons with the Phantom's words, the jumble of letters for the Witch Doctor's language. But if there's a message, I can't get it.'

Caitlin's heart beat harder as the woman methodically turned the pages, then finally closed it, peered over her glasses and shook her head.

'It's very clever, dear, but it's just a comic. You know, boys' games. I wouldn't get too het up about it. Just a nice keepsake for you.'

Caitlin stared at the old lady for a moment, felt her skin tingle. Struggling to get the words out, she posed the all-important question: 'Did the boys have a special language for themselves?'

Enid laughed. 'Funny you should ask. Yes, and quite fluent they were, the little rascals. It was something like Pig Latin. But I don't think … Well, this is different.'

'I know what Pig Latin is, but the native language in the comic is not Pig Latin. Perhaps it could it be some other form of code?"

Enid shrugged. 'I suppose it's possible Sean could have worked something out. Quite an imagination he had.'

'Do you have any of his work?'

'There's nothing here, unfortunately. I cleared out anything the boys left months ago.' She gestured to the mask on the table. 'That's the only thing left of anything Sean did. He thought up these clown masks and they've proved very useful, particularly in Tim's case. They make him smile and give him something to hide behind.'

A sudden twitch at the corner of the woman's mouth reminded Caitlin of someone swallowing a bad oyster. 'What is it, Enid?'

'Brother Loudé rang the other day. There's something unsettling about that man. Anyway, he wants to put together a scrapbook of Sean's drawings for Peter. I told him I had nothing.'

'That's odd. When I suggested the same idea to him, he thought it was nonsense. Can you remember the date of his call?'

'Yes, it was Yasmin's birthday: the thirtieth of May.'

Caitlin drew a sharp breath. That was the last day she'd been at the school, the day she'd found Sean's pencil drawings. Could there be a connection between Brian's wariness of the brothers, Sean's unhappiness and the cause of his death? She spooned sugar into her tea, slowly stirred it, then dipped it into the large sugar bowl again.

'That makes five,' Enid said. 'Just blurt it out, dear. I'm a tough old bird.'

Caitlin dropped the spoon onto the saucer, focused on a jug of daisies on the pine dresser. 'Is it possible Sean committed suicide?'

'That's preposterous. Is that what they're saying?' Her glasses slipped down her nose. She pulled them off, walked over to the window and stared out into her jungle of a garden for a moment, then swung around.

'After their mother died, the stepfather's physical abuse became intolerable. There weren't any other relatives, except eighteen-year-old Brian, so the court decided Sean and Peter should be fostered.'

Enid fiddled with her glasses for a second, then closed them. There was a pensive note in her voice when she said, 'They were happy here, but going to the orphanage was another matter. You shouldn't move children around like chattels. I was able to wangle some visits through someone I knew. Peter had settled in, but Sean … He worried me, but to kill himself? Not him. Those boys were inseparable. What one felt, the other felt. There was a special bond between them. Peter must be absolutely devastated.'

The woman walked back to the table and sat down again. 'My husband and I wanted to adopt them, tried for months, arguing back and forth with the Department of Community Affairs, even enlisted the help of our local member. Too old, we were told.'

'They said that?'

Enid nodded. 'So many things need fixing in that department. I've been working with a committee that's investigating institutionalised care for children and the one thing I've discovered is there's not too much true charity out there.'

Caitlin grimaced. 'Like sails without a prevailing wind.'

Enid nodded. 'Exactly. I don't think the government is really interested in improvement. That would cost money.'

'Do you think it's possible to change that attitude?'

'We must all keep trying, believe in a better world.' She rubbed her aged hand over the smooth table. 'I fostered a little girl some months ago, who'd been physically abused. She was also fond of drawing and made a picture of herself in what might have been a party dress, wearing a tiny crown. In the drawing she seemed to be levitating. When I asked if it was her, she murmured, "Yes, that's me, a princess."

'I found her quite inspiring, I had to do more, so when a friend suggested I offer my experience to Richard Brinsmead, the Leader of the Opposition, I did. And so, I became a member of his committee. Richard's a wonderful man,' Enid said.

'Richard!'

'Do you know him?'

'Quite well, actually. He opened my first exhibition. I'm an artist.'

'Well, he's a rarity. I don't know how he survives in that world of power play – he's a bit of a contradiction, an honest politician. And I'll tell you another thing, if the committee uncovers anything serious, he won't flinch from exposing the facts or who's responsible, no matter who or what they are.'

Caitlin glanced across to the window. Delicate pink clouds marbled the sky.

'Has anything disturbing … I mean, is there …' She looked back at Enid.

'Oh, yes, plenty of allegations, but it's so hard to get proof. We have to be very careful. You see, it's just a private committee. It's not a parliamentary committee, where there's protection from defamation.'

'I thought you said it was.'

The woman looked grim. 'You wouldn't find a government setting up a committee like Richard's. Too much wrong with its own institutions. It's an Opposition committee made up of a few like-minded politicians, but mainly people from the community trying to protect young children. We've received about thirty-five submissions so far.'

Those last few words quivered in Caitlin's mind, triggering a memory that remained elusive. What was it? Something recent … Oh, God! Brian's words, 'Them men, watching me,' took on a more sinister meaning.

'And Saint Anthony's?'

There was silence for what seemed like minutes.

Gently, she took one of the woman's hands. 'Enid, I know this is hard for you.'

'Do you?' Enid stared at Caitlin with grey eyes, wintery as a June day. 'It has come up. There have been rumours.'

'Rumours about what?'

'Abuse.'

13

Brother Purcell and Peter were ten minutes late.

What if they didn't come? Peter was her only hope of deciphering the code she suspected Sean had hidden in the pages of his comic book. She checked her watch, glanced up at the clock suspended opposite Sydney's Central Station's destination board – wishful thinking; her watch kept perfect time.

Perhaps Peter's appointment at the Dental Hospital had been cancelled. Or had Brother Purcell mentioned their meeting to Brother Finbar and the principal vetoed them coming? A picture flashed into her mind of the principal in his office the day he'd fired her, sitting in his tall, straight-backed chair, eyes shadowed with guile. It was drilled into her subconsciousness as a Baconesque image, a popish study of power, negating all compassion. Brother Purcell would be a welcome companion today for Peter; his warm, friendly spirit would surely help ease the boy's loneliness. But he'd be no match against the principal.

She couldn't afford for her plan to fail. The other schemes that had flitted in and out of her head were useless; even the rash thought of going back to Saint Anthony's, conjuring up more lies to see Peter, would be futile. She'd reached a dead end.

They have to come. They have to. Like a mantra, the words formed silently on her lips while she scanned the people coming from the suburban platforms.

Her heart beat faster. She wanted to go out and pace the concourse, but she had to stay put. It would be too easy to miss them. Brother Purcell mightn't trust her again if he thought she was placing too great a demand on his friendship.

And if he discovered her lies …

She remembered someone once saying, 'Competent liars tell lies with plain words.' She was selfishly inflicting her lies onto a grieving, six-year-old boy – they needed some dressing up. Inside her bag, she fingered the present she'd brought for Peter, supposedly from his half-brother, Brian. Even worse, she'd gone so far as to suggest she might be able to arrange a visit from Brian.

How would she broach her real reason for requesting the meeting with Peter? After all, she hardly knew the boy. More lies would mean navigating a mental minefield. Could any guardian angel erase such black stains from her soul? Desperation can be a demanding ally when you're not too sure of the rules. Yet she couldn't ignore the rumours of abuse at the orphanage, or her growing conviction there was something sinister in Sean's death.

A sudden smile spread over her lips. She'd spotted Brother Purcell's brown shaggy head coming up the escalator behind an elderly couple. She hurried towards him.

'I thought you might have left,' he said with his sweet, lopsided grin as he limped to meet her.

Caitlin shook her head, then looked down at Peter standing close to the brother's side. The boy had never been in her art classes; she'd only seen him in the playground. Except for their difference in age and height, Sean and Peter could have been twins, each with dark navy eyes, thick black eyelashes and fine black eyebrows sweeping up towards straight blond hair.

'Hello, Peter,' she said.

'Hello, Miss.'

No welcoming smile, only silent scrutiny, before his gaze seemed to go past her.

She glanced at the brother, who shrugged.

'Come on, Peter' – tapping the boy on his head – 'we'd better get you a drink.'

The choice at the service bar in the Refreshment Room made Caitlin cringe, but watching Brother Purcell was a treat. Skilfully, he guided Peter past sickly looking doughnuts and iced cakes with silver cachous on top. He ordered a chocolate milkshake for Peter and tea for himself and Caitlin. Caitlin paid for the drinks, which they took to a table in a corner of the large, almost deserted room. Peter chose a seat close to the brother.

Before she'd even stirred her watery tea, Brother Purcell said, 'We can't stay long, Mrs Preece.'

'I'm grateful you came,' she said, opening her bag, which she'd placed on the chair beside her. She took out the comics and slipped them onto her lap. She placed Peter's small, brightly wrapped present near his glass.

His eyes swivelled towards it.

'It's for you, Peter, from your brother, Brian.' Deceitful words to give strength to her plan.

He stopped sucking on his straw and let it slip out of his mouth. He looked quickly from her to the brother.

'That's kind of you, Mrs Preece,' Brother Purcell said.

Under his steadfast gaze, she blinked rapidly, feeling her cheeks flush. His words seemed tinged with something else, his eyebrows pushed into a slight frown. His gaze rested a beat too long on the elegantly wrapped present. But whatever Brother Purcell was thinking, his face was a mask of innocence. Two minds shadowing one another.

'Aren't you going to open it, Peter?'

The boy nodded, his attention fixed on the wrapping. He moved his glass to one side and carefully unwrapped the paper. Dropping his hands onto his lap, he stared at the Matchbox car glinting under the lights.

The brother leant towards him with a smile.

'Peter?'

Caitlin would have missed the 'Thank you' if she hadn't seen the boy's lips move.

She laid the comics she'd brought for him on the table, Sean's on the bottom.

'Do you like comics, Peter?' She heard the grating forced cheerfulness in her voice.

The boy said nothing, his eyes sliding towards the small pile.

'They rarely see them,' said the brother.

'They're harmless.'

Remembering the Batman doll on Sean's grave, not daring to look at Brother Purcell, she said, 'Brian thought you'd like these ones: Batman and Robin, Superman, Spiderman – heroes who solve mysteries.'

She put them next to the car.

The boy stared at her a moment, looked down at the comics, then back at her again.

'They're for you,' she said again.

Peter looked at Brother Purcell.

'To share with your friends,' said the brother, but she could see there was little warmth in the young man's words. He had the protective instincts of a mother hen. His wariness was invading her artless plan. Hedging around him would not be easy.

There was another faint 'Thank you' and a small, dutiful smile from Peter – a smile that illuminated the unique colour of his eyes, and that she hoped might dim the ugliness of her lies.

He fingered the pile, spreading the bright illustrations and titles into a bizarre fan beside the car. She saw him pause, his eyes riveted to the last one, and watched as he pulled Sean's Phantom comic out of the pile.

'When I was little,' she said, 'that was my favourite comic. The mysterious grey Phantom, the skull cave in the jungle and the Witch Doctor with his funny language. Brian was telling me you and Sean had a funny language of your own.'

She waited for his reaction, his blond hair screening his eyes as he inspected the cover of the comic before starting to turn the pages.

Caitlin prodded again, as gently as she could. 'Do you like the Phantom?'

He shrugged, closing the comic, and began to scrape the edge of a fingernail along the table.

Undeterred, she turned back one of the pages and pointed to a balloon with the witch doctor's garbled words. 'Do you know what this one says?'

Peter stared at the paper for what seemed an inordinately long time, as if he was trying to understand what she wanted from him. In the end, her intentions must have seemed as mysterious as the words in the comic. Finally, he shook his head.

'Whatever the witch doctor's saying, it's gobbledygook to me. And I'm sure it is to Brother Purcell.'

'It certainly is,' he said, peering closer. 'I suspect it is just so much nonsense. Who did these drawings?'

But she wasn't listening. All her attention was on the boy.

'I bet you're clever enough to understand what he's saying. And wouldn't it be great to solve the mystery before the Phantom?'

'I don't think there's any mystery to solve. As I said, it's probably just some nonsense.' Brother Purcell looked anxiously down at Peter, at his hands tightly clinched in his lap.

Her opportunity was slipping away. She quickly leant over the table, lowering her voice. 'Shall I tell you a secret, Peter? I think Sean made this comic especially for you.'

But the boy scrambled off his chair. His face had taken on a pinched, set look. Brother Purcell put a protective arm around him, bent down to say something to him, but she couldn't catch the words. Peter nodded. Brother Purcell straightened, pushed his chair back and stood up. His warm and friendly manner had disappeared.

'We have to go,' he said. 'Thank you for the drinks, Mrs Preece. Come on, Peter, we'll get you home.'

She stood up. 'Brother Purcell, you don't understand, I –'

'I'm afraid I do,' he said, picking up the car and dropping it into Peter's pocket. 'Lucifer can still surprise me by the way he charms the most unexpected people.'

'Me too.'

He glared at her. Peter reached for the comics; she intercepted to hand all but Sean's to him.

The boy looked up at her and held out his hand for the last comic.

'Peter, I'm sorry, but I need to keep it for now because I'd like to work out the mystery. I will post it to you.'

Peter went to snatch it from her, but she quickly withdrew it.

'I'll make sure you get it later, Peter,' Brother Purcell said.

When the boy didn't move, the brother took him by the shoulder and firmly turned him towards the tall glass doors.

She called out to apologise again to the two of them, but she was talking to their backs.

14

Caitlin hesitated in the doorway to Richard Brinsmead's office in Parliament House. When she'd rung the day before, Esther had told her he would be back that night from a week campaigning on the far south coast, supporting the local candidates, and that tomorrow would be the first day of a four-week parliamentary sitting.

For a moment, she felt a flush of guilt for barging into his working day, but events had moved quickly since he had invited her to join his Children's Custodial Care Committee. After the debacle with Brother Purcell and fruitless hours trying to decode Sean's comic, she could think of no other person to whom she could turn.

Waking with a start that morning to the first streaks of dawn, her initial recollection was of a masked child. Had it been the end of a dream or the beginning of something else? Throughout the morning, sifting through the gauzy trail of her subconscious, the image of Tim kept haunting her: a little boy with a cherubic face who hid behind a clown's mask. Why was he in foster care? Could there be any connection between his behaviour and what she now proposed to put to Richard? Why had Tim been placed with Enid?

It would be invaluable for his committee to follow the case of a boy like Tim; to get information on why Sean and Peter had been taken from Enid and placed at Saint Anthony's; to perhaps even gain access to the school, and if necessary to challenge the Government on the floor of the of the House. Enid had said that Richard would not flinch from exposing the facts or who was responsible, no matter who or what they were.

Yet Caitlin knew that talking to Richard was a risk. Getting this close to the charismatic politician could stir up emotions she'd pushed to the background when she'd married Martin.

Quelling her hesitation, she entered the outer office, where there were three desks attended by staff. Ahead of her was a door with a metal plate that bore Richard's name.

One of the doors to her left opened and Esther Fisk came out. She greeted Caitlin warmly.

'Richard told me you were coming in. By the way, he has a meeting with a Catholic priest after Question Time. He has arranged for you to sit in on it. He's busy, but I'm sure he'd like to say a quick hello.' She knocked softly on the door, calling, 'Mrs Preece is here.'

Richard glanced up as Caitlin entered the room, his intent expression melting into a smile. 'Caitlin!'

He pushed back his chair and came out from behind the desk. She walked towards him – another twinge of guilt when she saw how tired he looked.

'Not a good time?'

'Question Time's at 2.15, and I've just got notice the Premier's making a ministerial statement on the building industry. I have to reply.'

'Don't mind me, I'll wait.'

His telephone rang.

She silently cursed the object. There was an edge to the shorthand sentences he dealt to the caller, his hands sorting through papers while he spoke.

A bell suddenly rang through the large office, making Caitlin start.

Richard hung up the phone.

'What was that for?' Caitlin asked.

Before he could answer, the bell rang again.

A frown pinched between his eyes. He raised his voice over the din. 'Fifteen minutes to Question Time; there'll be one more. You can stay here or come down and sit in the Speaker's Gallery. On second thoughts, I'm not sure what Eccles – he is the Member who has brought Father Griffin in – has arranged for him to do while he is waiting. I think Eccles had him in for lunch. But if so, he is in for a rather tedious wait, so if you see him – there surely can't be too many priests around – chat to him, would you? Make sure he doesn't leave. I need the information I hope he'll give me, urgently. Time's running out to raise this in the House before the election is called.'

He gathered his papers and, to the sound of the bells ringing out a third time, strode towards the door.

She followed him. 'But Richard, I –'

A staffer rushed in, holding out a sheaf of papers. 'These are the figures you wanted.'

Caitlin squeezed back from the doorway to let the young man pass.

'Good work, John,' Richard said. 'Let's go.'

She was almost running to keep up with him; sweeping past cream walls, open doors, shut doors. Between shortening breaths, she said, 'Are your days always so frantic?'

He shook his head, grinning at her as they descended a broad flight of stairs. 'Today's a holiday compared to some.'

Down the stairs, across the main vestibule, through an impressive set of glass-panelled doors, she found herself outside the Legislative Assembly Chamber.

'I'll stay here,' she said. 'You won't forget me?'

'How could I?' he said, drawing her away from the open doors to the Chamber.

Politicians jostled, laughing, crowding past them to enter the Chamber: Government to the right, Opposition to the left.

Richard moved closer to the doors but turned back when a dark-suited man gripped his arm, manoeuvring himself between Richard and Caitlin. Caitlin couldn't hear their whispered conversation.

Richard's staffer, John, suddenly joined them again. 'The Premier's coming, Mr Brinsmead.'

Richard nodded and entered the Chamber.

With a sharp stare, as if she were deliberately keeping him from the scene of battle, John said, 'An attendant will take you to the Speaker's Gallery, Mrs Preece. If you'd like to sit down, you can wait over there.'

He nodded in the direction of a priest sitting on a green leather bench, then followed Richard.

At that moment, a loud voice from somewhere nearby called out, 'Make way for Mr Speaker' – as if God had spoken.

The milling figures still in the vestibule pushed her back against the cream walls. The black-uniformed figure of the Sergeant-at-Arms, with the long, gold mace over one shoulder, marched out from a door to her right, followed by the small, bewigged, black-robed figure of the Speaker. The brief, theatrical parade disappeared into the Government side of the Chamber.

Gradually the crush of bodies cleared. Caitlin went and sat down near the priest. The dark-suited politician who'd spoken to Richard seemed to be placating him.

'Father, I have to go into the Chamber,' she heard him say, 'but Mr Brinsmead's staffer has organised a time for you to see him. Don't worry … Yes, this afternoon. Yes, I'm sure, you're doing the right thing. No, you can trust him. His Children's Committee is doing excellent work. If you have any other questions, you can see me before you leave.' The member smiled, then nodded absently at Caitlin before walking away.

She glanced at the priest. About forty, with anxiety etched on his chiselled face. His eyes were fixed on the Chamber's now closed glass-panelled doors, which restricted vision and muffled most of what was being said. However, being seated directly opposite the doors onto the Opposition side of the chamber he could easily see Richard when he was on his feet and was clearly willing whatever was happening inside to finish quickly. Any movement beyond the glass panels triggered a fluttering counter movement from his thin hands. After ten minutes or so when Richard rose to speak, presumably to answer the ministerial statement, the priest stood too, as if time was battling patience, and began pacing the vestibule.

Minutes later, when Richard had finished speaking, the priest sat down again, rubbing his hands up and down the shiny black weave of his trousers as if to shave off some neurosis within.

Caitlin desperately wanted to speak to him about Richard's committee, but it didn't seem like the right moment.

Eventually, the doors leading to the main vestibule swung open and an attendant approached her. 'Mrs Preece?'

'Yes.'

'I'll show you up to the Speaker's Gallery.'

'Is there somewhere more private I can wait for Mr Brinsmead? Perhaps somewhere more comfortable where we can both wait?' She smiled at the priest. 'I understand you're also waiting for Mr Brinsmead?'

The priest remained silent.

'Well, there's a tearoom at the top of the stairs,' the attendant said.

She looked at the priest. 'Would you like a cup of tea, Father? Question Time will be at least another forty minutes.'

He hesitated, as if the question were full of problems. Then, with a nervous smile, he said, 'Yes, thank you, if the attendant tells Mr Eccles' staff where I am. I'm Father Griffin.'

The attendant nodded and together they left the vestibule.

But halfway up the stairs, the priest stopped. Caitlin glanced at him. He was gazing at her with a quizzical expression.

'Do you also have an interest in Mr Brinsmead's Children's Custodial Care Committee?' The words tightened with every syllable.

'I'm a member of the Committee. What particular aspects of custodial care are you interested in, Father?'

His eyes slid away. Perhaps the question was too complex for a simple answer.

At the top of the stairs a waiter showed them to a table in the small, empty tearoom. It was a welcome interruption.

■

In the dreary room, Father Griffin seemed uneasy, shifting on his chair. After desultory conversation, during which Caitlin had drawn extensively on her school years at Saint Brigid's, she went to Richard's office to ask whether he had returned from Question Time, only to be told that he had been delayed by an urgency motion. An hour was dragging into two. If Richard didn't come soon …

Seated back in the tearoom, she tried another smile of reassurance. 'Mr Brinsmead shouldn't be long now, Father. His staff told me he knows you're waiting and sends his apologies.'

She cast her eyes around the small room, but there was nothing left of interest – certainly nothing aesthetically inspiring, unless she were to repeat her thoughts on the sepia photographs on the cream walls depicting Macquarie Street with carriages and early model cars. And what can you say to a person who seems to be consumed by some inner demon?

This priest, after his first attempt to find out who she was and where she fitted in, had kept silent counsel. She had responded politely and diplomatically, mentioning her work at Saint Anthony's, leading on to Enid's foster work and Richard's committee. Now, it was as if she were talking to a ghost who had stepped out of those ageing photographs.

She peered into her china cup, contemplating the pattern of the dregs.

'Would you like more tea, Father?'

He shook his head. Tea the great reviver, but not for words. She could feel her smile falter as Father Griffin suddenly reached for his mackintosh, pleating his hands into its folds.

She stood up. 'He will be here soon, Father.'

But the priest pushed back his chair and stood up.

'I'm not sure I can wait much longer. Perhaps I can come back another time. I thought Mr Eccles said I would see Mr Brinsmead after Question Time. He said Question Time took about forty-five minutes.' He looked at his watch. 'It's well after that now.'

'Wait, Father. Please wait. I'll see if I can find Esther Fiske. She's Mr Brinsmead's researcher and the secretary of the Children's Committee.'

He stared at her. 'I know who she is. Mr Eccles mentioned her.'

Her hands gripped the back of her chair.

'Yes, Father, but Esther will know where to find him. Please wait, it won't take me a moment. He knows how important this meeting is to you – as important as it is to him.' She took a deep breath. She could hear herself gabbling. 'You've been very patient. Mr Brinsmead will appreciate it.'

The priest's hand dropped away from his mackintosh.

'I won't be long, Father.' She ran out, mouthing silent curses all the way down the long corridor. Reaching Richard's rooms, she glanced at the woman working nearest the door. 'Esther Fiske's office?'

The woman looked up, startled. She pointed behind her. Caitlin zigzagged around the desks, pushed open a half-closed door. Esther saw her and smiled, holding up a hand. Caitlin, trying to slow her ragged breathing, gestured with two fingers to cut the telephone call. Esther frowned and nodded.

'Doesn't matter if it's still in draft form. Just send it up anyway.' She put down the telephone.

'Come quickly, talk to this priest.'

Esther raised her eyebrows. 'Father Griffin?'

'Yes.'

Esther stared at her. 'His appointment is for 4.30, so Richard's only a few minutes late. How long has he been waiting? Are you alright?'

Shaking her head, Caitlin flattened her palms on the desk. 'He's been here since before Question Time. Came in with a Mr Eccles. He's about to leave, won't wait.'

Esther gestured towards the papers strewn over the desk. 'I'm swamped. Tell Judy on the front desk to put him in Richard's office. He certainly wants to talk to him.'

'No, Esther, you have to come. He's been waiting nearly two hours. I'm sure he thinks Richard's fobbed him off. He might even be gone by now.'

'Damn! Eccles shouldn't have got him in so early.' Esther swung her chair away from the desk. 'Where is he?'

'In the tearoom down the corridor,' Caitlin said.

By the look on Esther's face, asking her to sweet-talk a jittery priest might not have been such a brilliant idea. Caitlin willed the thought away as they hurried back along the corridor.

She stopped in the open doorway of the tearoom, Esther cannoning into her.

'Oh, Christ!' Her heart lurched as her eyes fixed on the priest's empty chair. She spun around. 'Esther, he's ...'

With relief, she caught sight of the priest standing in the opposite corner, peering at one of the sepia photographs.

■

Looking just like two old friends deep in conversation, Father Griffin stood with Richard at his office window overlooking the Domain Park behind Parliament House.

Caitlin marvelled at the agility of Richard's mind. Within the last three hours, the man had responded to a ministerial statement, debated an urgency motion on the intricacies of a government tendering process, then held a press conference, convinced Father Griffin to agree to her sitting in on their meeting (insisting she was a highly valued member of the committee, et cetera), and was now skilfully settling the man down in preparation to probe whatever might be drawn from him. She listened as Richard told the priest about Governor Macquarie's ideas in the days when open space was not a high priority; how dedicated parks would civilise a disparate population, steer them to a social order of streets and buildings … All this while waiting for the tea and coffee he'd ordered from Room Service, instead of using the kitchenette in the office.

She couldn't see the priest's face, but already his shoulders seemed to have relaxed under his black suit. His voice, as he asked the odd question, had lost the hard edge of anxiety.

The door opened and Esther entered the room with a waiter. When the men turned from the window and sat down, any observer would have thought they were indeed good friends: a priest and a politician working together to stop one of the most heinous crimes against humanity.

As Esther poured tea and coffee and offered biscuits, Caitlin studied Richard. Do politicians need to be actors? A provocative thought. He spoke as if he were pulling a curtain closed on one idea and opening it to reveal another. What was the psyche behind that face? A false persona?

She realised her tangential thoughts had drawn her attention away from what was happening in the conversation.

'Saint Barnaba's Orphanage,' Richard was saying, 'not far from Brisbane?'

'About a mile,' said the priest.

'How long was your chaplaincy there?'

'Nearly five years.' He hesitated, grey eyes contemplative, before lowering his head. 'Until I became an embarrassment to my bishop.'

'Bishop Declan?'

Father Griffin looked up. 'You know him?'

Richard nodded. 'Not as a politician; one of my aunts lived in his diocese.'

'Then you understand,' the priest said in a quiet voice.

Richard nodded again.

'The bishop kept saying he'd look into my allegations. After months, his answer was to send me to Sydney – to Surry Hills.'

'Ian, we've gone through dozens of cases, and I can assure you the abuse is not confined to the Catholic Church,' Richard said, 'although the percentages are higher than in any other Church or group we've canvassed.'

Caitlin looked at the priest, at the darkening grey of his eyes that seemed to veil many thoughts.

'Since hearing of these allegations' – he stole an uneasy glance at Richard – 'putting this collar on every day, standing in the pulpit, facing a sea of parishioners who view us as Christ's ambassadors, I feel a fraud. I think of the exceptional degree of trust placed in us broken, with fearful consequences.'

'This abuse of children's innocence is seeping into society like an epidemic,' Richard said, 'yet the Church hierarchy does nothing, takes no legal responsibility.'

Caitlin followed the priest's gaze, out to the canopy of Moreton Bay fig trees on the perimeter of the Domain, to the elegant, white ibises with their long, curved beaks picking at the grass in their darkening shadows.

'That is true – a very long tradition of covering up horrific acts, leaving boys suffering depression from assaults, rapes. And the suicides.' The priest's pain seemed ingrained in every word he uttered. 'I can't condone the Church for the harm any priest has done, for abrogating its responsibility to God.'

Anger shook Caitlin's voice as she said, 'You mean like moving priests from parish to parish, where the abuse continues?'

He looked down at his hands, which were again kneading his trousers. 'Yes, well, perhaps the perception was that it's a moral –'

'Father, it's a criminal one,' she said, softly this time.

Stunned silence.

After a moment, when he stared at her, a look of steel glinted in his grey eyes. 'That's why we have to stop it, this dogma of power and sex! For a thousand years, the Church has been dominated by notions of power – power that lies in the secrecy surrounding its innermost workings, secrecy that is used to protect the good name of the Church when it should be used to purge the problem.' A surprising, sardonic half-smile flitted over his face.

'There must be others motivated to do something?' Richard said, grimacing.

'Yes, but sadly we are the heretics. Exposing the problem is seen as attacking the Church, sensationalising something they see as an occasional problem.'

'But it isn't,' Caitlin broke in again.

'No. Things must change. And Catholics should look to the Pope for these changes,' the priest said. 'Yet on sexual abuse of minors, there has been an appalling lack of guidance, a shield for those who do not want to face the truth and for those who see facing the truth as not being in the interests of the Church.'

'So, children suffer.'

Father Griffin gazed at her. 'I was a very immature fourteen when I entered the seminary. As an adolescent in such an environment, I had my first experience of predatory priests. You have to learn to out-fox the foxes. But at that age, I didn't really understand. In Indooroopilly, in Queensland, I became aware of priests who should never have been ordained, priests with unhealthy ideas of power and sex.'

He leant forward to take a quick sip of his coffee, the cup clattering against the saucer, his spoon.

'There were rumours about a priest, a school chaplain from a neighbouring parish. A mother, whose son was abused by the priest, through the intervention of a mutual acquaintance, came to see me. I couldn't believe it.'

He paused. Two deep lines creased his forehead.

'Then the mother told me of another family who wanted to talk to me. Their nine-year-old son was abused by the same priest. It had been going on for five years. He was the wolf; I was the gatekeeper. The parents broke down and wept ...' There was profound sadness in Father Griffin's voice as his words trailed away.

'In my calling,' he said, 'many people, even those of the Catholic faith, think we're simple minded, taking on what they see as a cosy sinecure from normal life. But it's not; it can be challenging. When I spoke to that priest, of course he denied everything, but I was finally convinced those mothers' claims were true. Over time, by discreet inquiry, others came forward. More priests were involved. That's when I decided to speak to Bishop Declan.'

In a quiet voice Richard said, 'Did you say "priests"?'

The father stared at him; his hands clenched into fists on his knees. With an abrupt nod of his head, he looked away, perhaps thinking of secrets too shocking to reveal.

Caitlin glanced at Richard, then Esther, their faces mirroring the priest's distress.

Richard broke the silence. 'Ian, we know this is very difficult for you,'

No response.

Richard's voice fell to a murmur. 'Why did you come to me?'

The man cleared his throat. 'I heard you could be trusted.'

'Then you have to trust that I will only use whatever you authorise. I can shield my sources, Ian, but unless I can name names, reveal the circumstances, provide factual evidence, it will have no credibility. I'm protected by parliamentary privilege, but that doesn't protect you or anyone else. We need something to give to the police; they're the ones who can take this further.'

In her imagination, Caitlin traced a ghostly paintbrush over the priest's face: those fine contours, the dark hollows under those wide grey eyes, full of anguish. She understood now he was far more of a warrior, a warrior for the children, than she had first assumed. *Yet …*

Tiny beads of perspiration glistened in his russet eyebrows as he bowed his head.

She leant towards him her voice charged with emotion. 'Father, what you have been describing is a scandal of individuals. But the cover up is the greater scandal, one which involves the Church at every level. It is greater than the individual crime. Children live every day, every night with fear, shame and degradation. If people who think like us don't do something, what sort of people are we?'

Richard stood up and walked to the window. Caitlin followed his gaze across Woolloomooloo Bay, the rays of the setting sun transforming the windows of the buildings on the ridge beyond into pinpoints of gold. Behind that gold veneer lay the drugs and prostitution that festered in Kings Cross every night.

'We search for truth, yet the tragedy for many children is that it manifests too late.' His words were barely audible. 'But the seekers of truth need to be careful. Those who abuse children are not run-of-the-mill criminals. Outwardly they seem to lead ordinary lives; they're priests, businessmen, civic leaders – legitimate roles masking evil.

'A colleague I've been corresponding with sent me reports from a Baltimore paper covering the unsolved murder of a twenty-six-year-old nun. Sister Cathy Cesnik died of blunt-force trauma to the side of her head and another to the back of her skull. She was dumped on a garbage heap in November 1969. She was a teacher at a Catholic high school.'

The anger in his voice resonated throughout the room, seeming even to silence the frenetic birdcalls in the Moreton Bay fig trees outside.

'The chief suspect was a Father Maskell who served as chaplain at the nun's school.'

No one spoke.

Richard turned back to his visitor with a grim expression.

'Three or four girls who were being abused by a priest had gone to Sister Cathy for help. She knew of the abuse taking place. No question.'

Father Griffin's face had turned deathly white.

It seemed like minutes passed before the priest spoke. 'Yes, you're correct. It is a failing of the Church hierarchy, but I can only deal with the priests I know about. I lost track of one, Donald Taylor, after he left his parish at Toowoomba. But I know of one here in Sydney at Enmore, Saint Anthony's Orphanage. Ted MacManus.'

15

Martin waved a hand towards the breakfast things spread over the kitchen table. 'What brought this on?'

'I thought it'd be a nice change to sit down together and eat a civilised meal,' Caitlin said. 'We've hardly seen one another these last few weeks.'

'True, but I did warn you, this is what it's going to be like for the next few months, with the preselection and the election – in November, probably.'

Deep in thought, she poured him a cup of tea. It slopped over the saucer, marking a dark patch on his tartan placemat.

'Damn!' She grabbed for a cloth from the sink.

When she turned back, Martin was watching her with a quizzical expression, as if waiting for her to pick up on what he'd just said.

She sat down, leaning an elbow on the table to look out at the garden clothed in its winter garb, at the large azalea bush with its white bouquet of flowers. Feeling her husband's eyes still on her, she glanced across at him.

'What is it?' she said, jerking her head up, as he reached over to lift a strand of hair off her cheek, hooking it behind her left ear.

'Darling, your face is a printed page.'

'It's nothing, really.'

Nothing, when her mind was obsessed with what she had heard in Richard's office, Father Griffin's shocking revelations. The chilling fact that MacManus was a known paedophile confirmed at least some of her suspicions about Sean's death, though she still doubted he could be directly involved. But if not him, who else? She was beginning to share Richard's concerns that her amateur sleuthing could put her life in danger.

Martin shrugged and returned to his newspaper; his face relaxed. Even the tiny lines of tension between his eyes, which had almost become a permanent feature over the recent busy months, were gone.

For a moment, she felt misgivings about destroying his sense of calm. How could she tell him about the murky waters she was delving into? But she had to take advantage of an opportunity that might not come again for weeks. For now, talking with him about politics, no matter how much she detested it, seemed the only path open to her.

'Have they set a date for the preselection?'

'The twenty-sixth of July at head office in Ash Street, or it may be at Hunters Hill RSL. That's where Marjorie would like it to be held.'

'I suppose she's ringing you every day?' A slight waspishness caught the edge of her laugh.

He sighed. 'Well, you know what she's like, a great heart and a diligent secretary for the Electoral Conference, but you do need earplugs to get any peace. Marjorie, politics – not good subjects at breakfast. How's the work going for your exhibition?'

'I'll be lucky if I'm not touching up some of the paintings while they're being hung. And to complicate matters, Lexy told me yesterday that Jan de Vere is stopping off in Sydney on his way back to London. He wants to talk to her about being his Australian agent to promote the work of Clifford Possum Tjapaltjarri. And' – there was a lift in her voice – 'he wants to see my exhibition.'

Martin looked puzzled. 'Who's de Vere, and this Clifford Possum what's his name?'

She closed her eyes for a second. With a shadow of a smile, she said, as if speaking to a child, 'De Vere is the Rothschild among European art dealers. And Possum is one of the most exciting talents to come out of the Papunya Tula School of Aboriginal "dot and circle" painters.'

'I see. So, when is this de Vere coming?'

'Lexy said around mid-July.'

'Not the fourteenth, I hope.'

'Why?'

'There's the possibility of a fundraising dinner at the Hilton for the State campaign. If so, we'll be on the Prime Minister's table.'

She gazed at her husband. Was this to be her future, her own career crushed between his legal and political landscapes? She'd go to the dinner, but …

'Well,' she said, threading out the moment to lend maximum impact to her concession, 'If you really want me to go.'

'I do. I know it won't be easy, Caitlin. There'll be little wit or wisdom; politics and sport will dominate the table conversation. But Richard will be there. You can talk about your work and discuss your next exhibition with him.'

His words had slipped out with no thought of what they might mean to her. All morning, stressful thoughts of Sean and

MacManus had crowded her mind. Now, Martin's attempt to encourage her to view the dinner with more enthusiasm triggered emotional thoughts. His reference to Richard brought memories flooding back of a time when her parents were still living, when the world seemed bright and hopeful.

Six years ago, at her first exhibition, welcoming light had spilled from Lexy's Rossiter Gallery, embracing the people thronging the pavement as they pushed their way into the noisy, crowded rooms of the Paddington terrace. Caitlin wove in and out of the patrons, looking for Lexy, who when she found her, assured her no one had thrown wine at her work or screamed 'pornography'. The lesbian tag was inevitably simmering away, although with all that naked flesh adorning the gallery walls, it was to be expected.

Lexy had invited Richard, as both the newly elected Member of Parliament for the area and a good friend, to open the exhibition. Caitlin's first memory of Richard was his easy smile that brightened his eyes to the azure of a summer sky, transforming his pleasant face into one of extraordinary charm.

Fragments of his speech lingered with her: 'Caitlin's passion to create canvases confronting the sensibility of the eye, the spirit …'

He stood next to the huge figure of a nude woman sprawled open-legged on a canvas, tiny men running across luscious, cream-tinted thighs in tendrils of ant-like queues, up into her dark forest of warmth.

His speech finished with the immortal quote from Delacroix: 'The last brush stroke of a painting is done by God.'

Silence had hung in the air for a moment before appreciative murmurs rose from the crowd. Surprise, embarrassment, perhaps even disapproval, were washed away by the good humour stimulated by wine and the evening's bon vivant.

It was at that moment she'd first wondered, is this a man I could truly love?

Back at the breakfast table, intrusive bodily sensations seeped from the recesses of her mind. The rustle of his newspaper brought her awareness back to Martin, his eyes fixed on her.

'Caitlin? Away with the fairies?'

'Wishful thinking.'

She fiddled with the fringe of her placemat. She couldn't put it off any longer. It was a simple question, a question about evidence, but she had to be careful not to betray Richard or Father Griffin's trust, careful to avoid being trapped in the minefield of her husband's legal jargon.

She glanced across at him, trying to appear as if a flash of thought had just come to her. 'Martin, if someone tells you something, which if true could constitute a serious criminal offence, how would you assess its credibility?'

'In my territory now,' he said, raising his eyebrows. 'What are the facts?'

'Well, say there are allegations of sexual misconduct. What sort of evidence would you need to prove an act or acts had taken place?'

He shrugged. 'You'd have to be more specific. Without knowing the full facts, or at least some of the facts, I couldn't even begin to address the question.'

He took a sip of his tea.

Oh, God, he's not going to like this. She took some quick breaths to soothe the fast beats of her heart.

'Say it's about the abuse of a child.'

He spluttered tea into his cup. She inwardly flinched as his brown eyes pierced hers like searchlights.

'Caitlin, I hope this isn't another crazy crusade of yours. I haven't forgotten what you said at our dinner party a few weeks ago. You sounded the regular little zealot. Is this what you've been up to?'

'Please, just listen,' she said, gripping one of his hands, digging crescent moons into his skin.

He nodded, gently pushing her hand away. 'Well, go on. Tell me. It has to be something more than just a vague assertion.'

'I was at a meeting the other day,' she said, fiddling again with her mat.

'And?'

'It's confidential. I can't name names.'

He raised his hands in a gesture of mock submission. 'Go on.'

'During the discussion, someone spoke about certain Catholic priests in Queensland who have been identified as paedophiles.'

He sighed. 'Caitlin, you realise your commitment to confidentiality makes this very difficult.'

'Yes, I know.' She paused for a second. 'Say one of those priests has been relocated to Sydney, which seems to have been the response from the Church. Shouldn't they be stopped from offending again, brought to justice?'

'The only advice I can give is to tell you again that I would need to know exactly the nature of the allegations: who these priests are, what they have done, where they have come from, where they are now; what, if anything, has been the Church's disciplinary response? And who is acting on behalf of the Church?'

'I understand most of that is documented.'

'Well, the next step would be to make a formal complaint so that a proper forensic investigation of the facts can be conducted, and that's a role for the police. But I warn you, Caitlin, and whomever you've been talking to, tackling the Church is a formidable task. They command a wide and powerful sphere of influence.' He smiled. 'The flock has a presence in every level of government: in the Labor Party, the public service, the law, the police, you name it.'

'The Liberal Party?'

'Only recently. It's been entrenched in the Labor Party for years. The Irish connection.'

'I feel I have to do something. What should I do?'

'There is nothing you can do. Whoever claims to have this information is the only person who can place it before the appropriate authorities.'

'But you just said that even in the police force there could be people who would obstruct any investigation.'

'That's right, but there is no other way. You see, many lay Catholics believe the Church must be protected from scandal, from the failings of the odd priest.'

She was overcome by a wave of depression. She knew everything Martin had said was reasonable. Yet to follow his advice would mean abandoning Sean, the other children, and giving up her 'crusade', if that's what it was. Utter emptiness grasped her, a feeling in conflict with the normal tenor of her existence. Until recently her life had been rich and full. 'And if no one does anything, what happens to the victims?'

'History tells us that every society, through every age, despite every endeavour, has thrown up too many victims.' He pushed his cup away. 'The good people in society do everything they can, unfortunately it's never enough.'

A gust of wind shook the azalea outside and a shower of petals fluttered down. Were the children to be abandoned as easily?

16

Caitlin stood on the verandah of MacManus' presbytery, unsure of what she was going to say. Questions tumbled around in her mind, clouded by shock and anger. Having learnt of his paedophile activities in Queensland, she had to challenge him again over his obfuscation of his knowledge of Sean's scarf, force him to admit that he was one of the last people to see the boy alive.

Thoughts of Sean meeting a killer on that lonely mountain track, Richard's grim warning and Martin's cautionary advice argued for her to leave this place. But, after another second of hesitation, she placed a finger on the electric bell and pushed.

The muffled slam of a door echoed deep within, sounds of feet coming closer. A key scratched in the lock and the doorknob rattled. Caitlin fastened her eyes to it, watched its slow turn. The door opened a few inches.

A middle-aged woman in a floral apron stared back at her.

'Good morning, can I help you?' The expression on her plain, pale face with its faint pattern of broken veins suggested she wished to do nothing of the kind.

Caitlin smiled. 'I would like to speak to Father MacManus.'

The woman's eyes slid sideways, past Caitlin's shoulder to Saint Anthony's school, before returning to her. 'He's stepped out for a short while.'

'May I wait?'

She nodded, moving back to open the door just enough to allow Caitlin to enter.

The pungent smell of disinfectant and floor wax carried on a draught of cold stale air assailed Caitlin as she stepped into a bare hall, furnished with only a wooden hat stand and a tinted print of Saint Anthony for relief. The housekeeper closed the door quietly behind her. Caitlin wondered if laughter or even loud voices ever intruded into the space.

Opening the first door on her right, the housekeeper said, 'You can wait here in the parlour.'

'Will Father MacManus be long?'

'I'm not sure. He was in a bit of a flutter when he left, but I expect he'll be in for his lunch at 12.30.'

Caitlin nodded. The woman closed the door behind her. Caitlin listened to her footsteps on the linoleum fade down the hallway, then the muffled sound of another door closing.

She gazed around the room, feeling she'd entered a time warp: no comforts, austere, uninviting. She guessed there had been few changes from one parish priest to the next. Lace curtains like weary sentinels framed tall, narrow, Victorian windows. Four ageing stuffed chairs were grouped around a low wooden table set with a yellowing crotched doily. On a heavy oak sideboard stood a glass bowl of daisies, shrinking in discoloured water; alongside it, copies of *The Catholic Weekly*. Her eyes lingered for some seconds on the large, gaudy print of the Sacred Heart above the sideboard. Raising her eyebrows, she asked the long, sad face, 'Atonement?'

Silence pressed in on her. She slowly circled the room several times. On an impulse, she stopped at the door, opened it and peered up and down the hall. Faint sounds of clattering saucepans came from the kitchen. The housekeeper must be busy preparing lunch. From the smells, she dreaded to think what it might be.

She stared at a closed door on the opposite side of the hall.

Why not? she thought. Everyone has secrets, a vacant room. When he comes, he'll have me out of here fast enough.

Shutting the door of the parlour quietly behind her, she tip-toed across the hall, carefully turned the heavy, brass door handle and pushed. Softly, she closed the door behind her and scanned the room: his study.

That faint smell of disinfectant lingered here as well, accentuating the dreariness. On the far side of the room stood a small bookcase packed with books, to her left, positioned to catch the light from the only window, stood a plain oak desk. On each side of the window, more ancient lace curtains hung like thick cobwebs. Through the not-so-clean panes, she could see a stretch of grass and distant peppercorn trees screening the outline of Saint Anthony's.

Showing its age, the house creaked around her. Outside, she could hear the low-pitched but distinct sounds of normal people doing normal things. Standing there, an idea of what this priest might hide within those walls began to form in her mind.

She scanned the shelves of the bookcase: books of theology that appeared not to have been disturbed for years, passed on untouched by predecessors, perhaps.

Quickly walking back to the door, she opened it an inch or two. She listened, trying to interpret the noises of the house, weighing up her opportunity. The barely audible sounds of the housekeeper's culinary pursuits still emanated from the kitchen. She glanced at her watch: 11.45, getting close to the father's lunchtime? She hoped he wouldn't be back early.

She shut the door, crossed swiftly to the desk and dropped her tote bag on the floor. Pulling the brown, cracked leather chair out of her way, she saw three small drawers each side, with a wider one in the centre. She opened it and found it full of neat piles of paper, envelopes, a collection of ballpoint pens, stamps in a glass bowl and other paraphernalia connected with his parish duties.

She pulled out the drawers on her left. The tidiness didn't extend beyond the necessity of daily routine: back copies of *The Catholic Weekly*, pamphlets, odd bits and pieces of church detritus. The random array betrayed the faltering processes of a weary mind.

She started on the other three drawers. The top one was empty except for tiny, itchy-looking balls of fluff. With grim irony the thought flashed through her mind that this must be a *very* busy man, and she smiled and shook her head. When she pulled at the second drawer, her hand jarred at the shock of resistance. She tried the lower one. Nothing much there, either. She went back to the middle drawer, pulled at it again, hoping it was just stuck. It didn't move.

She listened for any sound in the hall before sitting in the chair to study the desk.

'You won't notice a few more scars,' she whispered.

Hoping to free up the drawer, she braced herself against the back of the chair and rammed a boot heel against one end of the drawer then the other in an effort to loosen it. She listened for a moment, then, leaning down, grabbed the drawer's curved metal handle and pulled hard. It still wouldn't budge, secure against prying eyes. *Christ!* She needed the key.

Her eyes swept the top of the desk. It was neat, almost bare: just a telephone, an inkstand with double inkwells, a couple of pens and more fast-fading daisies in a cut-glass vase. A brass lamp with a green shade stood beside a small pile of church newsletters. She lifted the lamp, the telephone, even the daisies. She picked up the pile of newsletters with trembling hands and gave them a good shake, tipped the ink stand far enough to run her fingers underneath. Nothing.

She turned her attention to the bookcase. Bloody hell, she thought, all these books. A hopeless task, with time ticking away.

Somehow, she needed to find her way into MacManus' mindset. How imaginative would he be? His habits suggested a dichotomy between neatness and carelessness: his hiding spot would be safe enough not to worry about an inquisitive housekeeper, but not so safe that it was difficult for him to access. She felt sure the answer lay somehow with the desk itself.

She rubbed her wet palms down the front of her jeans and took long, slow breaths, forcing herself to concentrate. It would be something obvious. She ran her gaze over each article on the desk again. She stared at the ink stand, then carefully lifted each inkwell from its recess to glare into the space underneath before replacing them. MacManus had been more creative than she'd thought.

Or had he? She peered closer. The tiny nob on the lid of the right inkwell was shinier than its companion. On opening it, the inkwell appeared empty, but when she felt inside, her fingertip met the coldness of a key.

It took three tries before her shaking fingers could fit the key into the lock. Once in, it turned easily, as if familiar with the motion.

She lifted out a standard sized envelope. It was addressed to MacManus. She turned it over. Her eyes widened in surprise at the name on the flap. She looked at the Surry Hills postmark, dated the previous Wednesday. After almost tearing the envelope, it took only seconds to read the short note, written on a Saint Bonaventure letterhead:

4th July 1973
Dear Ted,

I have been in Sydney some weeks and had intended to contact you earlier. I am at Saint Bonaventure in Surry Hills and would very much like to catch up. Being a little out of my depth in this city, something urgent has occurred on which I would like to ask your advice before Saint Bonaventure's Feast Day. Please let me know when you can come and I will make sure I am here.

> *Yours in Jesus Christ,*
> *Ian Griffin*

God! What game was Father Griffin playing? But she didn't have time to think.

She picked up a large manila envelope, no writing on it. Turning it over, she drew out a bundle of glossy black and white photos. Her stomach lurched; she swallowed hard to force down the vomit bubbling at the back of her throat.

A naked young boy's eyes stared at her. He was on his hands and knees; thick fingers were tangled in his hair as a man sodomised him.

She jumped as the front doorbell shrilled through the silence. She heard the soft swishing of the housekeeper's footsteps coming from the kitchen.

Caitlin tried to push the photos back into the envelope, but her damp, shaking fingers fumbled with the flap, unable to properly grip its surface. She heard the housekeeper pass, open the front door; the low murmur of voices, a man's intermingling with the housekeeper's voice.

Grabbing her tote bag, she shoved the photos, note and envelopes inside, closing the leather flap over them.

She heard the housekeeper laugh, the front door close, footsteps coming down the hall.

Hastily, she pushed the drawer closed, turned the key and pulled it out, returning it to the inkwell. Dropping her bag to the floor, she crossed to the bookshelves and took out a book, returned to the desk, sat and opened the book.

The footsteps stopped at the door. She straightened as it opened, suddenly staring into the saturnine face of Brother Loudé.

'Hello, Brother Loudé, how nice to see you. I thought I'd read up on my theology while I wait for Father MacManus.'

17

At first, she didn't take much notice of the large, multicoloured footprints that covered the hallway leading to the stairs of her Rocks studio. But as she clambered up the winding staircase and saw more on the wooden treads, she had to grip the banister to still her shaking hands.

When she reached her studio on the first floor, she stood in the doorway for several seconds, taking in the scene of devastation. A kaleidoscope of colour spread up the four walls like some monster had left its claw prints; paintings despoiled, drawings slashed, paper scrunched into rough balls and tossed everywhere, worktables overturned, tubes of paint trodden into the century-old tallowwood floor.

She took two tentative steps into the room, stooped to pick up a damaged drawing, glanced at it, then let it float from her hand.

The magnitude of the destruction assailed her. She wanted to scream, rant and rave, but her body refused to react. She closed her eyes. When she opened them again and looked around the long room, questions burned into her brain. Why would someone do this? Who would do this? Vandals? But in this part of the city, vandalism was rare. This had to be the work of an entirely different breed of person.

Memories of the incident in the Sacred Heart Church resurfaced. There was no powdery dust on MacManus' suit. Had he deliberately moved under the choir stall, knowing the statue would fall on her? And the visit to his presbytery; was this savage onslaught a reprisal for her intrusion into the priest's dubious proclivities?

Stepping over palettes and tins, paper balls squelching beneath her paint-smeared sneakers, she picked her way to her Victorian writing desk, as if drawn by a magnet. With trembling fingers, she leafed through the pages of her large art books, into which she had interleaved what she had taken from MacManus' study.

'Please, not those,' she muttered.

She stared at a print of Titian's *Madonna and Child in a Landscape*. Griffin's note was gone. She quickly checked the other books. The bastards had taken everything. Sean's comic, his Judas drawing. And the pornographic photographs.

Secret eyes everywhere; *life as it is*. Scanning the silent room, trying to see it through the eyes of the intruders, she was puzzled at the dichotomy of the damage. It was as if two minds had been working out of sync: one calculating, the other seeming to delight in wanton destruction. What had begun as an isolated incident involving a priest now encompassed a wider circle of malevolence. Icy apprehension engulfed her.

A shriek echoed up the stairwell; Mrs Mazzioni's strident tones were followed by quick, heavy footsteps on the staircase.

Moments later, two tall, burly policemen rushed into the room, guns drawn. They stopped abruptly, perhaps taken aback by the gamine figure that confronted them. The scene could have been out of the Keystone Cops, except the guns weren't props and the police were real – too real for Caitlin, who had become wary of the police after her experience with Detective Hurd.

'Who are you?' the older man demanded, lowering his gun.

She stared into his pale blue eyes, cold as marble pebbles; they seemed to want to penetrate her mind.

'Caitlin Cheney,' she said, giving her maiden name to assert her territory.

The policeman scrutinised the studio with an unreadable expression.

'I'm Sergeant Bollard.' He nodded to the other policeman. 'Constable Simmons. The lady downstairs said there was an intruder.'

'"Was" being the operative word. Past tense.' She wasn't sure if her touch of irony went down well with the sergeant. His eyes seemed to hold hers for too long as he roughly pushed his gun back into its leather holster.

He nodded towards her paint-spattered shirt, jeans and hands. 'And what exactly are you doing here, Miss?'

That last word was almost flung at her. She flinched. Did he think she'd just walked in off the streets? This studio had been the one place where she could shut everything out: her life's sanctuary. Now, it felt invaded, all order lost; its very reason for existence being questioned by a stranger.

She saw no kindness in the policeman's blank expression. If he couldn't lift his eyes to the walls, see the destructive images, well … She shrugged, turned away, flinched again as she heard something crunch under his shoes.

'Sergeant,' the constable broke in, 'I've seen Miss Cheney in the café. She's an artist.' His voice shot up a few decibels. 'She rents this studio from Mrs Mazzioni.'

For the first time, Caitlin took in the features of the young constable; they were vaguely familiar.

'Does she, now?' the sergeant said, staring at his colleague as if that idea had not occurred to him. He looked back at Caitlin. 'Do you keep anything of value here? Money?'

'Everything is valuable,' she said in an edgy voice.

'Sergeant, look at this,' the constable said.

Silently cursing Mrs Mazz for calling the police, she watched the sergeant manoeuvre around the debris on the floor.

'Is this yours?' he said.

She nodded.

'I'm no artist, but is that part of it?'

She stepped over to where the policeman stood peering at her largest easel. A low keen escaped her lips. She reached out a shaking hand towards the portrait of Sean that she'd been working on, curled her fingers into a tight fist.

A red cross had been painted diagonally across Sean's face. Each arm of the cross was slashed. A Stanley knife, the blade stuck fast in the wooden struts of the easel, conveyed a grim warning.

She reached out to grasp the knife.

'Don't touch it! We'll dust it for fingerprints.'

She backed away from the canvas. The searing heat of hate – unfamiliar – pulsed through her pain.

After a moment's silence, the sergeant turned his gaze past her, to the far wall of the studio where she had pinned several large charcoal drawings of Sean, along with studies for landscapes and other work for her exhibition. All had been destroyed.

'Is this the first time you've had trouble?' the sergeant asked.

'Yes.'

'Does anyone live on the premises, Miss Cheney?' said the constable.

'Mrs Mazzioni. She has a flat behind the café.'

'Well,' said the sergeant, 'whoever broke in, they weren't vandals. Old building, thick walls, so no noise despite the damage. Picked the lock, knew what they wanted. In and out. This was the work of professionals.'

His footsteps crackled through the debris on the floor as he came nearer.

'Got any enemies, Miss Cheney?'

'Perhaps a disgruntled critic?' the constable quipped, tip-toing over blobs of paint with ballet steps. A blush spread to his rust-coloured hairline as he caught a reprimanding look from his superior.

Shrugging, she asked, 'Are we talking about the art world?'

'Someone doesn't like you.'

A heavy silence fell over them. She looked steadily into the bleak eyes of the sergeant.

He raised his eyebrows at the young policeman, none too subtly. 'We'll file a report. This isn't the sort of crime we get around here. If you think of anything, even the smallest detail would help. And I would get a deadlock on your street door. Here, too,' he said, as he walked out to the landing.

After they'd gone, the studio felt eerily empty, stripped of everything she'd loved. She rubbed at her eyes. A jagged fingernail slid across the edge of one eyelid, catching at a miniscule piece of skin. She cried out at the sharp pinprick of pain. Or was it the pain of what had happened – menaced by faceless thugs who had shredded her life with their destructive search and ruthless threats?

She slumped on the couch, her head in her hands. Surreal impressions of MacManus and Brother Loudé flashed into her mind; photographs in a study desk, the brother's watchful, hooded eyes boring into her from the priest's doorway. Were they in some way responsible? She recalled what Rushton had said about being the Chairman at Saint Anthony's. Another link in the chain of circumstance? But she hadn't seen any reasonable likeness to him in the photographs.

Then, from a deeper layer of her memory, the vision of Sean's Judas drawing emerged. She drew a sharp breath. Could she recall a likeness to Rushton there? Or was she imagining it; was it a conceit driven by her prejudice against the man? She cursed the fact that she could not go back and check.

Caitlin couldn't expunge the thought that there was a connection. He would probably be too clever to be caught in a compromising situation. He was more the puppet master type, controlling the vices of others – an untouchable.

She'd entered a dark, alien world. She raised her tear-filled eyes towards the ravaged drawing of Sean on the wall above her desk.

'You'll never be forgotten,' she murmured.

Turning away, she sidestepped her destroyed work, treading a careful path to her desk. She needed to ring Richard, tell him what had happened: a déjà vu moment, conjuring memories of her call to him on the Monday after she'd left the presbytery. A long silence had filled the line after she'd told him of finding the photographs and Father Griffin's note in MacManus' study.

She had started to gabble something about having to wait longer for MacManus than expected, but her words were cut off.

'What did you do with them?' His words were clipped, with an almost unfriendly edge to them. 'Please, tell me you didn't steal them.'

Dear God! This was a Richard she'd never known: the politician on the attack.

Trying to allay his concerns, she'd said, 'The priest wasn't going to give them to me, was he? And I couldn't ask him. He wasn't there. Richard, it's evidence.'

An exasperated sigh from his end of the line. 'Don't joke, Caitlin. This is serious. What do you think would have happened if he'd caught you?' Another long pause. 'Is that everything?'

'Well, there was something else. Brother Loudé came into the study while I –'

'But you have them?'

'Yes.'

'Destroy them.'

She couldn't believe what he had said.

'Destroy them?'

'That's what I said.' His brittle voice suddenly softened. 'I'm sorry to be so blunt. Things are piling up on me. I'll ring you later. But please, destroy them.'

That was three days ago. And now, she needed his help again. But this time he didn't pick up and she could only leave a message: would he ring her urgently at her studio?

For the next few hours, she tried to clean up the mess, waiting for Richard to call back. By now the café would be closed. Mrs Mazz, after checking to see she was all right, had retreated to her flat.

As the hours passed without hearing from him and the day began to close into twilight, her thoughts became more confused. Richard was no fool. Nor would his passion to sustain the integrity of his

Children's Committee allow any compromise, even for her. Once he knew she hadn't destroyed those photographs and the note, her days on the committee would be over before they had started. Well, the evidence was gone now, but with what consequences?

Any further attempts to clear her thoughts were stopped by a ring on her studio's street door.

The moment she saw Richard, she realised that calling him might not have been a brilliant idea: just another irritant in his busy schedule. His brief hello was inscrutable; was he unsure whether he should be there?

As he stepped into the lit hallway, she noticed the tell-tale signs of fatigue imprinted on his face: dark shadows, lines under his eyes. Was it worry about the campaign or something else?

A strained silence hung between them as they climbed the stairs and entered the studio. The hush continued as his eyes swept slowly from one part of the room to the other, from those angry splashes of colour on every wall to the floor, the torn papers, the slashed canvasses she'd piled near the doorway. Finally, his eyes rested on Sean's portrait, which she'd propped on the sofa. It wasn't difficult to see how it had been damaged.

'What did the police say?'

'They'll file a report, but the chances of identifying the intruders are slim. Professionals, they said.'

She looked away to one of the darkening windows to avoid his sharp glance.

'Have you told Martin?'

Heavy silence.

'You haven't told him, have you?'

She turned to glare at him, not liking his sceptical expression.

'Not yet,' she said, 'but I will.'

'Like the photographs and Father Griffin's note, which I trust you destroyed?'

'I … I didn't destroy them. They've taken them.'

'And have you told him about the statue falling?'

'I haven't had a suitable opportunity. He's always in Chambers or in Court or campaigning. But I will.'

Weariness crept into his voice, as if he knew she was no truth-teller. 'Caitlin, you realise Father MacManus, even Brother Loudé, could be part of a paedophile ring?'

'I was out of the presbytery before the brother suspected anything.'

He was shaking his head. 'You're being naive. Look around this studio. Paedophiles rarely exist alone. Remember what I told you when you came to Parliament House, about the American nun? The priest in that case was part of a ring. Someone wanted those photographs, and they won the jackpot with that note.'

She felt heat colouring her cheeks. 'What are you saying?'

'I'm no detective, but if your intruders didn't know about Father Griffin, they do now.'

She ran her tongue over her dry lips. 'What can you do to protect him?'

'I'm not sure anything can be done. I can't believe you could be so stupid.'

She bridled at his blunt assertion. 'I thought you'd be the one person who'd understand.'

'I'm trying, but my will to eradicate this stain on children's lives doesn't extend to helping you break the law.'

Gazing at him, taking in the intensity of his words, she knew he wouldn't like what she was going to say. 'Well, we should warn Father Griffin.'

'No. We can't talk to him without revealing your role in this. And we certainly can't involve the police. Have you spoken to Quinn?'

'No. I've been flat out finishing the work for Lexy's gallery.'

'First the statue, now your studio. Caitlin, this is getting serious. I implore you: get in touch with Quinn.'

18

Caitlin's hand cramped again. She threw down her paintbrush and flexed her fingers, wincing with pain. She kicked at the boxes of books crowded under her easel.

'I need more bloody space.'

Two long weeks had passed since the intrusion; unfinished landscapes for her exhibition cluttered her home studio. Her studio at The Rocks was still chaotic, with tradesmen in and out like self-appointed tenants.

Martin had been furious when she'd told him about the break-in, his anger coming as something of a surprise. He'd never been that interested in her painting. But she was grateful for his concern and, in a way, it had brought them a little closer. He had even been supportive of her transferring so many of her canvases to her home studio. All the same, it was still a bloody nuisance.

'I need to take a break. Coffee, I need coffee,' she muttered.

She walked along the hallway, trying to ease the stiffness out of her legs. Halfway down the stairs, she paused on the landing to look out the tall feature window. Across the leafy canopy and sea of roofs stretching out in front of her, she could just catch a glimpse of the harbour. A white ribbon of birds stretched across the sky.

Glancing down, she saw Geoff's white van pull into the driveway, arriving sharp on ten o'clock to clean the pool: a refreshing breath of normality. But something caught her eye as she was about to turn away. She pressed her face closer to the windowpane, squinting through her pale reflection. The signwriting on the van was the same as Geoff's, but the driver was a stranger. She watched as he opened the rear doors to take out the swimming pool equipment.

That brief glimpse of an unfamiliar, downturned face triggered a sudden spasm of fear. The patio doors were wide open, her housekeeper and herself, unprotected.

Gripping the window ledge, she chastised herself: 'You're seeing devils everywhere.'

Somewhere outside she heard Sim bark. Not the friendly bark that always greeted Geoff's arrival; a fractious one. Maria's strident voice penetrated the house's silence: 'Sim, Sim, be quiet.' But the barking only became more frenetic.

Another wave of apprehension washed over her. She ran downstairs, her heart pounding, her throat hot and dry. Crossing the living room, she peered around the edge of the curtains. Sunlight on the window and the shimmering refraction from the pool hammered golden glare into her irises. She turned away for a second. When she looked back, shielding her eyes, she could see no sign of the man.

'Is something wrong?'

Startled, Caitlin half fell into a lounge chair, pressing a hand to her heaving chest. She twisted around to see her housekeeper with a wriggling Sim clasped in her arms.

'God, Maria, you gave me a fright.'

'Sorry. That fracas a minute ago was Sim trying to front up to the pool man.' She ruffled the poodle's fluffy grey fur. 'I'll keep him in the kitchen.'

Caitlin nodded. 'Good idea.'

But Sim, with another convulsive wriggle, was determined to jump from Maria's arms, He rushed to the open patio doors, barking furiously.

Maria ran after him. 'That's enough, Sim. In your basket until that man's gone.'

Scooping him up, she hustled the growling pup from the room.

Staring out into the garden, Caitlin saw the maintenance man come into view at the far end of the pool. He seemed more interested in surveying it than cleaning it. She walked outside and crossed the grassy sward to the edge of the water.

He glanced up with a slow smile. 'Beautiful pool, clear as gin.'

'What's happened to Geoff?'

He shrugged. 'They assigned this to me this morning. I'm Rafe.'

He looked around, taking in the sweep of the garden, the pool and the surrounding trees. 'He's got the pick of the jobs looking after this.'

'I'm sure he thinks so, too.' She was relieved by how light she managed to keep her voice.

His gaze finally settled back on her. For a few seconds, his muddy brown eyes stared unblinking into hers. She felt herself go cold.

He laughed. 'Right, better get on with it, hadn't I?'

He picked up a long-handled scoop, dipped it in the water and began to scrape leaves from the bottom of the pool.

Caitlin walked to the far end of the garden and plucked some deadheads off a small camellia bush before sauntering back to the house. Stepping inside, she closed the sliding glass doors behind her, hesitated, then slipped the lock into place.

In the dining room, she said to Maria, 'His name's Rafe. He's filling in for Geoff today.'

Maria nodded, flicked a duster towards the man outside. 'Just as well it's only for today; a stray cat would be friendlier.' She stared at the dust motes settling on the shiny, mahogany dining table. 'Watch out for Sim or he'll be out of the kitchen like a rocket.'

Caitlin made the morning tea, stringing it out to observe from the window what the fellow was doing. Trying to recall Geoff's routine, it looked as if he was competent enough. She had probably overreacted. Even Sim seemed calmer now, showing more interest in the morning tea ritual than what was happening outside, his nose twitching in anticipation of a biscuit or two. By the time they'd finished morning tea, he was sound asleep in his basket, warmed by a patch of morning sun.

Caitlin had just finished the washing up when she heard a low growl behind her. Sim was out of his basket, shattering the peace of the kitchen with furious barking. He rushed at the back door, scratching frantically as if hoping to tunnel under it.

She picked him up, clamping his muzzle with her hand. Walking to the window she glanced out. The garden looked empty, yet she hadn't heard the van drive away. She felt another quick pulse of fear. The fellow must be somewhere at the back of the house. But what was he doing?

Then she remembered, the last step of the maintenance routine was to check the heating equipment, which was in a corner of the garden. She sensed the pup relax in her arms. When she took her hand away from his snout, he didn't bark.

After checking the door to the garden was still locked, she felt the urge to go back to work. On her way upstairs, she looked out the landing window. The van was gone.

.

Caitlin's concentration was broken by a gentle knock at the studio door.

'It's 12.30. Are you sure you don't want me to stay?'

'No, Maria. Off you go, enjoy yourself. And thanks.'

'I'll be back at five. Don't work too hard.'

'Stop worrying, Maria.'

A short while later, Sim poked his head around the door jamb and gave a quiet woof.

'Hello, Sim' – rubbing at her tired eyes – 'ready for lunch?'

The phone began to ring in her study, next door to her studio. Stooping, she gathered the pup in her arms and went to answer it.

'Shush, Sim. Yes, hello?'

'It's North Shore Pool Service. I'm ringing to apologise for the inconvenience, but Geoff had an urgent job this morning. He'll be there about two o'clock this afternoon.'

19

Shafts of sunlight filtered through a grove of trees near one of the ponds set in the grounds of the Royal Botanic Gardens, a jewel of nature on the harbour's foreshore. Caitlin watched a raft of ducks swim towards her, rippling patterns across the water, before disappearing into the deep shadow of a small bridge. In the distance, the harbour's surface reflected the slate-coloured clouds that hung swollen on the horizon.

Nightmarish memories of the consequences of the pool man's ruse played in her mind. Later that day, when a young mechanic had collected her car for its routine service, the brakes had failed on the hill down to the Bridge approach, his act of courtesy almost costing him his life. The police found the brake lines had been cut. Feeling somehow responsible, she had told Martin. Given the damage to the car and the injury to the mechanic, it was hardly something she could hide. Strangely, rather than being angry, Martin was remarkably conciliatory.

For the tenth time that morning, she fingered the discreet business card of TE Quinn, Private Investigator. She imagined a cliché of a sleazy figure in a grubby raincoat, tracking down cheating spouses and insurance fraudsters. But Lexy and Richard had assured her Quinn was, well, unique. A supersleuth, Lexy called him, with a penchant for nutcases that stimulated his creative juices.

No matter how crazy the idea of a private investigator seemed, she did need someone to help solve the riddle of Sean's death. Someone who could go places and do things she couldn't.

But now at his designated meeting place, and despite Lexy's trusting endorsement, Quinn was nowhere to be seen. Well, another five minutes and she'd head home.

Caitlin watched as the ducks emerged from under the bridge into the sunlight reflecting on the main pond of the Lower Garden. As long as she'd been coming here, these identical ducks had followed the same sequence of movement around the ponds. She was reminded of Keats' line, 'Thou wast not born for death, immortal Bird!'

Hearing solitary footsteps at the other end of the bridge, she turned to see a tall, slim, neatly dressed man, a light breeze lifting fine strands of his sandy-grey hair. Certainly not Quinn.

Lost in contemplation of the ducks' movements, she almost didn't hear the whispering voice say, 'Don't look around. Follow the path to Lysicrates monument.'

She froze, struggling to quell her instinct to turn.

'Just keep walking,' the voice said, the words drifting on the cold July air, with the slight lilt of an Irish accent.

Like a robot marshalling its wired wits, Caitlin started down the path towards the impressive sandstone sculpture. Unable to contain her curiosity, she stole a casual glance over her shoulder. The man had disappeared. Perplexed, she wondered if she had been caught up in a Georges Feydeau farce.

She waited, time ticking away, and waited. Tired of his antics, she decided it was time to go.

She was about to leave when, from somewhere behind her, his voice came again, this time with a hint of amusement: 'You forgot what I said.'

'I like to put a face to the voice.'

'Just checking you have no shadows.'

'Have I?'

'See for yourself.'

She turned around. The man from the bridge. Was this Lexy's super sleuth? No wonder he'd disappeared so easily. With his grey suit, thin face, pale skin and fair hair, his shiny brown shoes the only contrast, this man would not attract a second look. Certainly not the sort you would expect to find, hat pulled low over his eyes, walking into seedy alleys, toeing aside rotting garbage, stepping over prone vagrants or strong-arming vicious criminals. This man was more reminiscent of Dorothy Sayer's British gentleman detective, Lord Peter Wimsey.

But all she could say was, 'You're very careful.'

'That's my job.'

They navigated their way through a group of young children with their mothers, the private investigator humming a snatch of Chopin.

'You love his music too,' she said, glancing at him.

'Poetry in song.'

They walked, two or three yards apart. Quinn turned his back to the water, propping his arms on the wall. He seemed to be keenly observing the children now chasing each other around the monument, but she was certain his grey eyes were taking an even keener interest in the landscape beyond.

She averted her gaze to admire the classical monument's proportions, the fine example of Corinthian columns used by the sculptor. To break the silence, she asked, 'Who was Lysicrates?'

'A wealthy patron of the arts in ancient Greece,' he said. 'The monument celebrates long gone choral voices singing in festivals from their graves. Have you heard of Sir James Martin?'

She frowned and shrugged. 'No.'

'Former Premier, Attorney General of New South Wales? No? Martin Place? … Yes. Well, the monument lived in his garden in Potts Point but was moved here in 1943.' He recited the words as if from a quirky textbook.

He suddenly straightened up, took from his jacket a small notebook with a ballpoint pen attached to its spine and, leaning a slim hip against the wall, his eyes still watchful, said, 'Miss Lipchitz and Mr Brinsmead gave me the general background of events to date; the circumstances of the boy's death, your visit to the cemetery, meeting Father Griffin at Parliament House, the falling statue, your studio ransacked, the incident with your car. But I want to hear your version.'

Staring at a Manly Ferry steaming its way to Circular Quay, Caitlin gave him a detailed account of all that had happened since the fateful day of the Katoomba excursion.

When she'd finished, he stared down at the water for a moment or two, observing a pooling of darkening oil carried in by an easterly swell. 'You've stirred up some dangerous people, Miss Cheney.'

Her eyes narrowed. 'If you don't want the job, say so, Mr Quinn.'

She was startled by the charmingly boyish smile that lit his face. He cocked his head to one side. 'Oh, I'm up for it. But are you?'

'I haven't come this far to quit.'

Another moment's silence.

Then, with a wry smile, as if her words had soured his thoughts, he said, 'Tell me more about your mysterious pool man.'

'Seemed quite efficient. A man of few words. Just a comment about the pool, did his work and left. Oh, and he rather upset my dog,' she said. 'But I do have something that might help you – it's a drawing I did of him after the phone call from the pool people.'

She pulled it out of her bag. He examined it critically.

'This is brilliant,' he said, slipping it into his pocket.

'Anyway, he didn't stay long. By the time I went back to my studio, he was gone. He'd clearly done his homework.'

Quinn shrugged. 'Child's play for a professional. Nicking the flexible brake hose with a razor blade would have taken less than a minute – in and out, leaving no trace. He must have known which car you drove. No doubt you were the target.'

'And the young mechanic …' Her voice faded; she cleared her throat.

'He was lucky he got off so lightly. An angel passing over,' he murmured.

She nodded.

'So, you need a bodyguard?'

She shook her head. 'No, I want you to talk to that priest MacManus about the photos. I think he is the catalyst that will encourage the police to look closer at Saint Anthony's.'

A startled gleam appeared in his eyes, as if an invisible hand had nudged a Luger pistol under his nose. 'You think the boy was murdered?'

'It's possible. Certainly not an accident, suicide very doubtful. The police, the brothers and MacManus are satisfied with the coroner's finding of suicide because that's what they want it to be: all the blame on the boy and none on the Church.'

He flipped through the pages of his notebook, scanning his shorthand.

'Those pornographic photographs you found, could you identify anyone?'

She smoothed out the black gloved fingers of her hands, conscious his eyes were fixed on her.

'I thought I saw some resemblance to Rodney Rushton, the prominent developer, but later, when I studied them properly, I couldn't be sure. All the camera angles showed were the back of heads or part of a profile.'

'Pity,' he said. He flicked through the pages of his notebook again. 'Those satanic symbols you describe on the boy's grave, paedophiles do sometimes use them in ritual acts to intimidate their victims. Strange things happen in cemeteries. Many tales are told of the Devil's Chairs at Rookwood.'

'Sorry?' Her eyebrows shot up. She wondered if she'd missed something.

'The Devil's Chairs – stone chairs. They occur in a few cemeteries around the world, but Rookwood is distinguished for having several. So, if you want to make a pact with the Devil, that's the right place for a cosy chat. If you can find them among all the other necropolistic monuments, that is. The human mind … Odd are its workings.'

His own mind seemed to snowball ahead. 'It's strange, the fascination some people have with satanic rituals. Take that bizarre instance about twenty years ago, in the fifties, of Eugene Goossens. Internationally renowned conductor who became the lover of Rosaleen Norton, the witch of Kings Cross. Not content with skidding into the seamy side of life, he gets himself arrested for importing erotic photographs. A glorious career ends in disgrace. Quite extraordinary, don't you think?'

She stared at the investigator as his pen tapped a gentle rhythm on his white teeth. Something in his eyes, in his voice, like a cat waiting to pounce.

'Suppose I track down this priest, uncover evidence that links the boy's death with paedophilic activities, and say there is a nexus between the orphanage and that paedophile activity. It's explosive.'

She glared at him. 'So, much easier to forget?'

'No, not at all. But trying to prove murder and abuse within the Catholic Church is like grabbing the end of a tiger snake's tail.'

'Are you Catholic?'

He laughed, shook his head. 'To me, the life here is the life there is, no frills. I'm not frightened of taking on the Catholic Church, Miss Cheney, but I have a wary respect for the ability they have to use their power to protect their reputation.'

She felt a growing frustration. 'As I said before, Mr Quinn, once you talk to that priest, the police will have to take a closer look at the young boy's death and what's going on at the orphanage.'

'Remember what Father Griffin told you at Parliament House. The Church has a way of making recalcitrant priests fade from the picture. The problem is greater than Saint Anthony's.'

'What are you saying?'

'Abuse is a disease that infects every facet of society.'

His expression had become exigent and suddenly she found it difficult to recall the vanished sweetness of his smile. In the littleness of her life, a life so protected, she'd never come across a man like Quinn: a chameleon.

'But for now,' he said, snapping his notebook shut, 'we will focus on the Church. I don't see any other starting point. The Vatican has been covering up this sort of scandal for hundreds of years. In Australia, it's the Catholic Irish immigrant police connection. Rotten as a month-old corpse. I'm not saying by any means that they're all corrupt, but they can and do coalesce in a dangerous liaison. I'll check out the Sacred Heart Church and Saint Anthony's Orphanage. Trust no one until we work out what's happening.'

'And Detective Inspector Hurd? I don't think he finds me too trustworthy.'

'You've got it the wrong way around. The barbeque set can be dangerous, especially in Hurd's division.'

20

At last, she was back in her Rocks studio. The pressure of work had done little to quell the shock of Sim's death. The horror of his brutal savagery, and its unmistakable message had almost taken her to breaking point, but somehow Maria's support and Martin's conciliatory concern had helped. The studio was almost back to normal and the demands of her work had brought back some sense of routine.

A knock on the door. Stepping away from her easel, Caitlin crossed to the door and opened it cautiously, as far as the shiny new safety chain would allow.

Bright late-morning light flooded the room. She stared at the apparition framed by the narrow opening: a man of indeterminate age with longish grey hair, wearing black framed glasses and a sixties style suit, holding a floppy felt hat to his chest.

'Can I help you?'

The eyes behind the glasses twinkled.

'Mr Quinn!' Laughter bubbled in her throat. 'Good disguise. But why?'

She slipped the catch. He gave a courteous bow before walking in.

'Professor Sturt, church historian and new parishioner to the Sacred Heart congregation.' He produced a photograph from behind his back. 'For your sentry downstairs, who I have observed doesn't miss much. I told her I want to commission a portrait of my grandmother.'

She laughed again. 'Watercolour, pastel, oil?'

'Oil would suit her perfectly.' Quinn slipped the photograph back into his suit pocket, took off his glasses and sucked thoughtfully on one wing of his glasses for a moment, before laying them carefully on her desk.

'I wandered into Father MacManus' church early yesterday morning and plotted the trajectory of the statue's fall from the scratch marks on the stone floor. Whoever it was in that choir stall didn't have you in his sights. I'm certain it was meant for the priest.'

She gave him a slow, sideways glance. 'No possibility it was an accident?'

'None.'

She was silent. His eyes bored into her so intently she had to look away.

'Miss Cheney, taking those photographs has changed their game plan. This is not just about a refractory priest. It points to something more sinister, perhaps a paedophile ring using the orphanage as part of its operations, with a leader who has access to considerable resources. A powerful and dangerous person.'

She walked to the window, pressed her forehead against the cold glass and closed her eyes. His words pierced into her brain. Knowing children were hostage to the callous destruction of their innocence, the silence of adults defiled her conscience.

Opening her eyes, she watched the seagulls gliding on a downdraft, then turned back to study him for a moment. Was she warming to this quirky man?

'Quinn, I want children to be as free as those birds in the sky, not clinging to scraps of human existence. Has there been any progress in identifying that criminal, Rafe?'

The PI shook his head. 'Your pool service is reputable, no dodgy blemishes. But one of their vans was stolen that morning, found later a few blocks from your house. Not much to go on, needle in a haystack stuff.'

'Prints?'

'Everything wiped clean, even the toilet seat next to your garage. Your drawing is the only lead. My police contact is still working on it.'

'And the orphanage?'

'God! That place is Dickensian. And Brother Finbar, the principal, wasn't too keen to meet a new member of the Friends of the Sacred Heart.'

'I'm not surprised. It would be difficult to find a kind bone in his body.'

'I was hustled out of his office, out of the orphanage as if it held an order of Hieronymite monks. However, I did manage to get past that excuse for a housekeeper at the presbytery, for all the good it did. I tried spinning exciting tales about hearing of the priest's valuable book collection. Told her how it would be of great assistance to Professor Sturt's work, preparatory to celebrations of the centenary of the parish in two years.'

She stared at him, seeing past the solemn expression on his lean face to the hint of something else in his eyes. 'But did the woman say anything about MacManus?'

'Not a bean. She hasn't seen him since Mass on Sunday three days ago. Even when I commented that a missing priest might raise a few worries, she made no response, other than it was none of her business. And her asinine remark about the books was that they wreaked havoc on her sinuses and I couldn't go into his study without his permission.'

She frowned. 'Waste of time then.'

'I talked to a few of the parishioners. No one seems to know anything.' He shrugged.

The coldness of the winter morning sucked the warmth from the room. She walked back to the window and looked down into George Street again, at the ceaseless traffic mapping its way in and out of the maze of Sydney's streets. Somewhere in that maze was MacManus.

She dragged a hand through her hair, half-turning to the detective. 'We have to find that priest.'

He didn't seem to hear her words. 'There has to be a link between those photographs and the raid on your studio. Whoever was behind the break-in was anxious to get them and send a sharp message to frighten you off. Brother Loudé is the only person who knew you'd been in the presbytery. He must have passed on that information to someone higher, not necessarily the top man.'

She nodded. 'The thing puzzling me is how they seem to know my movements. Someone could have checked my pool man's routine, but no one knew I'd be working from home that day.'

'How long have you been dealing with the pool people and the garage?'

'Years.'

'So, it's unlikely they were involved. How did you book your car in to be serviced?'

'The phone, of course.'

'This one?' Quinn said, sitting down at her desk.

'Yes.'

He tapped a finger on the phone. 'Shall we see if anyone's at home?'

'Sorry?'

But he'd already picked up the cream handset, unscrewed the mouthpiece.

'Someone has been busy.' He pointed to a tiny microphone. 'You've got a visitor.'

He screwed the mouthpiece back and replaced it in its cradle.

'Can you detect anything when you use it?'

'No, unfortunately.'

'Who are your neighbours?'

'There are offices on that side,' she said, pointing. 'I think the other one is empty.'

He glanced over at the window. 'They could tap into the line from somewhere outside, but if the tap is in that empty office, it could be attached to a tape recorder.'

She grimaced. 'Cunning as cockroaches.'

A mischievous smile suddenly lit his face. She took some comfort from envisaging her invisible enemies caught in Quinn's crosshairs. She listened for some seconds to the hiss of a whistle between his even teeth.

Finally, she said, 'Well, what is it?'

He shook his head. 'No, it won't work.'

'What won't?'

'It would put you in danger. Your husband would have my licence.'

'Just tell me, Quinn.'

'Alright. If we can draw them out into the open, we might just get the break we need. We'll let these thugs think they didn't get all the photographs. You'll pretend you want to get copies of the ones they missed. You'll ring me on a number I'll give you. I'll impersonate a sleazy photographer, Nicky Bail – a man who'll do anything for a price, like copying pornography. You'll say you don't want to come to his studio and instead arrange a place to hand them over. A park would be a good location; how about that little reserve next to the Maritime Services Building?'

'Alright, but what then?'

'You'll leave them in a large self-addressed envelope on one of the park benches."

'But why wouldn't they just come here again, or to my home?'

'We won't give them time. You'll ring this afternoon. The second you finish the call, you'll be out of here, do the drop and get to somewhere safe.'

Though it sounded simple enough, she had misgivings. She wanted to trust his judgement, but she'd only known the man five days. She looked down at the slashed image of Sean propped between two windows.

'Quinn, I'm not sure I can do it. I don't know if I have the strength,' she said. 'This morning when Martin went out to his car, he found our … our beautiful dog,' She paused trembling, as she recalled the terrible sight. 'He, he was lying on the front step … his throat cut. It was terrible.' She paused and wiped her eyes. 'How, how could anyone be so cruel? I'm feeling too vulnerable.'

Quinn's scraggy eyebrows disappeared into his long, grey hair. 'They certainly mean business. That's a classic warning: give up or they'll pursue you until they get what they want. But all the same, there is a covert element. I think they're too professional to hazard anything in a public place with lots of people watching. Hopefully, I'll get some useful photos and, if I'm lucky, I'll be able to trail whoever appears to collect the drop.'

She stared at the detective. 'I'm not too sure how pretty a picture I'd make as a corpse and I don't think Martin would be very impressed.'

'There won't be any slip-ups. I'll be watching your every step.'

'And if you can't?'

He shrugged. 'There's an inherent element of risk in everything. But you're the one who has to do the drop. More authentic.'

'It's still too risky.'

'I'm afraid that's the reality if you want to help those boys.'

She turned and stared down at the people walking through their ordinary lives. If only she could be one of them. But the hard, lonely truth was that she couldn't, not anymore.

'What time for the drop at the park?'

'Four o'clock. Ring me at three. Remember the name: Nicky Bail.'

He gazed at the large, damaged canvas. She wondered what Quinn thought of the ugly knife wounds slashed across Sean's lovely features, a sight that had become so painful to her. Perhaps she should turn it to the wall, for the image drew her into a downward spiral of self-recrimination, punishment for Sean's lost childhood, lost life.

When he noticed her watching him, he quickly looked away.

'We've got to get these evil bastards. I can't colour it any other way,' he said.

'Just make sure you watch my every step.'

He nodded, picked up his glasses and stood.

'Have a chat with your Mrs Mazzioni. When you get back, ask

her if you can stay with her, and keep the street door locked at all times once the café's closed.' He waved a hand towards the door. 'Don't forget this one. And whenever you use the phone, remember there are three on the line.'

As his light footsteps receded down the narrow stairs, his voice drifted up to her. 'Take very good care of Grandmother, won't you?'

Time dragged heavily after Quinn had gone. She tried to work, but concentration was impossible. Their plan gnawed at her. She called him at three and as she opened the door of her studio to leave, the phone rang, echoing through the room with shrill insistence. Slowly, she picked up the receiver.

'Hello?'

A gravelly voice. 'It's Father MacManus. Meet me at Saint Bonaventure's, Surry Hills, at 3.30, no later. It's vital.'

'Father? Father, what –'

But the line was dead.

She stared at the phone. Its silent indifference tied a knot in her thoughts.

Oh, God! She must talk to Quinn. She scrabbled for his number, rang it; no answer. She dialled again, the same monotonous ring.

She'd have to stall him somehow. A clock ticked in her head, a burring that wouldn't stop. Time was running out.

She wrapped her arms tightly around herself. What was Quinn doing? Of course, he'd be on his way to the drop point. As much as she needed to contact him, she couldn't wait any longer. She had no choice.

But were 'they' listening? Even if they were, she would have to go.

21

Saint Bonaventure's heavy wooden door whispered shut behind her. The cloudy afternoon cast deep shadows throughout the church's small interior.

Her high-heeled boots echoed in the icy silence as she walked towards the front of the church, haunted by a fearful rhythm of thoughts and a sense of déjà vu. Was she a fool to trust the words of a paedophile priest instead of waiting for Quinn to contact her? She hoped he would get the message she had left with Mrs Mazz, to follow her here to the church.

Near the altar, the glow of the tabernacle lamp enlivened the seraphic features of the statue of Saint Bonaventure, the thirteenth century Cardinal Bishop of Albano. She gazed into the statue's almond-shaped eyes. 'How good are you as an intermediary for resolving human hopelessness?'

She heard a faint murmur. Was that the saint whispering, protesting against using God's house for ungodly reasons? A human response? Or just her overwrought imagination?

The sound came again, no saint murmuring mea culpas but a distinctly earthly sound.

Quickly opening the ornate, brass gate of the communion rail, she ran towards the doorway behind the statue. Gloomy light from the small panes of a long, narrow arched window cloaked the walls. She pushed open the door. The dry mustiness of the room caught at her throat, intermingled with an acrid smell that stifled her senses. As she fumbled for a light switch, a groan from the far corner made her skin prickle.

Moving closer, the strong odour of urine came from what she'd first thought was a jumble of black rags half hidden under a rack of vestments. She pushed the rack aside and knelt.

'Father MacManus!'

No reaction. The priest's face was furrowed as if someone had made a plaything of it. Caitlin closed her eyes for a moment and inwardly wept.

She reached out to touch his hands, curled against the blackness of his jacket, then reeled back. These were not the stubby fingers of MacManus, but the elegant hands she recognised from Parliament House.

She stumbled to her feet, grabbed a white surplice from its hanger on the rack and, making a pad of it, pressed it against the priest's face to try to staunch the bleeding.

'You'll be all right, Father Griffin,' she said. 'I'll just try to make you more comfortable before I phone an ambulance.'

Pulling a heavy cassock from the rack, she tucked it around him, then took down two more surplices and folded them into a pillow to put under his head. Even before she stood up, blood had begun to seep onto the make-shift pad. She had to find a telephone fast.

Minutes later, when she returned to the sacristy, the priest was conscious. She knelt by his side. Her voice came as a whisper through ragged breathing, 'The ambulance won't be long, Father, not too long at all.'

He turned his head towards her, his swollen eyes seemingly fighting to focus. 'MacManus … Cemetery …'

'Don't try to talk, Father. We'll soon have you in hospital.'

His eyes closed. She bent over him. Nothing.

The walls of the room shrank in the suffocating stillness. What else could she do? She was desperate to keep him alive. A finger on his throat relieved some of her dread.

What had played out in this room? Had this nervy, hapless priest remained silent against the brutal assault of a psychotic criminal? Perhaps the same one who had destroyed her studio? Or her dog? Certainly this was no act of a fellow priest. But where was MacManus and how exactly did Saint Anthony's fit into this mayhem? How could the Church allow this sore to fester within its so-called divine purpose, tolerate such evil from its religious?

The stakes were becoming ever higher. As Quinn had warned, this problem reached beyond the local parish, condoned by the hierarchy, even the Vatican itself. She thought again of Richard's account of the American nun and the coterie of criminals and corrupt police that had left her dead on a rubbish heap.

For a long time, she'd been aware of rumblings about the ultra-conservatism of the all-powerful Curia in Rome that placed the Church's reputation above all else. What beliefs had evolved within the Curia to incite men of God, blessed with a sacred vocation, to profane Christ's most holy covenants? What tragedies had their lies induced; what evil lay behind the cloak of Holy Orders? Shielding men like MacManus, guilty of deviant behaviour in their pastoral duties. And Loudé; was he another soul carved by elusive sculptors working with two-way mirrors, their cloistered existence insulating them from the moral values of the rich stream of life they had sworn to uphold?

Heavy footsteps pounded the stone floor of the church and up to the chancel, breaking through her thoughts. She ran to the door and pushed it wide open.

The room became a cupboard as two ambulance men crowded into its space. Caitlin squeezed herself into the smallest part of the sacristy as they worked on the priest with quiet efficiency.

It seemed a long time, but probably only minutes before the older man said, 'Let's get him out of here.'

She followed them from the room. 'Will he be alright?'

He stared at her. 'Perhaps you should ride with us to Saint Vincent's?'

'I have my car.'

He nodded, shooting her another quick, penetrating look. They manoeuvred the stretcher down the stone steps of the chancel, out of the church.

She sat down on the cold steps, gripped her head in her hands, recalling the first time she'd seen Father Griffin: anxiety stamped on his chiselled features, his slight frame playing out unspeakable regret. Now, she was watching his battered body being carried out from his church.

What role did MacManus have in visiting such grief on this priest? Was Father Griffin providing sanctuary to a friendless fellow priest, hoping he would show remorse for his evil ways? Caitlin wondered. Now, perhaps even mistaken for MacManus, he had paid the penalty for his compassion.

But then, why did MacManus call her at her studio – more mea culpas or more lies? Lies, Sean's scarf, the toys on the grave. Or was it really McManus? It certainly sounded like him.

She could think of only one place MacManus might go to purge his sins, Sean's grave, and it seemed to fit with Griffin's stuttered message. She would ring Mrs Mazz and leave a message for Quinn to meet her at the cemetery.

22

Huddling among the cave-like roots of a Moreton Bay fig, Caitlin opened her jacket and pushed one hand inside to flick on her torch. Five-thirty. She looked back along the gloomy driveway towards the entrance to Rookwood Cemetery, 100 yards away.

Was that a car engine, or were her nerves strung too taut?

Yet, she felt sure that MacManus would return to orchestrate his power over his victim even after death. Or perhaps it would be remorse – she recalled the toys left on Sean's grave.

Another ten minutes. Despite her warm clothes, the cold seeped into her body. Her legs had started to cramp from her crouched position. The lightest of drizzles began to dampen the grass around the tree.

'Why am I doing this?' she asked herself again, thinking of Quinn and poor Father Griffin with a pang of guilt. And for all she knew, MacManus might be miles away, safe and warm.

She stood up, wriggled her feet, rubbed her hands up and down her arms, and recited some verses of *The Rime of the Ancient Mariner*. That must have taken at least fifteen minutes. She was losing track of time but dared not use her torch even though it was almost dark.

Her eyes suddenly fixed on the shadow line of the large bush not far from Sean's grave. The darkened leaves glowed yellow, as if someone was moving behind it with a torch.

She blinked rapidly against the rising wind that blew rain into her face. A bulky man was approaching the grave: MacManus. He walked back and forth several times, before melting into the shadows once more. Her time to talk to the priest was running out.

The wind, rain and snapping cold bit at her skin as she stepped out from the shelter of the tree. She hesitated, wiping at her eyes. She had only taken a few steps when another shadowy figure materialised from the bushes near where the priest had stood. She dropped to the ground, crawling back into the darkest cover of her hiding place.

Seconds passed before she raised her head again. The shadowy figure wavered, split into two. A moment later, there were three, the third was MacManus. Caitlin gripped the edge of a root, trying to think what Quinn would do. But she wasn't Quinn and nor did she feel herself; it was as if she was inhabiting another person's body. The three men had moved to Sean's grave and now stood clustered together, veiled by the light rain.

Suddenly, the priest fell to his knees, a pleading supplicant. She strained to catch any words, but the wind was too strong. A loud cry, perhaps of protest, then a sharp crack rent the air. MacManus toppled sideways.

She gritted her teeth to stifle a scream.

One of the men leant over the priest. Minutes ticked by as the man remained bent over MacManus – what was it: remorse, a warning, a strange act of compassion? – until the second shot.

She folded her arms round herself to stop her body shaking.

The two men moved away from the grave, their powerful torches flicking through the trees. Caitlin watched as they reached the edge of the drive and started to slowly walk in her direction. A stifling sensation clamped her throat. Had the criminals somehow linked MacManus' call to the possibility that she would meet him here? If so, it wouldn't take them long to find her. The wind ruffling the leaves, a canopy of whispering voices.

She twisted round, probing the darkness. The Moreton Bay fig was surrounded by open ground on every side, except for a few small bushes. She could see more shelter among the trees and bushes lining the boundary of the cemetery, but could she get to where she had left her car?

The two men walked past her and disappeared into the darkness. She heard a car engine fire into life. Then the sound of the car faded into the night.

She waited for what she guessed was another five minutes before pushing herself to her feet and cautiously circling the tree. The drizzle had stopped, but the wind was colder. She was alone in this land of the dead.

Half doubled, she ran across the drive towards the priest, falling to the ground beside him. She fumbled for her torch, flicked it on.

'Sweet Jesus.'

The widening red stain pulsing from his body glowed in the yellow torchlight. His face was grey, covered in sweat, his eyes closed.

The wind was like a freezing blanket wrapping round her. Don't think about it, just do it, she thought. Balancing the torch on a branch behind her, she pulled off her jacket and shirt, sucked in a deep breath and quickly shrugged her jacket back on.

Her hands trembled as she pressed the woollen material of her shirt over his stomach and genitals to try to staunch the bleeding. Those bastards had shot him in a way that ensured he would die but not instantly. Her day had become stained with the blood of priests. She shuddered. Evil was all around her. Human life meant nothing to these callous brutes! MacManus may have revealed too much of a Judas strain, become their weak link. But Father Griffin, what had he done to deserve his battered body?

If she was honest, MacManus would receive no forgiveness from her. His unwillingness to talk earlier might now have destroyed any hope of finding the truth of Sean's death.

Blood pooled over her hands as if she were washing in it. Glancing at his face, she saw his eyes had opened. Fixed on her, their colour was almost invisible between grey pouches of skin. His lips moved, his fingers grasping for hers as if to seek some comfort.

She forced a smile onto her mouth. 'You don't deserve to die, Father.'

He opened his lips again, made no sound.

She leant closer to him. 'Do you want to tell me something?'

She felt his fingers close over hers; he drew them feebly towards his chest.

The words came in a whisper: 'Tru … truth pa-aa, per, pocket.'

His eyelids fluttered; his lips seemed to be trying to shape more words even as blood dribbled from them.

'Paper, Father?'

She put her face close to his mouth, feeling his breath on her cheek. Then it was gone.

She raised her head, looked into his lifeless face. 'Try talking to your God now!'

Yet staring at the odd twist of the fingers that still held hers, as if he'd been trying to place them over his heart, she thought an inner calm had perhaps come to him – at an agonising price.

She started to unbutton his jacket then stopped, gazing down at her stiff purple fingers. She shivered. 'Paper -pocket, that was it.' His jacket had no pockets, his shirt two. She wriggled two fingers inside the pocket nearest his hand and touched something. Carefully, she pulled out a small piece of paper. Unfolding it, she held the black, spidery web of lines to the torchlight. Bronte writing, the tiniest she'd seen, impossible to read in the poor light, but it seemed to be a list of names.

She stared down at MacManus. Was this an act of redemption? Could it be the names of those in the paedophile ring?

The list wasn't long, but if she was right, her possession of this scrap of paper with its tortured handwriting was both precious and dangerous.

The wind had dropped and in the sudden quietness she became conscious of her vulnerability. Jerking her head up, she glanced around, listening. There it was again. The sound of a car.

She switched off the torch, scrambled to her feet, emotions misfiring. She ran for the shelter of the Moreton Bay fig. The headlights caught her crossing the road.

The car accelerated. She swerved to avoid it, almost tripping over the gutter at the road's edge.

'Caitlin! Caitlin … Stop!'

That familiar voice was one of the sweetest she had ever heard.

The car door opened and Quinn appeared in the beam of the headlights. Breathless, she longed to hug him, but instead glared at him. 'How did you know I was here?'

'The faithful Mrs Mazz. She stayed in the café until I arrived.

Said you were going to Saint Bonaventure Church in Surry Hills. I arrived just as they were putting the priest into the ambulance. I must have missed you only by seconds. They let me have a brief word with him, he said you would come to the cemetery, I put two and two together and took a punt. So here I am'

'You took your time.'

He shrugged. 'You didn't leave your exact address.'

She nodded towards Sean's grave. 'They … They shot MacManus. He's dead.'

'You sure?'

She nodded.

Quinn regarded her for a second. 'Are you alright?'

She was silent, then finally nodded again, pushing wet hair from her face.

Seeing his odd expression, she said, 'What is it?'

'You're hurt.'

She shook her head. 'That's MacManus' blood.'

Without another word, he bundled her into the passenger seat, wrapping his tweed jacket round her shoulders. He took a small flask and a handkerchief from his jeans' pocket and handed them to her.

She went to give the handkerchief back. 'I'm no weeping Winifred. Thank you. But I'll hold onto the brandy flask.'

'You've blood on your face, your hands,' he snapped, then slammed the car door and disappeared.

He was gone for several minutes. Returning, he threw something onto the back seat, slid behind the wheel, started the engine and swung the Riley through a sharp U-turn. The squeal of the tyres underscored his smouldering silence as they headed to the cemetery entrance.

His silence began to annoy her. 'Why are you so angry?'

'Forgive me if I'm slow, but what did you think you were doing? You could be lying dead beside MacManus.'

'I got a message from him to meet at Father Griffin's church. What was I supposed to do? I tried to call you twice, left several messages.'

'Christ, Caitlin, there was a police station on your doorstep.'

'He'd never have talked to the police.'

'He can't now, you've fixed that. One priest dead, another clinging to life, while I'm running around chasing false hopes. By the way, no one came to pick up the envelope. Where did you leave your car?'

'My car?'

'Where is it?'

'In East Street. Why?'

'Do you think you can drive?'

'Quinn, I only had a sip.'

'That's not what I'm worried about.'

'Sorry. Yes, I'm alright to drive.'

'By the way, what do you think I was doing back there – giving him the last rites?' Quinn said.

She stared at him, then muttered, 'Oh, shit.'

'Precisely. I collected your shirt, destroyed your footprints. Anything else you've forgotten?'

With sticky, bloodstained fingers she drew the list from her jacket pocket.

23

The crush of people around the gambling tables in Rodney Rushton's home had become unbearable. Caitlin squeezed between two overweight women, ignoring their indignant looks, still furious at herself for allowing Martin to talk her into this Liberal fundraiser in the developer's Northbridge home. Of course, Martin had disappeared two minutes after they arrived.

'Off to press the flesh, darling,' he'd said, grinning. 'Enjoy yourself.'

Enjoy herself? The faces around her seemed inured to greed, to power, to mindless nothingness. Had they donned masks for the night, masks that hid their inner personalities from the mirror of truth? Everywhere she went in the large rooms, as each minute crept by, the guests were milling, watching, shuffling and talking about money. Like a roulette wheel gone crazy, they gambled with an intensity she found difficult to relate to reason.

Why Martin was associated with the event remained a question between them. He'd taken the line that many charities made money from gambling nights. What was the difference? But for her, the difference was the morality associated with running for parliament, the principle of public office and public trust, and associating with illegal gambling, to say nothing of the possibility of drawing scrutiny from the press.

Their heated arguments over the gambling night merged with her inner turmoil over MacManus' death. Her memories of his dying moments, of the killer's brutality, were terrifyingly vivid. Waiting for a knock on her door from the police had left her mentally exhausted, not to mention enduring Quinn's silence. Learning that Father Griffin would recover from his injuries was the only good news she'd received all week. Quinn's simmering anger exploding into an interrogation as to why he shouldn't quit the case, had frightened her. With Martin's entrenched attitude that it was a police matter, it would be difficult to continue without Quinn's help. But in her mind, she'd crossed the Rubicon.

She'd expected the execution style killing of a priest would make headlines in all the newspapers, but the reporting had been brief: a couple of columns buried well in from the front pages, a small, grainy, almost unrecognisable photograph; 'police baffled … a priest well respected in his community … a sad loss'. The police suspected it was a case of mistaken identity. Their appeal for information had apparently yielded nothing. The newspapers had quickly gone quiet. A cover-up? If it was, it showed how far the influence of the paedophile ring could reach.

Three nights ago, Quinn had called her at home, his voice brusque as he fixed a meeting for the next day at his home in Glebe. Well, she'd thought, at least we're still talking.

Caitlin shivered at her recollections and desperately cast around for something less confronting to engage her attention. She studied her tense face in a heavily gilded mirror near one of Rushton's gaming tables. She was about to turn away, when in a corner of the mirror she saw the reflection of a tall, older man, standing on the other side of the large room. His gaze seemed fixed on her. When she swung around, he had gone.

She shrugged. Probably her overwrought imagination. In need of fresh air, she pushed past a huddle of cigar smoking men, only to be accosted by Helen Rushton.

'Come and join us, Caitlin,' she said from amid a group of be-jewelled women. 'We've just been talking about Martin's marvellous win in the preselection.'

'You must be so excited,' another woman said.

In the noise of the room, she lost another woman's words. They sounded like an echo of 'so excited'.

'What a wonderful performance, and that great speech. One of the best I've heard. I was so impressed by how cleverly he answered the questions,' the first woman said.

Nodding, smiling, Caitlin's attention drifted around the room. She caught sight of the older man again, close to the blackjack table, still watching her like a silent shadow but making no move to approach. Their eyes met; a sardonic smile stretched across his scarred face. A shiver ran down her spine.

'Helen, ladies, will you excuse me? I have to give Martin a message before I forget. The dutiful wife, you know.'

Manoeuvring through the crowd towards one of the open doors, she noticed Martin near a marble fireplace, brandishing his political feather duster at anyone who would listen. She stepped out onto the balcony overlooking the darkness of Sailors Bay and strolled to the far end of the sandstone terrace.

The fresh air cleared her head and cooled her skin through her velvet jacket. Gripping the railing, she stared into the garden below, smelling its rich moisture – too reminiscent of the night in the cemetery.

A burst of laughter erupted from one of the open doors. She smiled and glanced up at the stars in the navy canopy above; Van Gogh had called them 'dead poets' souls'. The thought seemed to highlight the distance between herself and the people inside.

'Escaping, Mrs Preece?' The voice had a heavy German inflection.

She spun around. The man's eyes glittered in the semi-darkness. She could see more clearly the disfiguring scar on his cheek that rippled into tiny seams of white skin, emphasising the arrogance of his smile.

'Have we met?' she asked.

He gave a slight nod. 'In a manner of speaking.'

She heard the click of his heels.

'Werner Brechtenshafft.'

Her fingers curled more tightly around the wrought iron rail. That name was on the top of MacManus' list.

'I have an interest in your work.'

'How nice,' she said. She couldn't take her eyes off his face.

He leant back against the railing, studying her as if she were a butterfly he was about to pin into his collection.

'Life's a risky game, there can be pitfalls in anything you attempt.' He glanced towards the open doors. 'I hope you had no heavy losses tonight.'

'I don't gamble.'

'Very sensible, especially in your position – the odds are always against you.'

In a tremulous voice, she said, 'Where have you seen my work?'

'It would have been some months ago, one of your exhibitions.'

'The Weinberg Gallery?'

A momentary spasm tightened the corners of his lips. 'Yes, that was it. The Weinberg Gallery.'

She felt a smile on her mouth. Her father always said a gambler needs to know when to hold his cards and when to fold them.

The Weinberg Gallery didn't exist.

24

Caitlin felt a little easier back in the relative safety of the crowded reception room but took care to keep away from anyone she knew until her nerves had settled. Taking a glass of wine from a passing waiter, she drifted to the edges of the room to examine the paintings adorning the walls: an odd collection of subjects, bought, she suspected, more for the status of the artist than as a reflection of the owner's taste. But then she would be hard-pressed to conjure up what Rushton's taste might be, or even Helen's, if she was given any say in such matters.

As she neared the foot of the staircase that led up to the private rooms, she glimpsed a small boy coming down. He seemed to be taking cover behind the elaborate banister rail. Instantly she recalled the boy at Enid Featherstone's house: Tim, or Rushy. Same size; same thick hair, long and straggly, an unusual shade of red, and heavy freckles like premature age spots over his white skin. A boy with a penchant for hiding behind a clown's mask, a boy who could easily be Rushton's son. Of course, Rushton – Rushy.

She put her hand on the stair rail. When he was three steps from the bottom, they were on eye level.

'Hello, Rushy.'

His eyes widened momentarily, before his expression returned to blank. Only when she mentioned the little girl Yasmin did she sense a second's flicker of interest. Then he fled, rushing down the stairs, disappearing along a corridor.

She was right, and she had to find him, try to talk to him. Easier said than done. From the moment he'd seen her, he'd clearly wanted to escape.

Caitlin hurried across to the corridor and arrived just in time to see him disappear through a side door, shutting it with a bang. Pausing only long enough to catch her breath, she started to walk towards the door as a waitress with a tray emerged from another doorway at the corridor's end.

'Can I help you? Are you looking for the bathrooms?' she asked.

Caitlin took a deep breath. 'No, Tim and I were playing hide and seek. I think I've lost him.'

She smiled. 'His favourite game. Well, he's not in the kitchen, so he's probably gone down to the cellar. Last door on the left before you get to the kitchen.'

'Thank you,' she said, hurrying to the door, praying Tim had not locked it.

The door opened onto a small, well-lit cavity and a few feet of wooden floor. Beyond that, at a right angle, a narrow staircase. At that moment, the light went out, but it returned at the flick of a switch to the right of the door.

A spasm of fear dried her mouth. Guests were certainly not supposed to go here.

She shut the door and descended the twenty or so steep steps to the bottom before she stopped to listen – no curious person had followed her. The brick walls had become rougher and a musty dampness itched at her nose. Was this the wine cellar Martin envied so much?

The fact that she was now an intruder in this passageway filled her with an ever-increasing anxiety. She could hear only her own slow breathing. She tasted dust, as if she were in a tomb. The absence of spider webs worried her, too: the passage was evidently well used. She had to get out.

She pushed forward until she came to another door, which opened to a dim room. As her eyes adjusted to the gloom, the shadowy outline of wine racks materialised: Rushton's cellar, just as she'd suspected.

To her left, pale light showed through the frosted glass panes of another door. She tried it, but it was locked. A faint glow caught her eye along the wall to her right. Illumination from outside?

Feeling her way along the wine racks, fresh air began to fan her face. Looking closer, she found a window, slightly ajar, and below it a wooden box. Clever little fellow, she thought. It was just big enough, she hoped, for her to use the same escape route.

Mounting the box, she pulled the window open and wriggled through, emerging onto a flight of wide, stone steps.

She scrambled to her feet and mounted a few steps. As her eyes drew level with the top one, she could see to her left a pathway sloping down to the water. To her right, it wound upwards through bushes and trees to the front of the mansion. The garden was deserted, no sign of the boy.

She meandered up the path; hopefully Martin was too busy glad-handing to have missed her. She glanced at her watch, but what seemed like ages had been crammed into fifteen minutes.

Reaching the corner of the house, Caitlin dusted down her clothes and stepped back beneath the luxuriant canopy of a weeping ash tree as a group of guests began to leave, their voices indistinct in the winter night. She waited for them to disappear down the drive before edging out from under the tree, nearly tripping as something caught at her jacket. Twisting around to free herself, a flash of colour swung towards her face, and a cold hand clamped over her mouth. She tried to bite, lash out with the heel of a shoe.

A voice hissed in her ear, 'Will you please stop that. It's me!'

She peered at the tree-shadowed features. 'What are you doing here?'

'Well, I was hoping you were still paying me.' Quinn tapped the camera hanging around his neck. 'Happy snaps of the guests. A Who's Who of people Sir Rodney Rushton is very unwise to welcome into his house.'

'Like Werner Brechtenshafft?'

Quinn whistled softly. 'Well, well, the rat has come out of his sewer? Rumours abound, but as yet, nothing concrete.'

'An interesting evening all round. The German and Rushton did not seem too pally tonight. And I have an inkling I may have been the problem.'

'You?'

'Brechtenshafft engineered a cosy little chat with me about half an hour ago. Oh, and by the way, I found a staircase from the kitchen that leads to Rushton's wine cellar.'

'You certainly have had an interesting evening.'

'And there's something else …' But all of a sudden, she couldn't explain to Quinn the unreasonable fear she felt for the boy wandering around in the night.

'What is it?'

'Nothing.'

Quinn was silent.

She waited until his silence began to irritate her then, pushing her face within inches of his, she said, 'I want to get back into that wine cellar.'

'Why?'

'Instinct tells me the cellar holds more interest than its stock of vintage wine.'

'So, what's stopping you?'

'A locked door.'

'A locked door didn't stop you from getting out.'

Caitlin gave a mirthless laugh. 'Getting out of that window in a long skirt is very different to getting in. You have to make some allowances for vanity and a bigger drop on the inside than coming out onto the steps.'

Quinn fished in his pocket and pulled out a set of odd keys. 'Would these picklocks help?'

They descended the stairs to the cellar door. Quinn flicked on the torch, passed it to her.

'Hold it steady.'

Cupping her hand around the torch, she focused the beam on the lock, watching as his slim fingers probed it with one pick, then another. The seconds dragged. Was that a promising click she heard? He glanced at her.

'Give me the torch,' he said. Switching it off, he pushed the door open, shut it behind them, and waited a few seconds before switching the torch on again. Its beam shone over a pile of wooden boxes not far from the door.

'So that's what I stumbled over.'

'Let's not make it twice.'

Quinn flashed the light around the cellar and back onto the boxes. Caitlin read, '*POMMARD REGION – Produit de France.*'

'Probably a nice Burgundy,' Quinn said. 'He certainly spends money on his wine.'

Swiftly, they crossed the cellar. Quinn opened the door. The beam lit another doorway on the other side of the passageway, a little further along.

'Hold the torch,' he said, slipping a pick into the lock, gently rotating it.

After a second, the door opened. Stale air, like bad breath, hit their faces.

The torch beam wavered over a pool table, sofas and what looked to be a bar stocked with soft drinks and small, brightly coloured packets – possibly sweets. Curtains covered a single window. In the far corner, a screen projector and a pile of movies in their metal cases.

'Hand me the torch.'

Quinn crossed the room and scanned the titles.

'Soft porn,' he said, lips curling in disgust.

'Soft porn? Well, well, are you thinking what I'm thinking.'

'And what are you thinking?' Quinn said.

'It's odd,' Caitlin said. 'Not too much money's been spent here, nothing like the cellar or the lavish furniture upstairs. Everything looks cheap, as if it's for less discerning guests. Perhaps "entertainment" for young impressionable boys?'

'Exactly what I was thinking. This is somewhere they can educate the boys, soften them up for what's –'

Without warning, Quinn switched off the torch.

'What are you doing? I was –'

'Quiet,' he whispered, pulling her back into the passageway. Its walls were illuminated by the light in the stairwell. Heavy footsteps echoed above them. She could hear the murmur of voices, and he pushed her towards the cellar, almost clipping her heels. He closed the door behind them, grabbed her hand and started towards the courtyard door.

But she pulled back. 'It must be Rushton and Brechtenshafft. Perhaps we can follow them, wherever that might be.'

She felt his breath on her face, his fingers tight on her hand.

'To where? We'll be like rats in a blocked pipe.'

Suddenly he clamped his hand over her mouth and, holding her close, backed away from the door, past the wine racks to the rear of the cellar.

When he dropped his hand, she whispered, 'If you ever –'

But he wasn't listening, propelling her behind a double wine rack just before the cellar light flicked on.

Around her, the dark, dusty bottles reflected the light, revealing the hexagonal pattern of the racks. Rushton's and Brechtenshafft's voices boomed down from the low beamed ceiling and rumbled from wall to wall around the cellar.

Quinn peered out from the end of the rack where they huddled; he nudged her arm and pointed across to the long rack opposite them. Caitlin nodded and followed him towards the rack at the far corner of the room, nearest the courtyard door.

She saw him lift out one bottle, his whole body balanced with an animal grace as if ready to throw it. She couldn't see anything, but heard Brechtenshafft say, 'No problems?'

'None. And arrived on time, last night,' Rushton said.

'We should start distribution at once.'

Low murmurs from Rushton.

Caitlin glanced at Quinn, laid her hand on his sleeve. Frowning, he turned his head slightly. She mouthed, 'Wine?'

He stared at her a moment, shrugged.

A sudden noise like a firecracker almost made her jump. Opening one of those boxes with something, she thought. After a moment, she heard Brechtenshafft say, 'It's a good product.'

'A robust product,' Rushton said, laughing. 'I've something special upstairs for you to celebrate your product, a 1962 Bin 60A Coonawarra Cabernet. If you like it, I'll get my vintner to send you a dozen. They've been personally signed for me by Max Schubert, the cellar master.'

He laughed again. The sound scratched at Caitlin's nerves.

'I prefer our Trockenbeerenauslese; a matter of taste.'

'Of course, of course. Now, I think I should head upstairs to see off some of my guests.'

She smiled. Rushton sounded as if he'd choke on his own generosity; humility didn't come naturally to him. His association with the German had to be a very beneficial one.

Brechtenshafft's accent became harder to understand. 'An impressive set up, Rodney. Expanding … Need a larger boat.'

The light was switched off, the door closed. Their voices faded with their footsteps.

She pushed herself to her feet, glanced at Quinn's thin face, pale in the torchlight.

'I think it's time you got upstairs too,' he said.

She shook her head. 'Not before we look in those boxes.'

Following Quinn past the racks, she added, 'It's odd, that comment from the German about a larger boat. Rushton's boat is as big as any in Sydney Harbour.'

'From what I've heard of Brechtenshafft, he doesn't think small.'

Quinn flashed the torch onto the boxes and Caitlin lifted the loose wood from the closest one. They stared silently at its contents.

Quinn pursed his lips. 'Well, Sir Rodney seems to have put himself in a rather indelicate and decidedly criminal space with this cargo.'

Caitlin lifted out several magazines that all featured graphic, pornographic images of children.

'Hasn't he,' she hissed through clenched teeth.

25

She found Martin talking animatedly to a small group of men, including Rushton. Most of the guests had left. Caitlin crossed to the group, ignoring the others, eyes fixed on her husband.

'I want to leave.'

His startled gaze flicked to Rushton, the three other men, then back to her. 'Caitlin, we're –'

'Now, Martin.'

With a tight smile he drew her close. 'Just give me a –'

'No,' she said, walking away.

Seconds later, she felt his hand grip her waist.

Leaning towards her, his voice betrayed rising frustration. 'You've embarrassed me in front of my friends.'

Through gritted teeth, she muttered, 'You'll be grateful later.'

Shrugging off his arm, she stalked to the far end of the room where Helen Rushton was holding court. Caitlin's cool goodbye to their hostess contrasted Martin's effusive thanks.

As their heels tapped rapidly over the marble floor of the entrance rotunda, he said, 'A charming performance.'

She shot him a sidelong glance. 'Don't fret. Another minute or two and she'll have forgotten we were ever here.'

'At least Rodney wasn't offended. I told him you were ill.'

'I don't give a damn what you said to that bastard.'

With a quick look back at the house, he stopped, grabbed her arm. 'What's wrong with you?'

Pushing him away, she took a few steps back to see his face more clearly. 'I discovered pornography in Rodney's cellar, boxes of it.'

His brown eyes were like two dark, piercing probes in the shadowed light, as if he were carefully turning over the words in his mind. A second later he was laughing, bending to kiss her lips.

'Is that it? Well, darling, we shouldn't dob in Rodney for having *Playboy* magazines. Though boxes do sound obsessive.'

She stared at him. Did he think her so naive?

'What about child pornography?' she snapped. 'Rodney and that German partner of his are shipping it in.'

The laughter vanished. He looked stunned.

'That's preposterous!'

Turning, he walked towards his car, got in, revved the engine. Rapidly, he reversed, gravel spraying from the tyres; the passenger door swung open.

'Get in.' His words sliced through the cold night air.

In loaded silence they drove along the winding driveway, headlights throwing shadowy patterns on the garden and the ornate, wrought iron gates. It was several minutes before Caitlin dared look at him. A muscle twitched in his cheek; lips pressed into a thin line.

She reached out a hand, laid it lightly on his arm. 'Martin, I know this is hard for you, but we have to –'

'Hard for me!' Pulling his arm away, he thumped the steering wheel. 'Christ, Caitlin, what the hell did you think you were doing breaking into his cellar?'

'It was an accident. I was playing with …' She shook her head. 'It doesn't matter. Those children in the magazines could be six, seven years old. Adults can do what they like, but these are children. We can't risk that filth getting into predators' hands.'

A marked silence.

'Martin? Martin?'

The lines around his mouth tightened. 'There's nothing we can do. You were there illegally. Even the police haven't the authority to search without a warrant. There'd be no grounds for that and absolutely no guarantee that whatever you saw would still be there.'

She looked away, stared at the grey road rushing by.

'Do you know that German well?'

'No, Rodney's mentioned him a few times. Tonight was the first time I've met him.'

'I wonder if Rushton knows the vice squad are investigating Brechtenshafft for importing obscene material.'

He turned to her. 'Who told you he –'

'Look out!' she yelled, catching a flash of colour, a cacophony of sound ripping through the air. A car slewed to miss them.

She slumped back into her seat, tried to still the hectic beating of her heart.

'Not the smartest of moves,' she muttered.

'Shit, where'd he come from?'

'Martin, you went through a red light.'

He grunted, slowing the car.

They turned off the highway, exclusive, well-kept gardens closing in around them. Minutes later, Martin swung the car into their driveway. Stopping in the portico, he switched off the engine and turned to her.

'Where did you get that nonsense about Brechtenshafft being investigated by the vice squad?'

She frowned. 'I can't remember. I overheard talk about it tonight.'

'You can't believe everything you hear. Gossip spreads like a bushfire on a hot day.'

Caitlin was silent. If she and Quinn hadn't heard that conversation in the cellar, seen those magazines, she could almost accept the implausibility of it all. She should have told Martin about hiring Quinn earlier, but to do it now would expose a trail of events she wasn't ready to share with her husband. Yet somehow, she had to convince him that his continuing association with Rushton would fatally damage any hope he had of a political career.

And where did Tim fit into the equation? Here was a boy, badly in need of loving attention from his parents, and yet shut out of their lives, condemned to the company of Rushton's domestic employees. For the moment, she would have to push that speculation into the background. But later, she needed to talk to Enid to find out more about the boy. For now, she had to drag her mind back to the present moment

'I know you will think what I'm going to say is improbable, but I believe a paedophile ring is operating from Saint Anthony's and Rushton is possibly implicated.'

He shook his head, laughed. 'No, it's not possible. You're seeing every little thing about the orphanage, about Sean, under a magnifying glass.'

'That's not true. The autopsy report on Sean showed recent abuse.'

'How do you know?'

'Detective Hurd told me. It was a key factor in the coroner bringing down a finding of suicide. I thought you would have known.'

'I did.'

'Why didn't you tell me?'

'You were already too upset without me bothering you with the sordid details. The coroner found no evidence of neglect on the part of the brothers.'

'Then who was the abuser? I'm sure it couldn't have been the older boys. Sean wouldn't have been frightened of speaking out against them. He would have done anything to protect his brother. But fighting the brothers, outsiders … Difficult for a boy of twelve.'

'Caitlin, you don't know what those boys can do, how vicious some of them can be.'

'The attacks on Father MacManus and Father Griffin were the work of men, not boys. There has to be a ring of outsiders involved; a powerful cabal with money, connections.'

'You don't think Rodney … You can't mean …'

She shrugged. 'He's on the board of the orphanage.'

'Caitlin, it's all circumstantial. You find a box of pornography and you come up with this. It's madness. Rodney might be a lot of things but he would never get mixed up in anything like that. He loves children. He's just adopted his orphaned nephew, for God's sake.'

'Has he?' No need to talk to Enid now, but the revelation created more concern than ever. Traumatised by the death of his parents, Tim had come into Rushton's clutches. It was too horrible to contemplate.

But now was not the time to pursue that matter. She was silent for a moment, then glanced across at him. 'I'm just saying, be careful,

Martin. Your political career could be stymied before it's started, all through your connections with Rushton, and by association with Brechtenshafft. He cornered me on the balcony tonight, threatened me.'

'What do you mean, threatened you?

'He asked me if I was counting my losses. He said in my position, the odds were against me.'

26

Parking outside what she'd assumed was Quinn's address, she'd been nonplussed. She stood on the pavement for a moment, staring at the building, checking the numbers either side. Shrugging, she decided it had to be Quinn's. Knowing a little of his quirky personality, his home didn't really come as a surprise.

She walked down a short path between two neatly clipped handkerchief lawns to an inconspicuous door in the shadow of a steeple-like porch. When she pulled the unusual antique bell hanging to the right of the door, she heard a happy, tinkling sound within. She was contemplating the dichotomy between the antique bellpull and the modern door when it suddenly swung open.

Quinn wore an unreadable expression. 'Welcome to the church of Saint Nemo.'

She stepped onto a colourful rug on the polished, wooden floor. Curiosity gave way to fascination as she absorbed the new face of what would have once been a conventional chapel. Light streamed through tall, stained-glass windows into every corner of the unusual open-plan space. Two huge plants stood in brass jardinières, shiny leaves luxuriating in the warm atmosphere, looking as if they'd been freshly transplanted from the jungle. The stark, black leather sofa and the brass lamp on a sleek wooden table were unexpected: not the hallmarks of economy but of an aesthetic bachelor life. Opposite the sofa, a cinnamon-coloured, double-sided bookcase jutted out from the blood-red walls; its shelves full of old and expensive-looking books. An iron spiral staircase led up to what Caitlin assumed was a loft. Glancing up the stairs, she caught a glimpse of a large telescope trained on a skylight.

She gazed at Quinn. Interesting addictions: words and astronomy.

'Who's the genius architect?' she asked.

After a moment's silence, he said, 'My brother, Julian.'

The secretiveness that flickered in his eyes only highlighted the weariness in his thin face. That word of 'welcome' might have come from another person, some other conversation; the jaunty movements of his lean frame from their meeting in the Botanic Gardens were gone. And why this meeting here in the privacy of his home? Had he regretted his bitter threat to quit the case?

As if reading her mind, Quinn led her around the staircase, past a black dining table, to a pristine white galley kitchen, reminiscent of a seaman's cabin.

'I thought it safest to keep our meetings below the radar.'

She took one of the black dining chairs he offered.

Drawing a thin file from a cabinet, he dropped his lanky frame into a well-worn Victorian armchair. Opening the file, he pulled out a sheet of paper.

'I ran MacManus' list past a friend in the vice squad,' he said, handing her the paper. 'He's ticked off some interesting people. I'm trying to set up a meeting with my contact, but he has to be careful. He's so honest he's a bit of a problem for some of his colleagues.'

Scanning the list, Caitlin pressed a finger down onto the only name she knew, saw a wry smile on his lips.

'A big fish,' he said. 'Hard to reel in.'

She nodded and stared out the window, recognising the verity of his words. She still felt the vivid shock that had run through her body as she'd read the name that night in the car as they drove away from the cemetery: Rodney Rushton. If the truth could shatter the secure opulence of that man's life, others might follow.

27

The tick-tock, tick-tock of the dining room skeleton clock marked the passing time. Caitlin stared over the remnants of her breakfast, out to the morning sunlight filtering onto the garden beds of bright, colourful tulips. The sweet smell of lavender wafted in on the breeze.

Since Friday night, their home had become a battleground; Caitlin accusing, Martin defending Rushton. She, driven by her intense dislike of the man; Martin, she suspected, by political necessity. Now, at the breakfast table, it seemed near crisis point.

And where did that leave Caitlin Cheney, her creative spirit and her concern for the boy, Tim, left in the clutches of a man like Rushton? It was almost overwhelming.

The bizarre chain of events embroiling Saint Anthony's, the carpet-bagging domain of New South Wales politics, the attitude of the police, and the web of Rushton's lust for money and power had infected her like a malignant virus.

Over the last few months, she'd begun to wonder what kind of man she'd married. A man who changed his manner and attitude to suit the circumstances. A barrister soon to take silk, yet driven by political ambition, blind to the inconvenient facts of everyday life, not pausing to consider consequences, betting his future on a game of chance.

She shook her head, picked up the morning newspaper and idly turned its pages, scanning the world and its gossip. All the warmth of the sunlight, the balm of the lavender fled as she stared at the cliched headline: 'LIBS BIG GAMBLE'.

"Liberal candidate, Martin Preece, was the major beneficiary of a recent gambling night attracting an assortment of colourful racing identities, racketeers from Kings Cross, a well-known Sydney hitman, and high rollers from the depths of Sydney society. Held in the harbourside mansion of millionaire businessman Rodney Rushton, it is another example of the dubious lengths our political parties will go to to fund their election campaigns.'

And there in the feature photo was a jovial looking Martin among a group of decidedly questionable characters, with the caption, 'MP's benefit night?'

She closed her eyes. That photo! How could he have been so stupid? Hadn't he learnt to be more discreet during his years at the Bar?

The door opened, and Martin silently walked in. Bending to kiss his wife, he caught the headline.

'Jesus Christ!' The words exploded into the quiet room.

'I told you so,' she said softly.

Maria, who'd just appeared in the doorway, hesitated.

'Coffee,' Martin snapped at her, grabbing the newspaper and striding out.

'I'll put it on,' Maria said, her voice sounding uncertain.

Caitlin hurried out into the living room and crossed to Martin's study. He was slumped in his chair, staring out the window, his eyes seemingly fixed on the breeze playing havoc with the leaves of the hedges.

Looking down into his taut face, his shadowed eyes, she kissed him and held him close, murmuring, 'All you can do is ride it out. What's that old political saying? "Today's headline, tomorrow's fish and chip wrapping."'

'Tell that to the General Secretary, the Hunters Hill voters.' Turning, he shoved the paper towards her. 'These left-wing journalists have their beady eyes open for every chance to attack.'

'I did warn you. Perhaps that's why Richard wasn't there.'

'Whiter than white, is he?'

She shrugged. 'Just politically astute.'

She sat down and began to read the article again, her anger fuelled by the journalist's self-righteous tone, but equally by Martin's inept responses, his words sounding a hollow justification.

'God, Martin, look at this.' She stabbed at the paper. 'They're saying there were criminals present.'

'Caitlin, I've read it three, four times. None of those wild assertions are backed with facts,' he muttered, weariness in his voice.

'And speaking of the people Rushton had there, haven't you forgotten something?'

For the first time since she'd come into the room, his eyes met hers, unfocused, as if he was not looking at her, but through her, to a completely different image.

'Oh? What's that?'

'Those magazines,' she said. 'The ones in Rushton's cellar. It looks as if your friend might have already landed you in deep shit. With an associate like Brechtenshafft, doesn't this put you in double jeopardy?'

Martin stood up suddenly, pushed his chair away from his desk, walked to the window.

A soft knock sounded on the door.

'Yes!'

Caitlin flinched at Martin's sharp response.

The door opened.

'Your coffee,' Maria murmured, barely looking up.

Without turning, he waved his hand towards the desk.

'Thank you, Maria,' Caitlin said, taking the coffee.

After Maria had closed the door, Caitlin said, 'You've upset her again.'

'You give her too much latitude.'

'And you give too little,' she shot back.

She looked down at the paper, lingering on the photograph of Martin.

Her mind skittered back to the first time they'd met, three years ago. He'd been standing on the steps of the Supreme Court, his barrister's gown billowing out like angel's wings, dark eyes regarding her with silent interest, while in the background her parents tried to stifle their apprehension for the days ahead in court.

Then, like a character from a comedy of manners, Rodney Rushton had blundered up the steps, shoving his huge frame through the crowd, piggy eyes ignoring any protest. Martin, undeterred, charmingly, skilfully manoeuvred her parents and herself into the courtroom, as if oblivious to the fact the millionaire businessman they were suing for fraud was in front of them.

She would never have imagined that little act of compassion, embedded in the memory of those terrible weeks during which her parents had wrestled with their demons and hoped for justice, would affect her so intensely. The collapse of her parents' business and the protracted court case had taken its toll. Her father was dead within months, her beloved mother eight months later. It seemed inevitable she should turn to Martin. Yet, sadly, the intimacy that so quickly developed had, after their marriage eighteen months ago, abated just as rapidly. Already, the flaws that at first were barely noticeable were becoming a yawning chasm.

She focused again on her husband's picture. Slowly, she traced his face with a finger, stared at his grinning companions who looked like the habitués of casinos and racetracks, as the article had claimed. An image carefully chosen by the newspaper to do the Liberal Party the greatest possible damage.

Suddenly, she pushed the newspaper towards him. 'Is this really what you want?'

Thrusting the paper away, his response was brusque. 'It's just a photograph. You know how it was that night, people crowded in everywhere, flash bulbs popping in your face every second.'

'Oh, I remember how it was. I was down in that cellar listening to Rushton and Brechtenshafft – criminals, Martin – indulging their base proclivities, discussing the destruction of children's lives like they were shares on the stock exchange.'

'Caitlin, you were there illegally. Nothing you heard or saw could ever be used in court.'

'Rushton has to be exposed for what he is: a paedophile. And is he the reason why Tim is like he is, has he been damaged by his uncle's unwanted attention? Sexual abuse of minors is just as big a problem within families as it is with those separated from their families.'

'If that's true, how do you think it can be done without any tangible evidence?' Martin said.

She ran her fingers through her hair, shook her head.

He sighed. 'Anyone who makes an allegation of that kind would face a defamation action that would surely destroy them and achieve nothing.'

'There has to be another way. He's pulling your strings. He wants to use you once he's helped you win a seat in parliament.'

He stopped pacing the floor, stared at her.

'What do you mean?'

Her mouth went dry, she stood up and gripped the edge of the desk. 'He wants to make sure the man he's backed wins, and it may be a worn-out cliche, but it's true: "He who pays the piper calls the tune." You only have two choices. Break with Rushton completely or withdraw your candidature.'

'Don't be ridiculous! Of course, in an ideal world, people like us should do something about this child abuse problem, but it is more difficult than you realise and we don't live in an ideal world. In the larger scheme of things, we are just little people. Now, as for Rodney, I need time to think that through.'

She threw the paper onto the desk, pages fluttering to the floor, and fixed him with a hostile gaze. 'Time is something those children don't have.'

Ignoring her words, he said, 'Your friend Richard hasn't helped. Clearly, he is in bed with the press, jumping in with this pithy comment about an inquiry and possible disendorsement – as if a party inquiry could establish that the function deliberately sought to raise funds from the criminal sector.'

She glared at him. 'What did you expect? Congratulations for the publicity?'

'He could have cautioned me.'

'Would you have listened?'

'Isn't he the leader of the party?'

Picking up his coffee cup, he started to drink, grimaced.

She studied him for a second, not quite sure whether the sarcastic expression on his face was in sync with his words.

'Isn't your obsession with politics blinding you to the obvious? Integrity depends on you being your own man.'

A frown creased his clear skin with tiny pleats. 'That's ridiculous.'

'Is it? Remember what Shakespeare wrote in *Hamlet*, *"To thine own self be true, and it shall follow, as the night the day, thou canst not then be false to any man."'*

The coffee cup clattered onto the saucer. 'And look what happened to the character that said it: a sword through his guts.'

'Can't you see what it's doing to you? Where's the man who fought for my parents' rights, and for children's in the Children's Court, who inspired me to seek justice for Sean's death, hoping to keep other children safe? Now I feel I'm living with a stranger, what we have together being slowly destroyed. If you love me, if you want a life with me –'

'Caitlin, politics is my oxygen.' The furrows deepened between his dark, unblinking eyes. 'How many times have you said you paint to live? What would you say if I asked you to give it up?'

'Nothing I have done has ever threatened your lifestyle.'

'Hasn't it?'

She walked over to the study door, opened it, hesitated, and gave her husband a parting glance over her shoulder. 'No, not yet.'

28

Sunday morning, after telling Martin she would work in her Rocks studio, Caitlin left home at eight o'clock. Another sleepless night had filled her with the urge to get out of the house, to talk to someone who could assure her she was not as obtuse and unreasoning as her husband believed, that her view of the world had integrity, purpose.

She trusted Lexy, even Quinn, but it was not a matter of trust. She needed someone whose experience and objectivity set them apart, someone who would be rock solid in a crisis. Last night, she'd decided she needed to talk to Richard.

She struggled to match Martin's legal brain, to pick a way through the morass of lawyer's jargon he cleverly inserted into their arguments. But Martin still wouldn't, or couldn't, see her dilemma. Where was his trust in her judgement? Even though what she had told him could not be proved in a court of law, it contained enough substance to make it imperative to break with Rushton. His position was morally indefensible.

Conflicting thoughts plagued her. Like prising up a stone to see what was underneath, she wanted to expose the concepts driving her husband's psyche to the daylight. But wasn't it true that every relationship had both partners keeping secrets? Secrets could hold power, an inner landscape; like her own creative watchfulness, invisible to Martin or anyone.

Parking outside her studio in an almost deserted street, she glimpsed her face in the rear-vision mirror: doe-like eyes caught in the glare of the dishonesty that seemed to surround her. She wound down the window, wanting the cold air to negate these painful thoughts, yet she could not reconcile the erosion of trust, each for the other, that was splintering her marriage.

Richard's car pulled up behind her. He climbed out and walked towards her. One day he might hate her for involving him in the darker corridors of her life, but he was the only one she could confide in and in whom she could place her ultimate trust.

Squatting down, he smiled up at her, 'Lovely morning, a little chilly.'

'I'm sorry it's so early. You probably needed more sleep.'

'True, but I'm used to it.'

He stood up, opened the car door, extended his hand to her. As she got out an unfamiliar warmth suffused her body. She pushed her shaking hands deep into her pockets, dropping her keys in the process. He bent down to pick them up and unlocked the street door.

While Richard inspected the restoration of her studio, she made them mugs of tea. She took them to the small table under the middle window, drawing two chairs into a patch of weak sunlight.

Looking at him properly for the first time that morning, she was conscience-stricken. The strain of vigorous campaigning around the state, like a political gypsy, was evident. Deep hollows in his cheeks made shadows of his thirty-eight years; weariness had etched lines down the sides of his chiselled mouth – one she longed to caress but didn't dare.

'You look so tired.'

Reaching across to draw one of her hands into his, he said, 'You look as if you need more sleep too.'

She dipped her head and took a sip of tea, feeling his eyes watching her.

Finally breaking the silence, he said, 'Nice as this is, I'm sure you didn't invite me here just for Sunday morning tea.'

Now he was here, she couldn't think how to begin. She turned her head towards the harbour. The twists and turns she'd put herself through since her discovery in the cellar over a week ago – all those nights arguing with Martin, the early mornings when she'd crawled out of bed, dazed from lack of sleep – had taken their toll. And all the long hours of pleading with Martin had given her nothing.

She rested a hand on the windowsill in a narrow band of sunlight. Warmth – so little, and Richard, so close. If only she could expunge from her mind the violence that had invaded her world and just hold onto this moment. But now she had to break the spell and somehow tell Richard what was happening. He was the only person who could make her husband see reason, get him to cut his ties with Rushton and bring some balance back into their lives.

Suddenly entwining his fingers in hers, he said, 'What is it you want to tell me?'

She stared down at their hands for a moment. 'It's about the gambling fundraiser Rushton had at his Northbridge home.'

'Not the best way to raise money for a political campaign.'

She licked her lips, cleared her throat. 'No. Well, it wasn't the easiest of nights for me, being in the house of a man I detest. I was so bored I decided to have a wander around the place. In the cellar –'

He raised his eyebrows. 'Since when have you been interested in wine?'

'There were a number of wooden crates brought in from France. Only they weren't filled with wine, but pornographic magazines. Child pornography.'

His hands slipped out of hers. 'And you just walked in, found them?'

'Not quite.' She briefly sketched her movements, from meeting Tim and the circumstances that eventually led to overhearing Rushton and Brechtenshafft in the cellar.

He let out a deep sigh. 'Have you any idea of the risk you took?'

'Quinn was with me. He'd been photographing some of the guests. Questionable guests, too.'

He pushed his mug of tea away, gazed around the room as if searching for words, then leant towards her, his face close to her across the narrow table. 'What the hell was Quinn doing putting you in that situation? The police suspect Brechtenshafft is involved with Asian brothels, opium and heroin smuggling, slavery.'

'Slavery?'

'Yes, slavery. I've heard he could be here to extend his criminal network, using young immigrant women. It could explain Rushton's interest. If you'd been discovered, you might not be sitting here this morning.'

He rubbed a hand over his face – concern or weariness?

'Have you spoken to Martin about this?'

'Yes.'

'What did he say?'

'That he'd heard nothing, but he'd find a way to somehow raise it with Rushton.'

'The pornography or Brechtenshafft's threat?'

'Both, I'd hope,' she said. 'Then his legal mind seemed to go into overdrive: concrete evidence, body of proof, et cetera, et cetera.'

'I'll bet it did. And I wonder if he gave a thought to the political implications?'

'I think he's terrified of losing Rushton's support.'

Richard's face took on a strange, closed look. He stared at her intently, giving her the feeling she was a piece of glass and he was looking through her, seeing something beyond that was decidedly unpleasant.

'Martin is mired in his obsession with politics, yet his association with Rushton could destroy everything he believes in. That's why I had to see you. You're his leader, he might listen to you.'

'Possibly, or then again, possibly not. Politics is a complex business and the only hard and fast rule is that there are none. You see, Rushton wouldn't be scrutinised quite like a politician, so we would have to be careful not to stir up something that might blow over. If the press gets a whiff of scandal, everyone associated takes a hit to their credibility.'

'That's what I'm frightened of,' she said.

He gently took her hand again. 'Caitlin, perhaps it's not as bad as we think; just a case of the paper trying to put some acid on the party. I find it curious that after that splash last Sunday there's been no follow-up. Rushton may have called in some markers. But it is a real worry. The person who wrote that article is a tenacious journalist. My concern is that if he decides to follow it with another story, this could blow up closer to the election when voter opinion is easily swayed. As for Martin, no doubt he believes the essence of politics lies in strong alliances, which it is to some extent, but it can also make you vulnerable.'

'In what way?'

'Loyalty in politics is fragile – it's not a one-way street. My party will not want to suffer because of Martin's misplaced loyalty. He should be careful or he could finish up in the political wilderness. There are certainly elements in the party that would be more than happy if he were disendorsed.'

She stared at him in disbelief. 'My God, he'd be devastated. He lives for politics!'

'Then he doesn't need Rushton hooked to his star.'

She scraped her chair back against the floorboards, stood up and walked over to the damaged painting of Sean still standing against a wall. She studied it for a moment, then turned around.

'The connection between Martin and Rushton could be even more of a problem. On the gambling night, the German essentially warned me to mind my own business.' She pulled the copy she'd made of MacManus' list from her pocket and passed the paper to him. 'Do you recognise any of these names?'

He scanned the list. 'About half, I would think. This is becoming more and more of a waking nightmare. Where did you get it?'

'From Father MacManus.'

'And what is its significance?'

'They're paedophiles.'

'How do you know?'

'He told me.'

'When did he give it to you?' The softness of his voice failed to completely hide his concern.

She shrugged. 'Oh, about a month ago.'

He stared at her without blinking. 'Caitlin, I've not been off the planet. I do read the papers. Father Griffin had been giving Father MacManus shelter. Two priests attacked, one now dead. Please, tell me, where and when exactly did that priest give you this list?'

She didn't, couldn't answer.

He stood up and paced the room. 'Then tell me, have you shown this to Martin?'

'No.'

'Thank God. The fewer who know the better. The men at the centre of this don't care who they hurt. You've escaped them twice. The next time they try – and they will if you don't stop – another innocent person, like your mechanic, could have an accident. Perhaps die.' He took her face in his hands. 'I don't want that person to be you.'

'I can't stop. You don't know …'

Suddenly his arms were around her. She tensed, went to pull away, but instead gave in to her emotions, clinging to him for a few long seconds before they stepped apart.

'All right. For you, I'll speak to Martin, but now I'm begging you …' Richard's voice was husky.

'What if he doesn't listen to your advice?'

He laid a finger against her lips. 'We all have our choices, don't we?'

She gazed at him for several seconds. 'Yes. The hardest part is living with them.'

29

Caitlin walked briskly along Clarence Street towards the warehouse Quinn had chosen for their meeting. She hoped the detective he had lined up to speak to her was not as obtuse as Hurd, or any quirkier than Quinn. She needed something productive to come out of this; her frustration was mounting.

She stood in front of the building, its dignified shabbiness crushed between more modern, taller, utilitarian neighbours.

She stepped into the narrow vestibule and, after a quick glance at the tenant directory, headed for the lift. A portly man pulled open its steel mesh door. His cheerful smile deepened the wrinkles on his chubby face. Closing the door behind her, he glanced over his shoulder, winked and said, 'Good afternoon for it.'

Unsure what 'it' was, she smiled back. 'It certainly is. Third floor, please.'

She watched as he thrust leather gloved hands into the rectangular hole beside him, grasped at a rope and pulled. The lift shuddered, emitted a few thumping noises and began to move upwards. At the third floor he pulled on the rope again, stopping the lift with another jolt. She stepped into a narrow corridor that ran the length of the building. The lift door squeaked shut behind her then began its slow, descending symphony.

She walked along the corridor until she found a door with a small, frosted glass panel embossed with black letters: *Lulu Enterprises*. Typical of Quinn's offbeat humour to choose a place like this.

The dull roar of traffic below evaporated into cathedral-like silence as the door squeaked shut behind her. She took a few steps forwards, glancing around. In the fading afternoon light that struggled through two grimy windows, she could see stacks of packed cardboard boxes.

Footsteps on the linoleum floor made her spin around.

'Welcome to my brother's world,' Quinn said, materialising from nowhere.

'Is the detective here?'

He gestured towards a dim passageway. 'In my brother's office.'

She sensed an odd bittersweetness in his words. Dodging the straw that spewed from the packing cases, she followed him.

In a room not much bigger than a cubby hole, the detective was sprawled in a swivel chair tucked between a battered roll-top desk and a steel filing cabinet.

'Detective Sergeant Scott Turner, Caitlin Cheney,' Quinn said.

Smiling up at her, the detective, younger than Quinn, unwound his tall, slim figure from the chair. His handshake was firm, but not the kind to crush her small fingers.

'Here,' he said, stepping away, 'take this seat.'

'I'm fine,' she said, shaking her head at Quinn's offer of a wooden chair. Instead, she leant against a small cupboard. Quinn propped himself against the door jamb.

Shrugging, the detective sat down again. His gaze seemed to roam everywhere.

Finally, he said, 'Quinn's given me what he knows. It's important I hear your version.'

She stared at him. His initial pleasantness had given way to something more serious and reassuring, yet slightly unnerving, as if he had stepped from one world into another.

'I'd only be repeating what Quinn's told you.' she said.

'Everyone's version is different. There may be things you didn't tell Quinn and now remember.'

'I didn't think that's why I was coming here. I thought we could be looking for a way ahead.'

'The way ahead isn't going to be easy, so we need to start from the best-informed past. From what Quinn has told me, you don't seem to quite realise the gravity of what you've been dabbling in.'

'With all the hush-hush of meeting in this place, I was hoping you'd found a link between Sean's death, Rushton and what might be a paedophile ring at Saint Anthony's?'

Turner raised his eyebrows, looked at Quinn. 'She doesn't mess around, does she?'

Quinn shrugged, giving Caitlin a sidelong smile.

'I told you there's no point trying to gloss over it,' he said to Turner.

She glanced at him. 'Gloss over what?'

'That the investigation into Sean's death has become another matter gathering dust in the police records,' the detective said.

Caitlin gave Turner an icy look. 'They've closed the case?'

'Such cases are not always completely closed, but they do go onto the back shelf. Tight resources mean we can't keep working on them. That's what happens.'

She turned, glared at Quinn. 'You said he wanted to help.'

'Just listen, Caitlin.'

Her words poured out, 'Is this helping? I knew Sean. His death wasn't suicide or an accident. What about those magazines, MacManus, Griffin? I want to know what's going on at Saint Anthony's. Is it part of a wider paedophile ring? To what extent are Brechtenshafft and Rushton involved? And what about Rushton's nephew, Tim, who may be living with a paedophile?'

The detective gave a tight smile, as if forcing it onto his face. 'We'll get nowhere with this tit for tat business. So, why don't you sit down, take Quinn's advice on where to go from here and let me give you some facts regarding another investigation? And I have to say, in doing so, I am exceeding my authority.'

She stayed where she was, folded her arms.

He leant forward, rested his elbows on his knees and stared down at the floor.

'Those magazines you found in Rushton's cellar are just a small part of a bigger operation, masterminded by Brechtenshafft. How much do you know about paedophilia? the way paedophiles operate?'

She shrugged. 'Very little.'

'If Saint Anthony's Orphanage is a part of a wider circle of paedophile activity, penetrating the underworld of that wider circle is a battle in which someone like you should not be involved.'

'Underworld? You make them sound like the Mafia.'

'A close relative. And like the Mafia, they will go to extraordinary lengths to protect their territory, support each other. The police? Like the curate's egg. For the bad ones, it's a honeypot where power and money become irresistible.' Turner paused, pursing his lips in apparent disgust.

'Does that mean you want me to do nothing?' She tried to suppress the frustration boiling within her.

'Miss Cheney, these rings are a law unto themselves. They're well organised, powerful. They have many layers and a strict hierarchy. Those at the top, those who reap the greatest rewards, can often be found among the elite of society.

'As for the paedophiles themselves, they are playing for the highest stakes and for them the risks are part of the attraction. This makes them the most dangerous. They'll do anything to keep their operations active, secret, and when and where necessary, they use professional thugs to do their dirty work, even to kill. The death of that priest, Father MacManus, is one instance – a weak link, dead. And Father Griffin, lucky to be alive. It's far wiser to leave it in the hands of the vice squad.'

'Wiser? Wiser to forget Sean's murder, the other poor boys in the orphanage and Tim, easy pickings, with no one to protect any one of them?'

'I hear what you're saying, but try to put yourself in my place, trying to question victims who live in a frozen, shutdown state, who flinch when someone tries to comfort them,' he murmured. 'An eleven-year-old girl who's been serially raped by a roomful of priests, a seven-year-old boy subjected to anal intercourse, children who have been threatened with physical violence if they don't keep silent, children who believe their own personal value in the world is only as a sex object.

'So many of these victims have been cast into a life of depression, self-mutilation, self-destructive promiscuity, suicide. The cases go on and on.'

His words numbed her. She saw the bleakness in his blue eyes, as if he were retrieving these thoughts from far-off places.

'Shining a light on the cockroaches who perpetrate this harm, I have to be careful. And many senior officers in the force are averse to rattling the Church's cage.

'The problem is much more complicated than catching and punishing the offenders. Many cases involve dysfunctional homes, the poverty trap. And what does society do to help them? Nothing.

'I know of one fourteen-year-old boy picked up at The Wall who was found to be living with a notorious paedophile. The boy pleaded with us not to intervene; he told us, at least he had a roof over his head, food on the table.'

Caitlin went to speak, but in a slow, troubled voice, Turner continued, 'There's something else you should know.'

She followed his gaze to a pile of papers on the desk. He carefully straightened them into a neat stack. She didn't know why but it unnerved her; her mouth went dry, her heart beat uncontrollably.

'A body was fished out of the water at Wisemans Ferry last week. An execution style killing. My contact got curious when the man turned out to be a foreman on one of Rushton's construction jobs who was about to give evidence to officers of the extortion squad. They've been investigating stand-over tactics in the building industry.

'Because of the similarity between this murder and that of MacManus, forensics matched the bullet from the foreman against the one they'd retrieved from Father MacManus.' The detective rubbed at one eye, then crossed his arms. 'They came from the same gun.'

30

'He should be back by now,' she muttered, glancing at her watch in a cycle of tedious repetition. It was already half past six.

She should have sat in Martin's comfortable chair, closed her eyes, practised some meditation. Instead, she began to pace the length of his book-lined chambers.

Returning to the window, she pressed her forehead against the cold glass, staring down in the forlorn hope that she might see Martin crossing Phillip Street. But how could she distinguish the figures huddled under their umbrellas, hats firmly clutched to their heads, buffeted by the wind and squalls of rain lashing the street?

Turner's words from a few hours ago haunted her, and as she looked into the darkened glass her imagination conjured up surreal images: Rushton transformed into a demon gambolling over Martin's partner's desk, clawing his law books from the shelves, ripping them to shreds, tearing his Daumier prints off the red painted walls, destroying his career aspirations. Exactly what would happen if they couldn't get him out of their lives. She folded her arms tightly over her stomach to ease the nerves that sparked like live wires.

Martin would think she'd gone off the edge if she told him Rushton could be involved in a double murder. And if she did, she'd have to break Turner's confidence.

She heard a sharp click behind her. Turning, she saw Martin standing in the doorway.

'This is unexpected,' he said, pushing the door closed.

Propping his umbrella in its stand, he placed his coat and scarf on a chair, crossed the room and put his arms around her.

'If you're looking for a dinner date, it will have to be another night. I've got material to prepare for tomorrow, then a meeting at the party's head office.'

She gazed up into his face. 'It's important.'

'It will have to wait,' he said, glancing over at his desk.

'No, it can't.' Her voice sounded very loud in the quiet room.

He was giving her that unsettling lawyer's look, the one she always imagined him inflicting on hostile witnesses as he imposed his will on them. Caitlin pressed her lips together, held his gaze.

'If it's about Rodney,' he said, walking over to his desk, 'I'm not in the mood for another lecture.'

'You'll want to hear this,' she said, following him.

'I doubt it,' he said, not looking at her. He sat down, pulled the pink tape off a brief and turned the pages to where he had left a marker. 'Unless you're going to tell me the police have magically obtained a search warrant for Rodney's house and found those magazines.'

He opened a volume of law reports and quickly traced his finger down the centre of the page.

Absently he muttered, 'But that hasn't happened, has it?'

'Martin, if you don't –'

'Sweetheart, how many times have I told you? Thirty, forty times? Without something concrete, your allegations are simply defamatory.' He paused, fixing that direct gaze on her again. 'If we breathed a word of this to the wrong people, Rodney would have no compunction in going after you, me or both of us. And don't fool yourself – he'd win, handsomely. Now, please go and let me finish my work. And ask Maria to leave me some dinner.'

'I can't, don't you remember, she's just left for Spain to spend a few weeks with her family. Or perhaps you haven't noticed.'

'Of course, I just forgot. Not to worry.'

He began to make notes on slips of paper, which he tucked into the brief, each time ticking off a line on the pad. He seemed to be willing her out the door with the intensity of his concentration.

For a minute she stood watching the controlled expression on his face, the tight line of his mouth, trying in this battle of words and silence to get the upper hand. She could babble away for hours and he still wouldn't listen. Somehow, she had to make him, had to shock him out of this obsessive cocoon he had spun around himself.

But she had to be careful. In her mind she went over and over her meeting with Quinn and Turner, wanting to tell Martin everything. She took a deep breath.

'Martin, the police pulled a body out of the water at Wisemans Ferry.'

'One of Rodney's foremen.'

'You know?' She glared at him.

'I read the papers.'

He swung around to select another couple of leather-bound volumes from the mahogany shelf behind him. She watched him open the first book at a page marked by a slip of paper, pick up his pen and start making more notes.

'I hope you're not going to blame that poor fellow's death on Rodney?' he said, with the ghost of a smile.

'It's interesting you say that. Whoever killed the foreman used the same gun that killed that priest, MacManus.'

He looked up, forehead wrinkled with deep lines. 'Where did you hear that?'

She sensed a dangerous chasm opening. If Martin knew she'd hired Quinn and been talking to Scott Turner, it would lead to a torrent of questions and inevitably she would find herself forced to tell him about Father Griffin's beating, her night in the cemetery. It would be the end of any hope of cooperation or understanding between them; there'd be no more talk of help for Tim or the boys at the orphanage.

'I didn't hear it, just another gem from the ever-vigilant press,' she said lightly, 'Extraordinary coincidence, isn't it?'

Martin raised one eyebrow. 'I must have missed it, but yes, extraordinary. But where's the link between these deaths and Rodney?'

She walked to the window to try to hide her emotions, and took another deep breath. 'Do you know him well enough to be absolutely sure there isn't a link?'

An amused expression lightened his face. 'Well, enough to know it's a line he wouldn't cross.'

'You can't ignore the fact that the same gun killed them.'

Martin shrugged. 'Guns pass from hand to hand in the criminal world like candy from a tuckshop.'

'Two men, Martin, apparently strangers, killed execution style with the same gun, both connected to Rushton. How many coincidences do you need before you start to suspect a link between Rushton's involvement with stand-over tactics in the building industry and a paedophile ring in the orphanage where he's chairman of the board?'

Martin leant forward over his books and papers and pointed his pen at her. 'For God's sake, Caitlin, can you hear what you're saying? You're obsessed with playing amateur detective. I implore you, stay out of it.'

His soft, pleading words seemed to come from a genuine place, as if he really cared for her. Should she listen to his advice? It had a strong ring of truth.

She was silent for a moment, recalling all the times she'd tried to understand how good people like her parents could ever have become involved with Rushton and how, just because he was a very competent lawyer, her husband had been pulled into his net. Rushton's friendship of two years may have given Martin an insider's run on his quest for a seat in parliament, but why couldn't he see the ultimate cost of that support? All her words of reason hadn't been able to open his eyes to the naked reality that someone else's lust for power can ruin a man of principle.

From somewhere out in the corridor she caught the murmur of friendly voices, a laugh.

She gripped the edge of the desk. 'Forget it, is that it? Forget the police have stopped working Sean's case because they don't have enough resources. Forget that every day more of those boys are abused, pushed into dusty pigeonholes away from the scrutiny of society?'

'And you're going to stop it, just like that.' He snapped his fingers.

He gazed down at his pen, twirling it slowly in his elegantly manicured hands. All of a sudden, he looked up.

'Let's say Rodney, in the most serious scenario, ordered these killings. It would be almost impossible for the police to establish any evidential link between him and whoever pulled the trigger. It could take years before it came before a court, if indeed it ever did. And as for your theories about a link with child abuse and the involvement of the Catholic Church, well, that's in the realm of farce.'

She stared at him for some seconds. 'In your legal world, say in the Children's Court, you must see many cases of abuse. Isn't there some form of judicial process through which they could instigate a broad ranging investigation into the causes of abuse?'

'It would take something like a Royal Commission with very wide powers to crack that one and I don't see any government, now or in the foreseeable future, having the guts to go down that path. Between that and stand-over tactics in the building industry, you'd be fighting on two unwinnable fronts. No one would win and certainly not the boys. Even if they survived, I doubt they'd live long enough to see justice. Caitlin, I really am sympathetic to what you would like to achieve, but you have to face reality.'

'Wouldn't you have a vital political edge if you were identified with these issues?'

'Not with the voters of Hunters Hill,' he said with a half-smile.

'I'd have thought your electorate would have a strong moral conscience.'

He laughed. 'Sweetheart, you are naive. Anyway, it could be too late. By tomorrow night I may be facing disendorsement over that damned gambling night.'

She looked down at him, startled. 'You didn't tell me.'

He sighed. 'I've been called before the State Executive to show cause why I shouldn't be disendorsed. Brinsmead might regret it.

Disendorsing a candidate with my reputation so close to an election won't help his chances. But I'll do my best to save him that worry.'

She could almost see the machinations in his mind, painted on his surly expression.

'You can't blame Richard. You've put the party in a difficult position by not splitting with Rushton.'

'I don't see why. The gambling story is dead.'

She laughed, shook her head. 'And I'm naive. Journalists have a nasty habit of dragging stories out in the last few days before an election. And it's not just the gambling night.'

He stared at her. 'You told Brinsmead about the magazines.'

She looked away.

His lips barely moved with the two quick words: 'You fool.'

'I had to.'

'Why?'

'You don't think he should have been warned? What if the press reveals one of the Liberal Party's high-profile candidates is being funded from the proceeds of child pornography?'

'That's absurd.'

'No, Martin, you're expecting me to forget those magazines exist. After all my pleading to get rid of Rushton, you still want to protect him, even at the risk of making Richard look an incompetent fool, undoing all the hard work he and the team have done to create the opportunity to win Government.'

'How many times must I tell you? It's not about protecting Rodney. It's simply a matter of loyalty.'

'And your loyalty to Rushton is more important than your loyalty to Richard?'

'It's bigger than that. It's a question of loyalty to the team, the parliamentary party, the party rank and file, and everyone else who supports us.'

He turned to replace the two books on the shelf.

'Richard's a good politician, not to mention your leader. In this situation, doesn't your loyalty to him go beyond any other?'

Martin gave her a quizzical look. 'I'm beginning to question whether your loyalty to Brinsmead is more important to you than your loyalty to me.'

'I thought we were talking about you.'

'So did I.'

She studied his intense expression, felt her face flush. 'You're twisting my words.'

'I don't think I have to.' He smiled his enticing smile, a smile that had always stirred longing in her. 'You keep saying Rodney's my problem. Well, Brinsmead's yours. You know he's in love with you.'

'Don't be ridiculous.'

'He's driven a wedge between us.'

'Stop this, Martin. Richard's not your whipping boy. Blame Rushton if you're disendorsed.'

His smile faded. 'Who's twisting words now?'

Caitlin closed her eyes for a second. 'Words, useless words. It seems that's all we have left. And you won't even listen to mine.'

She waited for him to say something, but instead he stood up, put on his coat and scarf and grabbed his umbrella.

She felt the strangeness of the sudden silence. She took a few steps toward him.

'Martin, wait.'

He glanced at her. 'Brinsmead's been using me to get to you.

And you're right, words are useless. Nothing will change that. Now, I have to go and try to salvage my political career.'

Before she could come to terms with what he had just said, the door closed behind him. She stared at its solid panelling, her husband's words like a tempest flooding her brain, challenging her to ask herself, did she want this arid existence? Or the possibility of a richer life with someone like … Richard?

She turned back to Martin's desk, picked up the telephone and, before she could hesitate, dialled Richard's number at Parliament House. When she heard the soft drawl of his 'Hello?' she said, 'Richard, it's me.'

'Good timing. I was just about to walk out the door.'

'Sorry.'

He laughed. 'Don't be. It's a momentary reprieve before the meeting I'm attending tonight. It's in Randwick Town Hall, marginal territory, so it's important. A good chance to gauge the response of the swinging voter.'

'I thought you'd be at the State Executive meeting. Martin says you're threatening to disendorse him.'

'That's not true. I argued against disendorsement, but some of the Executive, those who backed the person he's just defeated for the preselection, are worried about fallout closer to the election. They are the ones pushing for it; it's their initiative, not mine. It could be worse. At least he always has his law practice. In fact, he would probably be far better off in the long run staying with the law. And Rushton will soon find another stalking horse.'

Her mind went blank. She couldn't find the words to convey what she wanted to say.

'Caitlin?' Anxiety gripped his voice.

'Richard, I … I –'

'Are you alright? Where are you?'

'In Martin's chambers.'

A moment's silence. 'Is he there?'

'No, he's gone to meet the State Executive.'

She gripped the cradle. 'Richard, I think I've stirred up a hornet's nest. I must see you.'

'Why not come out to Randwick? 90 Avoca Street. Afterwards we can grab a coffee. Actually, I need to ask you something.'

'Ask me now.'

'Later. Promise you'll come. And I do really have to go.'

The phone clicked in her ear. She put the receiver down. The silence seemed to go on and on.

31

A bitter wind peppered dust and leaves against the windscreen of Caitlin's Mercedes. She swerved to avoid a deep pothole as the car vibrated over another corrugated stretch of dirt road.

The telephone call from Brother Purcell had been brief. He wanted to meet her at Saint Benedict's Monastery in an isolated valley off the Colo River, about two hours' drive north-west of Sydney. When she had asked if she could bring someone with her, the brother had said he trusted her but was fearful of what happened to Father MacManus and Father Griffin. It had to be just her, himself and his conscience.

The brother seemed to be going to extraordinary lengths to talk to her. But why? What had happened to make that conscientious, personable man break the rule of silence expected at a religious retreat? Guilt, sins of omission or commission? Did it have any bearing on Sean Tessler's death? Was his brother Peter now in danger? It was a strange request. When she rang the orphanage, however, they confirmed he was at the monastery.

They were to meet at 4.30 at the statue of Saint Benedict, which stood in a half circle of pines opposite the stables and barn. The brothers would assemble in the chapel for prayers at a quarter to five. It was just after four.

As she drove, shadows of trees etched cold, dark patterns on the high, sandstone hills between which the small, narrow valley was wedged. She turned her headlights on. Spots of rain spattered the windscreen as she wound up a steep hill. To her right, she caught occasional glimpses of the dark water of a swiftly flowing river. Casuarina trees, with branches like gigantic horsetails, brushed the car windows. She gripped the wheel tightly; to pass another car on such a confined road could be a slippery nightmare.

Relief washed over her when the hill ran gently down into a valley. Here the road was less rutted, though a single lane bridge with its wide, wooden planks jarred her nerves.

Her thoughts turned to Richard. She had gone to his meeting at Randwick, was thrilled with the reaction he received from the crowd, the way he handled their challenging questions. Then, over a supper that was something more than a cup of coffee, he'd asked her if she'd come to his electorate to open an art exhibition organised by a group of local artists. They'd approached him for a recommendation and he'd suggested her.

After the call from Purcell, she'd rung Richard to ask if they could catch up in his electorate that evening and was told that it was one of the few nights he would be home. He gave Caitlin his address and said he was looking forward to seeing her. A silver lining to her expedition to this remote spot.

The road's openness petered out and another hill slowed her down. The tiny clock on the dashboard showed 4.10.

Rain drifted in a light mist over wattle and gum trees. She turned on the windscreen wipers, trying to ignore the thought of being stranded out there alone. It wasn't too late to turn back. She pushed away that thought, too. If only she couldn't hear Quinn's angry voice like a painful drum beat in her head: 'What do you think you're doing in this place? It's crazy.'

A fork in the road loomed ahead. On the brow of the hill to her left she saw the bulk of a building penetrate the mist. Saint Benedict's, its isolation exacerbated by the misty rain that blurred the darkened trees.

Quinn's angry voice again: 'This is crazy. Take my advice, go home.'

But this was her only opportunity to talk to Brother Purcell, the only person at Saint Anthony's she felt she could trust to question on Rushton's involvement with the orphanage. She'd have no other chance since Brother Finbar had barred her from the school. Even Quinn had been frustrated by the silence that seemed to drain the Christian spirit from that place.

Reaching the fork, she veered to the left. Around the next bend, the monastery came into full view, lit by a single shaft of sunlight penetrating the heavy clouds. A good omen.

Within minutes, she was turning in through the open gates. A quiet oasis for a retreat, though she wondered what fractured personalities might seek repair or reprieve within its holy sanctuary.

Trying to recall Brother Purcell's exact directions, she continued along the tree-lined driveway, past an extensive vegetable garden, to the slab barn where the brother had told her to park. She turned and saw the large statue within a half-circle of pines. In the fading light, she could make out the figure of Saint Benedict, patron of the order.

She checked the clock on the dashboard: almost 4.25. Glancing up again, she noticed a dark-clothed figure step into the open from the shadow of the pines. The man had the awkward gait of Brother Purcell, but before she could react, he had disappeared beyond the arc of pines.

She got out and quietly closed the car door. Glancing up at the monastery she noticed it looked deserted.

She passed the statue and followed the path of the limping Brother Purcell through the trees, further down a slight slope towards a large dam, its water a sheet of black glass. A gust of wind whipped leaves into her face. She shivered, pulling her polo neck jumper over her chin. From somewhere close by, a cow bellowed.

The brother stopped, turned back. She stopped too. Something niggled at her brain. What was it? What was it …

Jesus Christ! He was trailing the left leg; Brother Purcell limped on the right.

She reeled around, almost losing her balance on the slippery ground, and ran.

She heard the scream before she realised it was hers. The cow in the distance joined in with a series of long, deep bellows.

She screamed louder, grabbing at the pines to stop herself from falling, tearing off shreds of foliage; her boots slipped on the wet grass and the mud and stones around the gap in the pines.

Saint Benedict's statue loomed in front of her – a commanding figure in the mist and rain. But she doubted it held any power to drive off the nightmare that threatened to engulf her. She knew the man wasn't far behind her; already she could hear his vicious expletives through the pines.

Sucking air into her lungs, she screamed again. The cow's bellows stopped as suddenly as they had started. Her stumbling footsteps were taking her too slowly to her car. She risked a glance back over her shoulder. The gap was closing rapidly.

As she reached her car a rumble of thunder and a flash of lightning highlighted the man running towards her, shedding the black habit, his face distorted by rage. She found the door handle with fumbling fingers and wrenched it open, groping in her jacket pocket for her keys, arms and legs shaking as if touched by electric wires. She fell into the seat and slammed the door, twisting to push down the lock.

But already he was beside her, pulling open the door, reaching in to grab her by the arm and neck. Shards of agony seared over her scalp as the man tore at her hair, his hot, quick breath on her cheek. Her neck felt like it might snap.

She screamed again. He clamped a hand over her mouth and nose.

'Save your breath. The monks are too busy with their prayers,' he mocked.

She swung to hit him in the face.

'Still trying to be smart?' he hissed.

Her fingers clawed at the soft leather of her passenger seat. Her knuckles rapped at something cold and hard. She gripped it and swung, saw the blur of the torch's shiny barrel twist through the air, the surprise on the man's square, flat face in the split second before it struck him. He staggered back, clutching at his bleeding nose.

She tried to close the door. It wouldn't budge. Anger fuelled her. She struck at him again, but the blow glanced off his wrist. The torch fell to the floor. His iron grip returned, tightening around her throat. She grabbed at his bloodied fingers. *Oh, God …*

For a second, his grip on her throat relaxed. She raked her fingers down his face, felt her head spin with the force of a savage blow across her mouth.

'Out you come, you bitch,' he snarled.

She heard a voice cut through the air: 'Hey, you, let her go! I said let her go.'

A tall, heavily built man in white overalls was striding towards them.

Stepping away from the car, her assailant whirled to face the man. 'None of your business, mate. Just a squabble between me and my missus.'

She slammed the door shut, pressed down the lock and peered through the windscreen.

Her attacker dropped into a fighter's crouch and lunged forward, swinging his fists. But he was no match for the big man, who landed a solid punch to the jaw that sent him stumbling back. Turning away, he fled, disappearing into the trees.

Her rescuer walked to the car, tapped on the window. She wound it down a few inches.

'You okay?'

She could only stare at the white-overalled man, every part of her shaking.

He sat on his heels, his face level with hers. 'Miss, are you hurt? You're safe now, he's gone. I'm the monastery's vet, they called me in for a difficult calving.'

A faint smell of soap clung to his skin. It comforted her. And he had an open, honest face that seemed to exude reassurance. She tried to smile, nodded her head.

'Are you sure you're not hurt?'

She nodded again.

'Well, you should come up to the monastery. I think you've had quite a fright and a cup of tea is in order. Brother Augustine will call the police.'

She shook her head. 'I'm okay, thanks.'

She went to start the engine. Her keys weren't there. She looked along the passenger seat, reached down, felt around her feet, retrieved the torch and shone it on the floor. Relief surged through her as she caught the glint of silver. It took her a few seconds to put the key into the ignition.

'You should talk to the police,' the vet said. 'It looked more than just a family spat.'

She shuddered. Hurd's surly face sprang to mind and the police who'd come to her studio. And Turner, could she even trust him? She had begun to distrust anything, and everyone.

She glanced at the vet. 'It was a stupid argument, that's all. But thank you.'

'Are you sure? I didn't like the look of that fellow. He could still be around.'

'I'll be all right.'

The vet shrugged and stepped back.

The car's engine roared into life. She wanted to get away, and fast. She switched on the headlights, reversed and sped back along the driveway. But she wasn't all right. She was petrified.

She scanned the road ahead, the rear-vision mirror, the bushes, the trees either side of the road, expecting to see him at any moment. In another part of her mind, she rolled back the last few minutes.

The impostor must have known Brother Purcell or observed him for days like a professional actor. That perfect mimicry of the brother's voice, the black habit, the jerking limp – his one mistake, thank God.

All thoughts merged into one. The viciousness of the attack, those hands tearing at her hair, and the fingers around her throat threatening to choke the life from her. Without the vet, she'd have been fished out of the monastery's dam like the body at Wisemans Ferry.

Any doubts of a paedophile ring involving the orphanage had been extinguished. Whoever had put out the contract must fear she was too close to the truth.

She drove as fast as she dared, navigating a series of tight bends. No car appeared in the rear-vision mirror. The stretch of road ahead lay empty.

A few more bends and then a straight stretch where the treetops met above to create a tunnel. Another quick check in the rear-vision mirror and she began to relax a little.

She had just driven through the next series of bends when a light flashed in her eyes, becoming brighter: a set of headlights on high beam hurtled towards her from behind. She glanced into the mirror before spinning the wheel for a tight, right-hand turn. Her car skidded a little in the mud, tyres spraying gravel onto the edge of the winding road.

The car loomed closer. She accelerated. Richard's house at Kurrajong – her only safe haven – was still half an hour away. She flicked the mirror to anti-glare. The car was now so close it flooded her interior with light, leaving her totally exposed.

32

Caitlin tightened her grip on the steering wheel, pressed harder on the accelerator and barrelled over a small bridge. Its rough planks juddered a staccato rattle.

In the rear-vision mirror she could see the dark bonnet all but touching the boot of her car. She imagined her attacker hunched over the wheel behind the brilliance of his headlights. Ragged nerves twitched her body. What if he tried to run her off the road? Her car zigzagged, as if possessed, through the leaves and broken branches sent flying through the air by the strong wind.

The misty rain that had persisted for the last twenty minutes or so now burst into a torrent of water that drummed a military tattoo on her roof; she strained to see through the windscreen. The dense bush either side of the road blurred. Sandstone cliffs appeared through the water as grotesque, monolithic shapes. The memory of her attacker's cold, black eyes, the vicious set of his features, seemed to spring out in front of her. The spirit of evil in those eyes was terrifying. Her hands slipped off the wheel, the cloying odour of perspiration coated her jumper, her skin.

The glare of his lights flashed in her right wing-mirror.

What was he waiting for? To run her into a tree on one of the many bends, or into the river on one of the more open stretches of road, to cause a spectacular crash she wouldn't survive?

She picked up speed as the hill ran down into an open valley. The river stretched to her left; a thread of black ribbon barely visible through the sheets of rain. Her vision blurred.

But as the valley opened up once more, she knew that narrow, low bridge must be coming up soon. Or had she just passed it? She shook her head. A few more bends and she saw a sign that read left to Singleton, right to Windsor: the main road. The car seemed to turn on two wheels as she drove on to the smooth surface of the highway, and she started to climb the steep hill out of the valley.

As they flew up the dark, slippery road, her pursuer accelerated, almost touching the rear of her car again. A hunter out for his prey. The throb of his engine tortured her brain, vibrating in counterpoint to the Mercedes, a black monster looming large behind her, the silver bumper bar almost touching her boot.

Suddenly, his headlights swung towards the right side of her boot, as if to overtake. The glare in the wing-mirror was intense, but there was nowhere to go: rock face one side, sheer drop the other. *Dear God*, he was going to ram her into the jagged cliffs.

Headlights from a vehicle coming around the bend towards them forced him to drop behind. In seconds they had cleared the bend and were driving away from the rock face. Fate was on her side, but for how much longer?

She closed in on a semi-trailer ahead of her, braking on the next bend. Taking advantage of the long vehicle's slow pace, she accelerated, the needle of her speedometer licking the 70-mph mark. She crested the next steep rise.

A minute or so later, her headlights picked up the sign indicating Blaxland Ridge Road and Kurrajong on her right. A surge of relief flooded through her. With luck, she could be at Richard's in ten or fifteen minutes.

But the slim advantage she had gained evaporated. Her pursuer's lights loomed bright behind her once more, the distance between them shrinking rapidly. Ahead, she caught the beam of oncoming headlights: a large truck grinding up the hill towards the intersection. Her mind raced. If she slowed to allow the truck to pass, she would be at the mercy of the demon behind. If she pulled in front of the truck … Either way, she risked her life.

The mass of approaching metal seemed to hover for long seconds, as if held by an external force. In a blinding split second, she wrenched the steering wheel to the right, pushing the accelerator hard.

A sudden, ethereal white light flooded the interior of the car, her head vibrated with the hiss of air brakes, the blare of horns. The truck's silver grill filled her vision. The Mercedes rocked from side to side as the steering wheel spun through her hands, the tyres crunching over gravel, spraying up a hail of shrapnel.

Then she was back on the road, heart pounding, breaths coming in short, painful gasps.

She sped along the quiet Blaxland Ridge Road, the speedometer edging up to 60-mph again. Scrubby trees, bushes, straggling fences flew past. When she dared glance into the rear-view mirror again, the darkness only slightly eased her tension.

But another frightening mind-spin wiped away any momentary relief: what had given oxygen to her attacker's uncanny ability to guess her movements? She knew about the tapped phone, but they had to have other surveillance. Nowhere was safe. Her home, her car, her life. What else?

She forced herself to take slow, deep breaths. Her attacker could still be somewhere behind her. Richard's home was her only hope of refuge.

Momentarily distracted, a sharp bend came up too quickly. She lurched in her seat as the car skidded dangerously, tyres tearing at the coarse gravel edge. She lost traction, slewing sideways. A large clump of bushes rushed towards her. Fishtailing towards the other side of the road, she managed to turn with the slide, easing it out of the wobble.

Richard's home, RMB 276, could not be far away. She glimpsed a roadside mailbox: 298. Her eyes shot up to the mirror: still an empty road. Two cars passed, going the other way.

Out there, someone wanted her dead. Images of Rushton sprang to mind, Brechtenshafft, even the brothers at Saint Anthony's. Were the police involved? Hurd? He'd been trouble from the beginning.

Again, she surveyed her reflection in the mirror: grey eyes narrowed into slits. She hit the wheel with her fist. *How can you accurately assess a person's character.* Perhaps it wasn't Brechtenshafft after all. What if Rushton was the mastermind? She could understand his desperation to keep the dark side of his life a secret.

The last mile passed beneath her tyres. Relief flooded through her when she saw the sign for Richard's property.

She slowed and with a sigh, Caitlin turned into the driveway.

A line of tall trees hid the house but through them she could see pinpoints of light. Overhanging branches created a tunnel of darkness, now shafted by the beam of her headlights. Nearby, the discordant notes of a frogs' chorus played through the night.

Halfway up the drive, she registered a car pulling into the driveway behind her. She continued up to the house. She could go no further. The other car stopped. A man's figure appeared, silhouetted against headlights. He began to walk towards her, and waved.

33

Caitlin settled back into the sofa, burrowing into the mohair blanket Richard had wrapped around her, still shivering despite the heat from the fire.

She heard Richard moving behind her, caught the clink of glasses.

'Here, drink this,' he said, sweeping his troubled eyes over her.

The fumes of brandy caught the back of her throat. She turned her head away.

'I don't need it.'

'You do.'

She sipped the fiery liquid, grimaced and held it out to him.

'All of it.' A command.

It smelt horrible, tasted worse, but soon she felt warmth suffusing her face, her body.

As Richard took the glass, his eyes fixed on the deep scratches on her hands, the bloody marks on her neck. 'Caitlin, what happened?'

She pushed her polo neck jumper up to her chin. 'It's nothing. Just a brush with a bush while I was out painting.'

He shook his head. 'Bushes don't leave finger marks. You've been out sleuthing again, haven't you? Well, if I can't stop you, the only course of action is to help. So, what can I do to help you?'

She remained silent, staring into the fire. Seconds ticked by, his gaze fixed thoughtfully on her.

'Surely you can tell me?'

She threw off the blanket, stood up. 'I should never have come.'

'That's up to you, but I don't think you should go home looking quite like that.' He pointed to a door that led off the wide entrance hall. 'That's the bathroom. You can find whatever you need in there.'

She smiled weakly. 'Are you always so diplomatic?'

A smile twitched at the corners of his mouth. 'No. It's just the first time I've found a woman at my front gate looking as if someone's tried to kill her.'

•

She leant against the cold wood of the bathroom door. A throbbing headache hammered her temples. Thoughts circled in and out of the pain. Her mind played out the attack again, her fingers curling in front of her face to protect it as if the attacker were in the room. But she was helpless to shut out those black eyes, eyes with no remorse, no humanity; images of being pushed into a dam, slimy weeds, filthy water lapping over her head, invading every orifice of her body.

She shook her head. She was safe in Richard's home.

But still a tiny voice whispered, 'You're not safe.'

Bile rose in her throat. She rushed to the basin. *Oh, God.*

She hung retching over the vanity for some seconds, then rinsed away the bitter greenish-brown fluid mingled with droplets of watery blood, swilled away the aftertaste, and splashed refreshing water on her face.

Gazing into the mirror, those same tense eyes stared back: eyes of a stranger, all alone. She shuddered. So close to death. She grabbed a hand towel and buried her face in its softness.

Christ, the risks she'd taken. After all those warnings. No one was to blame but herself. She had ignored all the advice to step back and let others handle the situation. From now on, she would look out for her own safety.

She dragged the towel away from her face and threw it, crumpled, onto the vanity. She opened her eyes with flickering resolve and challenged the stranger in the mirror.

Beyond all thoughts of her own safety, the plight of children caught in the web of abuse haunted her; their faces, particularly Sean's, were imprinted on her soul. Everyone – the brothers, the police, the justice system, even God – seemed to have failed them. A wall of silence dogged each living day. If she kept fighting, there'd be more risks.

'But I can't add my own failure to a list that is already far too long,' she muttered to herself.

Several weeks after Sean's death, she'd explored that fatal pathway at Echo Point. The ground beyond the three-foot-high wire fence was wide enough to stand on, but someone like Sean, frightened of heights, would never willingly have climbed over. There was no doubt it was murder.

Could MacManus, a priest, one of God's anointed servants, really be his killer, or was it the man she'd just encountered? Or someone like him? Perhaps there was a web of anonymous killers. And where did the orphanage fit into this network of evil?

She paced the small room, rubbing her hands up and down her

arms, stared from the mirror to the white tiled walls. Confronting herself in the mirror again, her first rational thoughts emerged. You are a fool if you think you can do this alone, she decided.

But she hadn't heard from Quinn for days. And with the election campaign in full swing, she shouldn't expect too much from Richard. Yet she did need him; she needed his analytical mind to talk her through the quagmire that bedevilled her. But if she told him too much, would he want the incident at the monastery reported to the police? Would he tell Martin?

The idea of any interaction with the police burnt like acid on her tongue. Nor could she further involve Martin.

It pained her to think of the hurtful words they'd hurled at each other a few nights ago in his chambers. After his innuendos about her relationship with Richard, being here in his home only made things more difficult. There wasn't a deeper relationship, they were good friends, nothing more, but would Martin believe her?

Good friends, nothing more. Those last four words, echoing through her thoughts, wreaked havoc with her emotions. Like a film rolling back six years, she saw Richard on the first night they'd met, moving effortlessly through the crowd in Lexy's gallery; heard his infectious laughter. His charm wove a spell over those who thronged the rooms and, even more devastatingly, cast a spell over her, too – one that had never left her.

She tried to imagine what life with Richard would be like, living in the Hawkesbury, far from … Dear God, what was she thinking?

She had loved Martin: his intellect, his compassion, his humour. But over the last year, they'd seemed to have less and less in common. She'd tried hard to understand the pressures in his life, that perhaps even a successful law practice might not be enough. She knew how obsessive she could be about her own work. Obsession seemed to rule their lives. And now she had a new obsession: the boys at Saint Anthony's.

And Richard? Rising to Opposition Leader so quickly was due to more than chance. Politics was his raison d'etre, too. Her affinity with Martin had been a retreating high tide, leaving debris in its wake. Would her chemistry with Richard survive the tides of time any better?

All of a sudden, she felt she could not trust her vulnerabilities. She'd go back to Sydney, shut out this longing for Richard. Break the spell. Simple friendship would be easier. And she'd try harder to reconcile her differences with Martin.

She looked in the mirror again. The stranger had gone.

34

The circle of light thrown by the fire illuminated Richard's sitting room in mellow tones. Her eyes flicked over the panelled coachwood walls, the high, heavy beamed ceiling, simple lamps illuminating small stacks of books on two solid wooden tables, and a magnificent pair of bronze horses. A man's room, but with a woman's touch; bowls of flowers beautifully arranged, no doubt, by his housekeeper.

Her gaze finally rested on an old-fashioned roll-top desk in the far corner. Above it hung her charcoal study of Chinamans Beach, which had been sold at that first exhibition in Lexy's gallery. Her friend had told her it had been bought by an anonymous collector. Why had Lexy not revealed the name of the buyer? Lexy and Richard had been more than friends back then, Caitlin knew that. But why not tell her this? Perhaps, she thought with a smile, Lexy felt the need to conceal that his interest was in the artist as much as the painting?

She heard sounds from the kitchen, smelt the aroma of minestrone soup. To stay was tempting, but she had to go.

When Richard walked into the room with a tray, she said, 'I'm sorry, I need to leave.'

He put the tray on the coffee table. 'First, sit down and eat.'

She looked from him to the large bowl of steaming soup, brimming with vegetables, a serviette folded around hot bread. She'd only had a light breakfast and skipped lunch to finish the canvas she was working on.

Richard dropped another log on the fire. Bright sparks shot up around it like minute fireworks. He picked up the fireiron, prodded the log deeper into the flames. She noticed his sideways glance at her orange jumper with its vestiges of blood, her stained jeans.

She took hold of the spoon, but her hand shook; the spoon clattered onto the tray.

Richard put the fireiron down, walked over to the sofa and sat beside her. 'Demons?'

She turned to stare at him.

'What really happened, Caitlin?' he said.

She looked down at her hands, now entwined tightly in her lap.

'I got a call from Brother Purcell. He was attending a retreat at the Benedictine Monastery up in the Colo. Wanted to see me. But it wasn't him, it was …' The words died on her lips.

'You went there alone!' He shook his head. 'Did you forget about MacManus? I'm ringing the police.'

She grabbed his arm. 'No. What will they do? Detective Hurd treats me as a meddlesome fool. When the police came to my studio, they took one look and decided they had other priorities.'

'You'll never give up, will you?'

'Richard, every day I relive that weekend at Katoomba, trying to work out what really happened. I've walked that last walk of Sean's short life, along the cliff face, again and again, and can only imagine the terror he must have felt. If you had my nightmares, you wouldn't ask that question.'

He strode over to the fire and grabbed the poker, prodded viciously at a log, then flung it onto one of the brass firedogs before turning back to her. 'If you won't talk to the police, then please leave the investigating to Quinn. That's why you hired him.'

A strained, pinched look formed around his eyes, no charming smile now on that grim face.

'Why are you so angry?'

'Why? Because you're risking your life.'

She stared at him, her hands closing into fists of frustration. 'If I hadn't discovered the cellar and found that pornography –'

'Which could have ended in disaster.'

Without flinching, she said, 'Something has to be done for those boys.'

'Don't you understand, Caitlin, you can't help them if you're dead?'

'Do you have to be so brutal?'

'That is the reality.'

She had trouble focusing her eyes on the dancing flames of the fire. It was all getting too difficult. She had to get out of here. Picking up her keys from the table, she stood up.

'Don't worry, hopefully your guardian angel, Quinn, will keep me safe.'

'And keep you away from Saint Anthony's? And cemeteries? And monasteries?

'No, Richard. There has to be a link between the orphanage and that thug, for him to be able to mimic Brother Purcell so cleverly.'

'If the brother is not involved, it's unlikely he knows your attacker. But if he does, you'll be walking straight into the dragon's lair.' He closed his eyes for a moment. His voice cracked with emotion. 'I'm not asking, I'm telling you: someone wants you dead. Evidence taken by my committee confirms paedophiles include powerful businessmen, judges, politicians and police. These ruthless men will do anything to protect themselves. It's a bonfire waiting to be lit.'

'I know that, but the children, Richard. They are just helpless children. Sean's brother, Peter, is only six years old. Some are even younger. And there's Tim. How will he finish up in a few years? A basket case at the best. Who knows what has been or will be done to any of them, destroying their chance to ever live a normal life? And isn't it true what they say, when people of good intent do nothing, evil triumphs?'

'For God's sake, please understand what you're up against. You don't have to be a Modesty Blaise to fight these men. You can fight them with different weapons. Do something more tangible. Take Martin into your confidence. He's a lawyer, he deals in analysing facts. Then pool your wits with Quinn. You mustn't be a martyr. Please, there are people who love you and don't want to see you hurt.'

A log shifted in the fire, sending a shower of tiny sparks up the chimney. A draught of hot air heated her face.

'All right, all right,' she said, fearing more words would push her further into the verbal whirlpool that swirled around them.

Richard picked up the tray and took it back to the kitchen.

A tiny voice inside her said: *Be a martyr if you will, but if Richard's committee exposes a paedophile ring involving Saint Anthony's, Rushton, Brechtenshafft and God knows who else, the whole situation could become so explosive it could even risk Richard's life.*

She had come to a fork in the road. There was a signpost: one side bore a question mark, the other a definite direction.

35

The chime of the grandfather clock in the entrance hall struck eight. Over the last hour, with Richard's patient assistance, Caitlin had systematically analysed all the events following Sean's death. Having told him everything, Richard neither criticised nor encouraged her, but helped draw out as much sense as possible from the tangled skeins of her knowledge. With sympathy, he had sought to balance the moral and the immoral, duty and responsibility.

She looked into his troubled face. 'What should I do?'

'You are a woman of strong moral responsibility and determination. It would be difficult to step back and ignore all that's happened. On the other hand, it would be extremely dangerous to go ahead with what you feel is your moral duty. You must follow your conscience.'

She gazed into the mesmeric light of the fire, a new turmoil engulfing her.

If only she could hold onto the wondrous freedom she had just felt, in talking without reservation of her fears for the boys; if only there was the possibility of talking about what she wanted out of life, about her desire for a relationship with a kindred spirit. If only she could lift those things that had burdened her spirit and free her soul. If only …

But that was just a dream; it could only ever be a dream. She had to force herself to break the spell, face the unfortunate reality.

'I have to go,' Caitlin said.

'Why?'

'I've stayed too long. I must get home.'

'Let me drive you.'

'No.' Her reply was sharper than she intended.

'Why not?'

'Trust me.' She forced a smile and wondered if he knew the things she left unsaid, if he held such powers of understanding.

He sat beside her. She smelt the fresh citrus of his cologne. An exasperated look passed over his face, then retreated.

'Is it Martin?'

For a moment she could not answer him.

'Why would you think that?' Her words sounded remote, as if spoken by someone else.

'Perhaps Martin knows me better than I thought,' he said, a wry smile on his face.

'Martin isn't –'

He put a finger to her lips. 'I understand the boundaries. Let me worry about Martin.'

'Richard …' Her voice faded again into silence.

She was on dangerous ground. But suddenly, the words came. Words she never thought she would speak aloud; until this moment locked in the distant recesses of her mind.

'I don't want to be disloyal, but Martin isn't an easy person to live with. Neither am I. Now, with this political life he wants …'

She paused to collect her thoughts, select the right words. 'I'm not a nine to five artist who changes into a Chanel gown for the political social whirl. In the first year of our marriage, I thought he understood, and he never demanded what I couldn't give.'

She stared past Richard to her drawing on the far wall. Suddenly she laughed at the irony of it all.

'I know everyone has things from their past they wrap their feelings around and can't forget or ignore, but why have you kept the drawing? It's nothing, just one of the many sketches I did for *Chinamans Beach*.'

'It means a lot to me. It's as simple as that.'

'Well then, if that's the reason, knowing you have it means a lot to me.'

'I'm glad.'

'Why of all things did Martin have to become involved in politics, and drag me into it? I'm totally unsuited to the political life. I don't have the talent. Having to work a room full of people – I can't be bothered with that sort of thing. My talents don't go that far. What I put on paper, on canvas, is the only way I can truly share my feelings with others.'

'That's not true. You have qualities that endear you to many people. You're unselfish. You've shown that by reaching out to help those less fortunate.'

'It *is* true. When I'm at functions with Martin, Chambers functions, Bar Association dinners, they're an ordeal. I never feel I have anything to contribute.'

Restless, she stood up and walked to the window, looked out into the dark night. The stars were so much brighter here than in Sydney.

She turned back to Richard. 'One of my art teachers used to say we're just a blink in infinity, more minute than any of those dots of light up there. We strive to fend off the reality of how little we matter, how little difference we make to anything.'

'We all make a difference. It's the sum total of our efforts that drives real change,' he said.

'I suppose so.'

She walked to the fire and spread her hands to feel the comfort of its warmth. Stooping, she picked up a pinecone from the basket of wood, smelt its earthy smell.

'Have you ever wondered why people go into politics?' he asked.

'Often,' she said. She dropped the pinecone into the fire, watched it burst into flames. Then sat down on the sofa. 'I'd like to think it's to help others, but I'd say it's mainly for themselves, for the power.'

'It's both, but sometimes there's another factor. Some choose the life because of its sheer intensity, perhaps not even consciously. Perhaps they need to lock out the demons that inhabit their subconscious.'

Her eyes moved over his face.

'Let me tell you a story,' he said. 'There was this young fellow studying law at Sydney University.'

His voice sounded soft and distant.

'He followed student politics with some amusement, their so-called idealistic, socialist principles, but he never joined a political party. He fell in love with a political science student, Rachel, with strong conservative views, and this put a certain strain on their relationship.

'His interest in the socialist ideals of equality and social justice was promoted by academics who were disengaged from the everyday life of the majority of Australians. Rachel believed in advancement through enterprise and a strong economic system. She argued that without the wealth of large companies, taxes and endowments couldn't be raised to support those genuinely in need.'

He'd turned away from her to stare into the fire.

When he spoke again his voice was thick with emotion. 'One night they had a fierce argument. She told him she loved him but couldn't decide what was more frustrating for her in their relationship: his obsession with a flawed ideology or her stubbornness in believing she was right. They parted that night on an angry note.'

He stood up and went to the mantelpiece to pick up a small, bronze statuette of a boy in medieval costume, one of the figure's fingers touching his lips as if asking for silence.

Caitlin looked into the fire. 'What's the point of this story? Where are you taking me?' she wanted to say.

His demeanour had changed, even his voice, like a leading actor shifting out of character. The young, charismatic Richard had become a Richard she'd never known.

'That night, Rachel was raped and murdered. A senseless, brutal attack. A serial killer who preyed on students in Prince Alfred Park.' He put the statue down.

'Devastated, the student abandoned his studies and for the next eight months struggled with his demons. The only way he could fight his remorse was to immerse himself in projects dedicated to righting wrongs in society. It took him into politics. Because he knew it was what Rachel would have wanted, he joined the Liberal Party.'

'And now,' she said, 'he's the Leader of the Opposition.'

The fire crackled. Caitlin wanted to reach out and touch him, but she held back.

In a choking voice, he said, 'Along the way I began to discover others like me, trying to ward off unhappiness, doing what they do because of something in their personal life they found difficult to manage, striving to increase their sense of self-worth in a world that values achievement above all else. The need to attain the acceptance of many, even at the expense of a sense of value to a few.'

He turned back to her.

'After Rachel died, my capacity for affection seemed to shrivel up. It was as if part of me had also died. I became an island. My parents were dead, no siblings, no relations. Then I met Lexy.' His laugh was dry. 'She'd hate to hear it, because she likes to believe she's a roving, free spirit, but she taught me that everyone needs to reach out to a kindred spirit, has a need to love and be loved.'

She jumped off the sofa, leant down and picked up her bag.

'Caitlin, what's wrong?' he said, moving close to her.

She watched the fire spit, then looked up at him.

'Why are you telling me this?' Her voice was heavy with tears.

'I thought it would help. We can't go through life carrying unbearable burdens alone.'

'Who is it helping?'

'We're alike, you and me. We survive on the surface, playing the game of life, wearing masks, trying to push back the pain that never leaves us.'

She stared at him. 'Well, as you said, we all have our demons.'

She went to edge past the coffee table, trying not to touch him. Richard flung his arms around her.

'Tell me you don't love me.'

She turned away. 'You said –'

'Look at me. No, Caitlin, look at me.' Clasping her chin, he forced her head around. 'Tell me.'

Tears stung her face. 'But Lexy?'

Richard smiled, shook his head. 'I thought she might fill the void, but we realised it wouldn't work. Our friendship was what we loved.'

With a finger he wiped at her tears, bent down.

'Stay,' he whispered, his lips close to hers.

Her arms encircled him, her mouth pressed hard against his. She fell back into the softness of the sofa's deep, burgundy cushions, her car keys pressing sharply into her side. She forgot everything, everyone. The world was this lovely room; she was floating in the fire's warmth, every fibre of her body relaxing till it was weightless. Her fears melted away in the miraculous protection of their sudden intimacy, as if their hearts and souls were as naturally mingled as their breath.

He ran a finger lightly over her cheek, then lifted some strands of her black hair, spreading them out on the cushion. She caught hold of his hand and kissed his long fingers, plaited them through hers. She studied the intent expression on his face, his soft, sensual lips, warm, quickening breaths. Her body melted into heat.

But suddenly, she couldn't look at him. She untangled their fingers and sat up.

'I'm sorry, I can't do this.'

She wanted to say 'My life is not yours; we travel separate paths. I'm not brave enough to make mine any different.'

He put his arms around her. 'Is it Martin?'

She shook her head. 'No. I don't know.'

'I know if a man or a woman loses love, it can cause a suffering beyond anything else. I never thought I would find love again, but I feel, deep in my heart, I love you. I realised it the night of the dinner party. I came to see you, not to please Lexy or anyone else, and the moment I saw you, I knew I loved you. And I felt you loved me. And I sensed the tension between you and Martin.'

'You think fate has marked us out for each other?'
'I'm not sure I believe in fate, but I do believe in us.'
Seconds passed. She felt a chill creep into the room.
'I have to go.'

36

After the long drive home the familiar landmarks along Caitlin's street were a welcome sight. The wind was blowing harder, whistling high pitched tunes through the trees and overhead power lines. Lightning slapped the sky bright as the dawn.

She turned into her driveway. Her home was sealed in darkness. Martin must still be at the Hunters Hill Primary School P&C meeting. A blessing. He'd been out every night since the State Executive had rejected the call for his disendorsement.

But she was still worried about the silence from Quinn. After leaving Richard's, she'd tried calling his office at Chippendale and his home in Glebe several times, stopping whenever she could find a phone booth. Without Quinn's help, how could she put any plan into action, even get close to Brother Purcell? Richard and Martin would think she'd lost her senses if they had any inkling of her intentions.

Her cold fingers fumbled with the front door key. The flickering lightning lit the columns of the portico, ethereally white in the bleak enchantment of moonlight. A drumroll of thunder heralded the impending storm. Shadows danced out of the trees. She slammed the door shut, locked it.

The house was freezing. She immediately missed the warmth and light of Richard's home. She slid her fingertips along the wall, reaching for the light switch. In the stairwell's darkness, a cold spasm shivered over her skin. Shapes writhed, contracted. She found the switch, flicked it on. The images vanished in the light, leaving nothing but the faint, whistling wind outside.

Her first thought was to change her clothes. She didn't want Martin asking awkward questions if he suddenly came home.

Feeling better for her fresh clothes, she walked down the stairs to Martin's study, clicked on the desk lamp, picked up the phone and started to dial Quinn's home number again. A clap of thunder reverberated through the room, rattling the windowpanes. A silvery slash of lightning flashed through a chink in the curtains. Heavy rain began to batter the windows.

She dialled again and listened to the all too familiar ring with increasing frustration. 'Where the hell is the man?'

'Caitlin. Caitlin!' The words ripped through the turmoil of her thoughts.

She swung around, dropping the phone, one hand clutching at her throat. Martin was standing in the doorway. She saw his lips move but his words were lost to another clap of thunder.

He crossed quickly to her, took her in his arms and went to kiss her, but she buried her face in his chest, hands over her breasts to still her thumping heart. It took a few seconds to get her breath.

'Don't do that to me again.'

'Sorry, darling. It's just that Marjorie, who was at the meeting, told me recent party polling puts me ten per cent ahead. Isn't that great news?'

She put her arms around him, kissed him.

'All this rain, day in, day out, makes everyone nervy,' he said.

She averted her eyes to the shelves of law books that lined the study. Words, too many words, too many cases, traumatic times in the lives of the needy, the greedy, the guilty and the innocent. And which one of them am I, she wondered?

'I'm sorry.' He looked at her intently. 'I really didn't mean to startle you. Has it been a productive day, working here in your studio?'

She flinched under his steady gaze. Was that a trick question? She felt how she imagined some hapless creature might feel in the witness box. If Martin knew what had happened today, her trip to the monastery, nearly being killed, seeking refuge at Richard's, and if he knew the seeds of her feelings for Richard had, by some strange alchemy, flowered into the beginnings of love ...

'Caitlin, you're shaking. You haven't been home all day, have you? What've you been doing?'

She broke from his embrace, folded her arms and paced the small room to avoid his puzzled face.

'If I tell you, you must promise not to be angry. Just listen until I finish.'

She stopped pacing, looked at him.

He nodded. 'I promise.'

She gnawed at her lower lip for a second, turned away, paced again, felt the force of his sharp-eyed scrutiny.

'You see, Brother Purcell phoned me, wanted me to –'

'I told you –'

'Please, you said you would listen.'

'All right.'

'He wanted to talk to me. He was on retreat at a monastery up in the Colo Valley. But it wasn't the brother –'

'Jesus Christ, Caitlin!'

She shrugged. 'I know, it was madness.'

She stopped in front of him, staring straight through him; the vision of her attacker's black eyes haunted her.

'I had to go. It had to have something to do with Sean's death. Otherwise, why the secrecy? I wasn't to know it was a hoax.'

He shook his head. 'You were convinced someone tried to kill you before, and yet you …' His voice tailed off.

'Twice.' Another roll of thunder; she waited until it subsided. 'Today was the third time.'

Lighting pierced through the opening in the curtain. Martin seemed transfixed by its white brightness.

'Do you think you have some kind of avenging angel of divine providence shielding you? You must stop this, now. Concentrate on your work.'

'For now, this is my work. Adults are the ones who should care for children. They are vulnerable, helpless to protect themselves. The police have done nothing. They've closed the case on Sean, and probably on MacManus. Well, Martin, like it or not, I'm going to blow the dust out of those policemen's eyes, particularly that Detective Inspector bloody Hurd.'

'Good God, Caitlin, do you have a death wish?'

She sank into the armchair that faced his desk, gazed at him thoughtfully. What could she say to persuade him?

'You have a brilliant, forensic brain, Martin. You can make sense of scraps of information that bewilder me.'

Martin sat at his desk, steepled his fingers against his chin and stared into space. 'Does this mean another attack on Rodney?'

'Not necessarily, although there is sufficient circumstantial evidence to implicate him. But if you can prove to me that he isn't involved, I'll be happy to accept your finding.'

'All right. Let's look at what we have. No admissible evidence that the pornography exists. Nor will I be party to a defamation suit. The junior on his legal team could spit you out like a pip. You're a thirty-year-old painter, not an intellectual Amazon.'

She hoped he hadn't seen her flinch. She was sure she was making some ground, she just had to hang in there to find out.

'I accept that something's going on. You're being targeted for a reason, strong enough to put a contract out on you. So, let's work on finding evidence to support that angle and see where it takes us. There has to be a lead somewhere.'

Caitlin took a slow breath. 'I'm sure Rushton's involved, though I don't know how deeply. What about the young boy who is living with the Rushtons?'

Smiling, he shook his head. 'Darling, I can tell you all about him. Timothy Guy Rushton, born 7 October 1966. Mother's name, Beryl Jane Rushton, she was Rushton's sister. I can give you any other details you'd like, except his father's name, it's not on the birth certificate. As far as I can make out, they were killed in a car accident. Does that show a lack of compassion on Rushton's part?'

Caitlin looked across at her husband.

'Did you also find out that this boy had been taken into care six months ago following possible abuse from an unknown, or at least unidentified, person? It could only be Rushton,' she said.

'What? I don't believe it.' His voice was hard. He glared at her.

'How do you know what to believe?'

'Who told you this?'

262

She hesitated, reluctant to involve Richard or Enid Featherstone.

'Quinn,' she said. 'Apparently, there was a complaint to the Department of Youth and Community Services from one of Tim's teachers. He was placed in foster care with some woman called Featherstone while the matter was investigated. Three months later, the department's officers decided there was not enough evidence to sustain the complaint. So, Tim was returned home.'

'Who is Quinn?'

'A policeman in Hurd's section.'

'How long have you known about the boy?'

'A few weeks,' she said, trying to keep her eyes steady on his, lying her way to the truth. 'I'm sorry. I should have told you before, but you got so angry every time I mentioned Rushton.'

A clap of thunder shook the windows behind her.

'It's a pity you didn't.' Looking down, Martin shuffled some papers on his desk, ran a hand through his hair then looked up.

'Well, the department sent him back to his uncle and aunt. A few slaps on his backside doesn't make Rodney a paedophile.' He gave her a sad smile. 'Forget Rodney for a moment. Why don't you write down everything you know that might have some relevance? As you said a short while ago, I have a mind trained to see what others don't. Give me the chance to do that. And could you do a sketch of your attacker at the monastery?'

He rose, walked around the desk and took her hands. He held them tight.

'That's the greatest assistance you can give me, to help you. Tomorrow I'll organise some protection for you. And please, do nothing more. On no account go off on any more hare-brained escapades. For the moment, work here in your studio.'

She sat silent. It was hard to believe that after all their arguments and harsh words, he had agreed to help. Perhaps the compassionate side of his nature and his respect for the law would win out and he would do what he'd promised, even if it meant losing Rushton's friendship.

37

Ghostly shadows of children lost hung like gossamer threads in every corner of her mind. She recalled the solid comfort of Martin's study, the overpowering effect of the rows of legal books. Eventually she picked up a pen and began to write. It was a bit like climbing Everest. But as Edmund Hillary once said about that mighty mountain, you climb it because it's there.

After spending a couple of hours trying to commit to paper all the detail she knew, she stayed awake most of the night, her thoughts making it impossible to sleep. Despite Martin's injunction on leaving anything out, there were some things she could not tell him. Still, it had been a useful exercise.

She gave him her notes in the morning, and he scanned them quickly. 'Good, that's something to start with,' he said. 'We'll go through this together tonight, after I've had a chance to study it all thoroughly.'

In her mind, she had gone over everything that Richard and Martin had said. Despite their logical approach, she knew something was wrong. Was her conundrum a missing Quinn?

Martin left for Chambers at seven o'clock. And Caitlin drove off soon after, speeding along streets that would be clogged with traffic within the next quarter of an hour, through the tall, cold, steel avenue of the Harbour Bridge, before turning down towards The Rocks.

Martin would be angry if he knew she was ignoring his advice. But the germ of an idea had come to her during the night, an intuition that an elusive clue lay hidden in her studio.

Climbing the winding stairs to her studio, she imagined she was already breathing in the heavy scents of oil paint and turpentine. Sunlight flooded the room with a bright warmth as she opened the door. Canvases leant against walls with drawings tacked above them and finished paintings hung above those, creating a crazy tapestry that drew her into a welcoming embrace. Seeing the workbenches covered in the paraphernalia of her art, she felt she'd been away for weeks rather than days.

Her eyes lingered on the drawings and paintings intended for her series on abused children. Prominent on an easel in the centre of the studio, Sean's navy blue eyes stared back at her from his unfinished portrait. An imaginative boy who had held too many secrets.

She was struggling to establish the tangible connection between his death and the chain of events that followed. Could she weave the scraps of information into a fabric of knowledge? Expose the truth, translate knowledge into action? If she could, perhaps Sean's covert efforts to reveal the terrible secret of Saint Anthony's would not be futile. She'd failed him in life; she must not fail him in death.

Her mind flashed back to a time when she had been on playground duty at the school. Now, that was something she'd left out of her statement for Martin. She had noticed Sean in a quiet, sheltered part of the quadrangle. Normally one or two of the younger boys would have been milling around, asking him to draw their favourite cartoon characters, some football hero, even themselves. It was unusual to see him drawing alone. It had been a very cold day; the other boys played games to keep warm.

Intrigued, she'd skirted the playground to come up behind him. He must have seen her shadow on the ground, because he shut his small sketch book quickly.

'What are you drawing, Sean?'

'Nothing, Miss, just doodles.'

He'd refused to look at her, his eyes framed by long, black lashes and the blond fringe that flopped over his high forehead. Everything about him looked fragile, as if the cold wind whipping around the quadrangle could whisk him away.

She dared not say more. But she had seen something she was not meant to see.

With the expressive power of Toulouse-Lautrec, not a twelve-year-old boy, he'd drawn four figures grouped together in black charcoal. A few lines, shading, and the figures on the edge of the white page, had a sense of foreboding that paralysed her with their menace.

But this was not the only image seared into her memory; there was also the collection of Sean's drawings the boy had given her in the art room the day she'd left Saint Anthony's. Among them, the portraits of the Apostles, with the half-naked boy drawn on the back of his portrait of Judas Iscariot.

Picking up a drawing book and a stick of charcoal, she began to block in the four figures from memory. When the phone rang, a discordant sound that threatened to break her concentration, she took it off the hook.

Her charcoal flowed into shapes, lines, shading. Who were

the figures? They were surely not subjects Sean would randomly sketch. Drawing them in black might signify they were some of the brothers. Could one of them be Brother Finbar, another Brother Loudé, perhaps even Brother Purcell? But what of the other two men in black? Perhaps priests, not brothers; MacManus? Even though she'd had only the most fleeting glance, she was sure she'd captured the details.

Propping her sketchbook on the workbench, she set up a blank canvas on another easel, squeezed black and white paint onto her palette and was about to start painting when she paused. Why was she doing this? Certainly not just to record the work of a boy who few had known and even fewer would remember.

She stared at her sketch again. Seconds ran into minutes. She stood, as if in a trance, drawn in by the essence of Sean's spirit, until she realised with startling clarity what he had done. He'd created a message in the only language he knew, a language fluent enough to portray the violation, the scouring trauma that engulfed and tormented him. He could never have found words to describe his ordeal, but he could try to reach out to someone who would understand, hopefully act on his behalf. Someone he could trust. And just as Christ had drawn to Himself the Apostles, Sean had chosen her as his disciple.

She knew her intuition had been right, the nagging thoughts that had kept her awake so many nights. Something horrific was being acted out in a supposed sanctuary for the innocent. And beyond that defiled sanctuary was a world in which the outward show was tainted by corruption and evil, perpetrated by the manipulation of laws, religion and Mammon.

Inspired by the power of Sean's intellect, infused with new energy, she began to paint in four men and a boy. She suddenly had the idea to reverse the black and white of the drawing, to create a more sinister and terrifying dynamic, as if the action was taking place in some dim corner of a nocturnal world. From a point at the top of the canvas, she painted a high raking light falling on the figure of a naked boy, highlighting his pale skin and the perfect form of his body. Above him, in a semicircle, she painted the faces of the four men looking down.

The smell of paint and the quick strokes of her brush gave impetus to her frenzy of creativity, driving her mind back to that terrible day of Sean's death.

'Make it happen,' she whispered to the paint, to the canvas, to the figures.

And it did, as if the painting, through Sean's spirit, was beginning to take on a life of its own.

But were her eyes playing tricks on her? She mixed flesh colours, and the boy's face, which might have been any child now took on Sean's features. Quickly, she blocked in the whole figure, portraying him as a broken doll, a puppet, depravity's plaything.

And what else? What else …

She ignored the paint dripping onto her fingers, blood red from the toy train she was shaping next to an outstretched hand, lifeless curled fingers. In the background, the grey, tangled wreck of a model plane. Enticements to cultivate interest, make entrapment easier; evil masquerading as love.

She stepped back, turning her attention to the men. Faces. Somehow, she needed faces. There must be faces. The faces of those responsible for his death? Although she knew she shouldn't be doing it, the force was irresistible; features resembling Finbar, Loudé, Rushton and Brechtenshafft emerged. Behind the men she painted a second raking shaft of light, drawing the viewer's eye down to

Sean's broken body, the innocence of his penis curled beneath one hand.

Caitlin flung her brush down onto the workbench, stepped back, glanced at her watch propped up on the desk. Two thirty, she'd been painting for hours.

She would try Quinn again. She listened to the frustrating ringtone in his home and then his office. Twice more she called, then left the phone off the hook.

Voices, a knock on the door. She slipped the safety chain, relieved to see Lexy and Mrs Mazz, their faces creased with worry.

'Where have you been?' Lexy demanded, striding into the studio, her grasshopper legs clad in bold, colourful Zandra Rhodes leggings. 'Richard's been trying to contact you. When he couldn't, he rang me and I tried ringing everywhere but …'

She spotted the phone. 'So, that's the reason.'

'I've been working. You worry too much.'

'With good reason, from what I hear.'

'I know you say not to disturb,' said Mrs Mazz, setting down a small tray on the sofa. 'You not eat enough, Catalina.'

The aroma of hot coffee and freshly baked bread sprinkled with olive oil and salt filled Caitlin's nostrils, reminding her she was hungry.

'You shouldn't do this, Mrs Mazz.'

Her landlady nodded her head, patted her cheek. 'You eat – now.'

'I will … in a minute. And thank you.'

'Now, Catalina. I'm watching you.'

Caitlin stared at the plate, glanced at the determined look on Mrs Mazz's face and sat down. Her landlady waited until she was satisfied Caitlin had begun to eat before leaving to return to her café.

While Caitlin ate, Lexy walked around the studio, pausing to stare at the painting of the four figures and the boy.

Taking the last slice of bruschetta and pushing her plate away, Caitlin walked over to her friend and put an arm around her thin shoulders. Lexy gently pushed her away to stare, for a moment, at the canvas, then turned to gaze at Caitlin.

'That is superb, like nothing else you have ever done. A Caravaggio. But darling girl, get onto something else. Still life, landscape, anything but this. This is torture. You're battering yourself against a stone wall.'

Caitlin stared at her. 'You want me to scrap the Abuse series? Is that it? You sound like Quinn.'

'Listen to him. He gives good advice. Richard told me what happened at the monastery. You may be looking to shock,' Lexy said, pointing to the men's faces, 'and I don't mind that, but if you use those, you'll be on a fast train to self-destruction. And I'm not anxious to get tangled up in a bundle of defamation proceedings.'

38

Twilight, a core of fear sandpapered her senses. It wasn't just Lexy's parting words. The transmutation of the boy's figure in the painting, the bleak despair of innocence lost, had forced itself deep into her psyche. Was this Sean's gift, to bring her face to face with the darker side of living?

The silvery glow of streetlights illuminated images around her studio. From every wall, every corner, her myriad selves watched her every movement. She critically assessed them. Drawings, paintings, months of hard work.

She flicked on the light and rubbed at her gritty eyes, walked back to her workbench. Reaching for a brush, she squeezed more paint onto her palette, applying all her critical faculties to – what had Lexy called it? A work in the style of Caravaggio. She stabbed thick, ugly streaks at the images of Rushton, Brother Finbar, Loudé, Brechtenshafft. Was one of them the mastermind Quinn had spoken of when they had met in his brother's warehouse? Or was there yet another figure even more monstrous, lurking in the background?

Rushton's face. She had caught the cruelty of his mouth, the cunning in those mean, piggy eyes that seemed to watch your every move, your every single gesture. Yet to orchestrate such a complex web of evil deception … She wasn't sure.

And the brothers? The Catholic Church had their Machiavellis. Was Finbar one of them? She stared at the principal's face. Ascetic, but behind it she sensed a weak spirit, a foot soldier, no leader. So, a question mark remained.

Loudé, her nemesis, seemed to have made spying an art form. She studied his face for some minutes. A cold, institutionalised man with rainy grey eyes, matching the tint of his greyish-white skin. He could have been hewn from the ancient gravestones surrounding the Sacred Heart Church. It was so easy to imagine him stalking the dimly lit corridors of the orphanage in the dark of night, his long, gaunt form moving in and out of shadows, his cassocked figure throwing contorted shapes onto walls. She shivered. It was not something she wanted to dwell on. He may have unhealthy passions, but to plot such heinous crimes?

She started to block in Brechtenshafft's face; those piercing eyes and the duelling scar gave him a demonic look. It was not hard to place him as the mastermind. Yet impressions could be deceptive. Was he but a cunning actor, affecting an air of sinister menace to scare off those who crossed him?

Of the four men, any one of them could be the mastermind, or none of them. She turned away from their faces, moved back to the window, leant her forehead against the cool of the glass.

Fleeting thoughts, fragmentary images skirted the edges of her brain. She watched the shadows of dusk surrender to night.

All at once she straightened up. She turned back to her easel, memories of her encounter with Brechtenshafft on the verandah of Rushton's house coursing through her head. The urge to pick up a brush, to try to capture his character on the canvas, was like an icicle piercing through her body. Never in her life had she seen anything like the scar that ran from under his left eye to his chin. And those blue eyes, those cold, calculating good looks. She tried to dredge up other features of his face, recall what he'd said to her that night – of the four he seemed the most likely to fit the shadowy mastermind of a paedophile ring.

She stared again into the emptying street. The heartbeat of the city was minutes away, tall modern office buildings looming over old sandstone shops, with people working, living, existing; yet here she was, alone on the stark plateau of her creativity, plagued by fears. An aphorism coined by the Elizabethan spymaster, Walsingham, sprang to mind: 'There is less danger in fearing too much than too little.' Empowered by the thought, she went back to work.

Minutes, perhaps hours, passed – nothing mattered, only those fine brush hairs and the paint on the canvas. She had absorbed Sean's spirit. But what of the other end of the spectrum? Driven by a fury of creativity, Brechtenshafft's face emerged above the others: the master puppeteer and his three puppets.

She threw down her brushes, stood back from the painting. This new juxtaposition had given the figures vital life, meaning. She stared at the German's face. What worried her? She shook her head, began to clean her brushes, gagging at the heavy fumes of turpentine in her nostrils and throat. She glanced into the man's icy blue eyes, the insolent smile that appeared from nowhere. She remembered the warning he'd issued on the verandah that night.

Where was Quinn to help her grapple with these fears? The room was weighted with silence.

She picked up her keys and bag, then hesitated in front of the painting. Little doubt, it was confronting. But wasn't that the purpose of the exhibition, to challenge complacent perceptions? If Lexy wanted something more pedestrian, she should have chosen another artist. Paedophilia destroyed children's lives – children who had no voices. Society needed to face its responsibility, needed to bring the perpetrators of these crimes to justice.

At the door, she turned out the light, glancing back for a final look at those faces visible only by the streetlight outside. She thought she'd succeeded in bringing out the boy's vulnerability, innocence, such an integral part of childhood. She shivered at those four faces above him, watching, waiting; deadly spiders creeping from their webs, their unearthly holes, poised to strike at their prey.

She was closing the door when she heard footsteps in the hallway below. Turning her studio light back on, she peered over the banister.

Martin appeared in the stairwell.

Her heart lurched.

'I thought you were supposed to be working from home,' he said, coming up the stairs.

'And I thought you'd be in Chambers, working on your commercial arbitration.'

'I should be. The other side have filed their statement of facts and contentions. There's a directions hearing on Wednesday, so I'll be working well into the night. But I've been worrying about you. I rang home, no answer; I rang here, the line was busy. So, I presumed you were here.'

She bent down and kissed him, tried to laugh. 'Everyone seems to be worried about me: Lexy, Mrs Mazz, you. But I do have a deadline to meet.'

'Sweetheart, you promised me …' Then, shrugging, he said, 'How's it going?'

'Come and see.'

She almost laughed again at the bewildered look on his face as he walked into the studio, so different to the tidiness of his chambers.

'Lexy's been here,' Caitlin said. 'You know what she's like, she rummaged through everything she could find.'

'What's this?' he said, walking over to the painting on the easel. 'Mrs Mazz would be doing Hail Mary's on the hour if she saw that.'

'She hasn't seen it,' Caitlin said.

He raised his eyebrows. 'If I were you, I'd keep it under wraps, here in your studio.'

She stared at him. 'So, you want me to do a *Dorian Gray*? Do nothing to scandalise polite society?'

'What are you talking about?'

'You haven't read Wilde's novel? An artist paints Dorian. Enthralled with his own physical beauty, he trades eternal youth at the expense of his soul. While Dorian stays young, the face in the portrait ages. To hide the terrible truth, he keeps it covered in the attic.'

'I'll need a drink to digest that.' He glanced over at the kitchen alcove. 'What do you have?'

'Coffee or coffee.'

He laughed. 'Either will do.'

'With or without milk?'

'Look why don't you just sit there and relax. I'll make the coffee,' He strolled over to the kitchenette.

Caitlin smiled at his concern. 'There's milk in the fridge.'

'Great, won't be long.'

Looking over at her he asked, 'What does Lexy think of it?'

'She told me to ditch it, said no way would it ever hang in her gallery.'

'Well, I'll give her this, she's astute.'

'Don't worry. In the end I'll change the faces, there'll be no defamation suits. It's just something I had to get out of my system.'

Martin took their coffee mugs over to the small table near the window. Caitlin followed him and sat down.

'Why did you paint in Brechtenshafft? He has nothing to do with the orphanage,' he said as he absently stirred his drink.

'If you lie down with dogs, you get up with fleas.'

'Is that what you think of Rodney and his friend?'

If Martin only knew how much she hated Rushton and the German; the menace she wanted to paint into those faces, into every line, every touch of colour, to capture the razor tone of their voices in the wine cellar when discussing the distribution of their pornography.

'Souls tainted with wrongful hungers. Like Dorian Gray,' she muttered.

'Rodney does have his virtues.'

She gazed at her husband. 'We can all manufacture virtues, Martin, put on an outward show, believe the lies we tell ourselves. People's lives are coloured by their environments.'

'Environments?'

'Social, political, religious.'

'I can see the social and religious, but where's the politics?'

She frowned. Was he being polite or did he really want to understand her ideas?

'You of all people should know there's politics wherever human beings are involved.'

She stood up and went over to the easel. She pointed to Rushton.

'How much do you really know about him? You know he's a successful businessman, he has a streak of ruthlessness, he supports the Liberal Party. But what else is hidden beneath his public personae?'

Martin scrutinised the painting again, then turned to Caitlin with a quizzical expression. 'I still don't get the political angle.'

'Everything Rushton does has a political angle. Take the gambling night. He was raising money for the party, but when you look at the people who were there, many had interests very different to the Liberal cause. Who knows what shady deals were being done by some of the people there that night?' She paused. 'How many branch members went?'

'Not many, I have to admit.'

Staring at the portrait of Brechtenshafft, she added, 'Don't forget his connection with Rushton, their close relationship. If you had been with me in the cellar that night, you would understand what I mean, how little either of us know of them.'

She sat back down at the table and picked up her mug.

Martin continued to stare thoughtfully at the painting.

'I said I would help you. I've been making some discreet enquires, calling in a few favours that may or may not be paid.' He turned his cup full circle in its saucer. 'So, Cate, how far are you prepared to go with this crusade?'

Caitlin was silent. Her husband rarely used the nickname – only when he was in a quiet, philosophical mood.

'As far as I have to, to get justice for the boys.' She studied the painting of Sean on the wall behind her easel. 'I want to give the children more of a chance than they have now, and hopefully that chance will lead to other chances. This is about survival for children who can't help themselves. The cost to me, to you' – she pushed her hair back from her forehead and shrugged – 'why count it?'

'You look tired.' He drained his cup. 'I'm taking you home.'

'What about your work?'

'It can wait until tomorrow.'

39

The sound came to her again, a soft, rhythmic slapping. Perhaps she was dreaming. She rolled her head from side to side. But it was still there. Do we dream taste, like the sour, dry taste in her mouth? she wondered. Or sensation, like the dull throbbing in her head? What about smell, like the deep, pungent odour that clogged her nostrils, as familiar as her oil paints, only stronger? A darkness in her mind prompted a sudden fear of being buried alive. She tried to drag her eyelids open, tried to move any part of her body, but the darkness closed in on her again.

What finally forced her eyes open? No other sound but the rhythmic slapping; only the smells and the dawning sensation of motion, a growing claustrophobia. She stretched her hands above her – felt no soil, no wooden coffin. But still this unfamiliar darkness.

What is happening to me? Where am I?

Her last recollection was of being in the studio with Martin.

'Martin, are you here?' Caitlin waited seconds, then called out again, 'Martin?'

Silence.

She reached out into the space to her left; nothing. Her hand hit something on her right. She slid her palm along it: smooth, almost silky to the touch; a wall, a curved wall. She certainly wasn't in her bed at home, but where could she possibly be? She was lying on something narrow, a bit soft. Odd.

She slowly pushed herself up into a seated position, her mind groggy. After several seconds, she swivelled sideways, and her feet dropped to the floor. She realised then she was still wearing her boots and the clothes she'd worn to the studio.

Caitlin waited a few more seconds, trying to orientate herself. Then, hands outstretched, feeling the way with her feet, she stepped into the darkness. A short step, then another, and – 'Bloody hell!'

She rubbed at her shinbone, then, with her fingers, felt something hard on a level with her knees; above it, something soft, then space. She ran her hands over the surface: a bunk. She cursed the darkness. No wonder she hadn't been able to identify that rolling motion. She was on a boat.

Oh, God. Every discovery only raised more questions. She needed answers.

She ran her hands along the bunk until she felt a bulkhead. Then her exploring fingers touched what seemed to be a door, a handle. She tried to open it: locked. She banged on it with her fists, shouted till her voice was hoarse. Nothing.

She stretched out her hands again, took a few steps to her right, climbed onto the first bunk and started to slide both palms over the wall, finding nothing useful. She moved over to the other bunk. The same. All smooth surfaces of wall, until her fingers caught something hard, cold, circular. She traced it – a porthole, sealed tight. Whoever had locked her in this cabin had planned the perfect prison.

Was it night or day? She couldn't tell. Her last memory was of leaving the studio. And Martin. What had happened to him? She slumped onto the mattress, trying to think through how she came to be there.

Suddenly, the thrum of an engine rumbled through the cabin. The smell of oil and seawater pervaded the stuffy air. She grabbed hold of the mattress as the boat surged.

Her world had contracted to this small cabin. Beneath her was the sea, dark, cold, its depths unknown. And she held no illusions: soon she was to be part of that sea, jetsam for its alien creatures. Every minute brought her closer to her last breath.

She slipped off the bunk, moved to her left to feel for the door, and, balling her fists, hammered on it again. I must make them hear, she thought, I must. She waited. Nothing. No feet moving above her or outside in the passage, just the rumble of the engine.

She held her head in her hands, straining to plumb the possibilities.

'God, you stupid woman!' she muttered.

She lay down, pounded her boot's heels against the door. Again, nothing.

There had to be a way out.

She pulled the mattress off the second bunk. Suppose the base of the mattress was the cover for a storage compartment; perhaps something inside could help her force the door? Sliding her fingers under the edge, she felt the board lift. Gingerly, she probed the space inside. Within seconds she felt heavy netting; from the odour, she realised she must be on a fishing boat.

Sweat ran into her eyes, mixing with tears of disappointment. She was trapped as effectively as if she were already dead and whoever had planned it had left nothing to chance. What planted such evil in someone's mind?

Her hold on reality was collapsing. In this narrow cabin, she felt bereft of hope. Her life, along with all its promise, would end here in this ugly emptiness.

In another time, another place, the rhythmic chug of the engine might have been soothing. But now she would have other company: a choir of mermaids to sing her to a watery grave. She laughed sourly at the thought and then stopped, listening. She knelt on the bare bunk, stared up at the ceiling. Her heart beat faster.

'Hello? Hello? Can you hear me?'

She kept still. All she could hear was her own ragged breathing.

She shouted again, 'Is anyone there?'

Nothing broke through the throb of the engine. She was desperate to hear a human voice, any voice.

Caitlin swung down from the bunk and sank to her knees on the mattress, muttering over and over, 'God, let me have my life, let me have my life. God, are you listening?'

40

The engine idled. Caitlin lifted her head. From somewhere above her, she could hear men's voices.

She pushed herself off the mattress, felt her way along the floor until her fingers traced the line of the door. She banged on it with her fists, yelling until her voice cracked. She could smell the unpleasant sourness of her perspiration. She began to pound on the door with her boots again. Soon her feet, legs, every straining muscle felt like rubber.

She lay back, exhausted, and stared at the ceiling.

The voices above became louder. Was that an argument?

Heavy footsteps thudded closer. The door flew open. She scrambled back to the far bulkhead. In the dim light that entered the cabin, she made out two men, Mediterranean, their dark features unshaven, grinning down at her.

The older one, his arms covered with tattoos, spoke first. 'This is a nice catch we have here, Vinci.'

She smelt the pungent body odour of the tattooed man when he straddled her, his greasy, pockmarked face hanging inches above her. He reached down and grabbed at her, his grip tight as a vice, and pulled her to her feet.

Caitlin kicked at his shins. 'Don't touch me.'

A sharp, stinging blow sent her reeling back; the side of her head struck something hard.

A snigger came from Vinci. 'Leave something for the sharks, Beppi.'

'Ours first.'

One of Beppi's hands gripped her jaw.

'No more trouble, you hear?' He pushed her towards the younger man. 'Get her up on deck.'

She tried to kick out at them, but Vinci wrapped his left arm around her waist. His right hand crept up to her breast. She felt his warm breath on her neck.

'My rudder is restless,' he muttered, rubbing himself against her.

'*Pazienza*,' Beppi said.

She squirmed away. 'Let me go, you bastard.'

She tried to kick at his legs. He jerked one arm viciously behind her back, spinning her round to propel her out the door. She tried to dig her heels into the floorboards, but his flat palm struck between her shoulder blades and she staggered into the passageway.

'Keep moving,' he snarled into her ear, pushing her arm further up her back till she thought it would break.

'You can't do this,' she screamed, trying to twist from his grasp.

'How you gonna stop us?' he said, grabbing at her hair and ramming her up the steps, onto the deck.

'My husband … He'll …'

Her words were smothered as Vinci planted his hands on her buttocks and heaved her up the last step.

'You're gonna be down with the fishes, so what's he gonna do, eh?' said Vinci.

Caitlin landed on the deck on her hands and knees. Wind and sea spray blew through her matted hair, stung her eyes. She looked wildly around her, saw the surging swell of the ocean, tasted salt on her lips. Heard the wind blowing further out in the ocean. In the dim glow of dawn her eyes travelled across the greasy planking and up to the face of a third man leering down from the wheelhouse: a man with a square, flat, sardonic face, no longer framed by a monk's cowl.

All her fears from the monastery flooded back.

He jumped down from the wheelhouse. She yelled as he grasped a handful of her hair and dragged her to her feet.

'Remember me?' he said.

She spat at him, but he jerked his head away.

'I see you do.'

He grinned at his two companions. 'She has fire in her blood, this one.'

He shoved her towards Vinci.

'Let's see what we have.'

Vinci caught her in his arms and ripped open her shirt.

'How's this, Joe?' Vinci said with a laugh.

'*Molto bene.*'

She tried to close her shirt, break away from them.

'Careful, she's slippery. We don't want any accidents until we've finished, Vinci.'

Caitlin stared at Joe. Finished what? But she was more worried about Beppi's fingers caressing the slender knife sheath on his grimy belt.

'Get her down on the deck, Vinci. Get those boots and jeans off.'

Beppi laughed as he planted one foot on her stomach while Vinci roughly pulled off one of her boots. She tried to kick out at him with the other.

'You won't need this one either,' he said, grabbing it and throwing it overboard.

Beppi's deft fingers pulled at her jeans. Caitlin tried to pull away, yelling with pain when Beppi grabbed at her hair.

Her fear turned to horror when she caught a glimpse of the knife in his hand, its evil blade catching the silvery light from the wheelhouse. His fishy fingers that would be so adept at gutting and filleting the catch, slid inside the waistband of her jeans. In an instant he'd sliced through her belt. In one quick wrench, Beppi tore the jeans open. Vinci pulled them off and swirled them above his head. With raucous laughter, he sent them sailing into the wind with the grace of a matador swirling his cape.

Beppi stepped back, his breath ragged, eyes shooting up and down her body.

She felt the boat heave; without anyone at the wheel, it had swung broadside to the swell.

Vinci pulled her to her feet, twisting her arms painfully behind her back.

She screamed at him, 'Let me go, you bastard.'

Joe spread his arms wide. 'Captain's prerogative. Come on, my little lady, give me a taste of what's on offer.'

He waggled his fingers at her. She felt a hard shove in her back, staggered across the deck and fell into his arms.

'She's certainly willing,' he shouted above her head, then swung her around. 'Or would you like Beppi to go first? He's the impatient one.'

He flung her across the deck.

'But he won't keep you long.'

The wind whipped more hair into her eyes, blinding her. She tried to scratch Beppi's face, but he hugged her to him. Joe twirled his hand to point to himself again. Beppi spun her around, thrust her back to him.

Stop, please, she screamed in her mind; she had no more breath to scream out loud.

Joe's hairy arms encircled her. He whispered in her ear, 'The fellas like a little foreplay.' He pulled her around, fondling her breasts.

Caitlin felt the boat roll and heave. She braced herself. Joe's fingers ran down over her stomach to her crotch, scoring into her shivering skin. Tears of pain blurred her eyes, but they meant nothing to these brutes. Scavengers in a moral wasteland, they would take whatever they could get. Caitlin could see that human lives were just gravel on the road of their survival.

The boat wallowed; a wave swept over the rail. The deck heaved again.

'Vinci, get the wheel you fuckin' prick,' Joe yelled.

But the boat bucked like a wild, panic-stricken creature. Vinci slipped in his scramble to get hold of the spinning wheel. Joe flung Caitlin aside and leapt towards the wheelhouse.

She staggered, tried to regain her balance, stumbled backwards, and in a second felt the edge of the boat dig into her spine. Instinctively, she threw herself back and somersaulted into the cold, dark water.

41

Iridescent bubbles surged around Caitlin as she arched her body and pushed herself up to the surface. Vague shouts came from the boat. She filled her lungs, then, feeling the sea was her friend, dived again into the dark depths. She swam strongly to put distance between herself and the boat before resurfacing.

Setting a gruelling pace, she pushed tiredness and fear out of her mind, ploughing through the choppy water like a robot. She had only two choices: to live or to die. To live, she just had to keep the rhythm of her body going. *Distance is only distance. Think you're at home, swimming in your pool.* Except this was a black pool with no tiled boundaries.

She dived, as deeply as she dared, unsure whether to strike out strongly or conserve her energy.

She resurfaced, treading water and looked around her. The boat had circled and was perhaps thirty, forty feet away from her. Now, it turned. The beam of a spotlight swung back and forth. The engine throbbed, foam frothing high under its bow. On one of its sweeps, the roving spotlight picked her out, pinning her in its deadly beam. The boat swung towards her.

Wait … Wait …

It was holding its course, straight towards her.

At what she hoped was the last moment, she dived below the surface and struck out sideways. The cold water slid faster over her body as she pushed all her energy into every stroke. Soon her lungs were fighting with their cage of rib and skin. She would have to surface.

Her arms cleaved the surface, then thrashed air. The water bubbled and churned, swirling her body upwards.

Blinding flashes of light; an ear-splitting roar. Fireballs rocketed up into the sky as pieces of the boat flew in all directions. Heat hit her face. A fireball larger than the rest shot into the misty sky. Waves pounded her face; pieces of debris plummeted from the air. She began to swim away, desperate to put distance between herself and the falling missiles. One hit and she would be food for the sharks.

She swam until her arms felt like lead and could take her no further. She swivelled around, treading water. Black and grey plumes of smoke reflected the red glow of the burning wreck. The acrid smell of oil and petrol stung her nostrils. A garish pall of smoke slowly spread across the water.

Caitlin tried to decipher some semblance of detail through the mist. Shapes formed, then dissipated; there one moment, gone the next.

Then silence fell, the burning hulk losing its brightness, until only her tired body existed, trapped in this vast expanse of water. The dark outline of the boat's hull, crowned by fire, was a ghostly, Turner-like image. Poor souls.

And now she was conscious of another glow that warmed the mist some distance away. She blinked, shook her head. It was gone; not a boat. She waited. But there it was again, disappearing into the mist, then reappearing.

If she could have, she would have laughed. The beacon from the lighthouse on South Head! *Thank God, what timing!*

She'd been swimming out to sea.

Heaviness dragged on her arms and legs, as if floating seaweed were wrapping and tangling its greasy, black tendrils around her, entrapping her alien body in its mysterious world. She rolled onto her back and floated to conserve her energy. She closed her eyes, shutting out the immensity of space and distance around her, telling herself it was only a bit further and a bit further and a bit further …

Guided by the beacon on South Head, clearly visible above the mist that hovered over the water, she pushed herself in long strokes towards land and safety, Camp Cove and Watsons Bay.

But she was so tired and the cold wind and the swell that ruffled the surface of the water were now so painful. Soon, hypothermia would set in; all too easy to fold herself into the anonymity of these deep, dark waters. Fear swam with her every stroke. *It's only water, it can't hurt you; just keep your head and concentrate,* she told herself, though deep within, she knew it could.

She began counting her strokes in batches of ten. The lighthouse seemed as far away as ever. She rolled onto her back to rest once more, gazed down the length of her body. She felt she was partially invisible, as if she was already slowly dissolving.

To die like this, among the fish … She gritted her teeth, forced the thoughts out of her mind. *Remember your two choices: to live or to die.* She wasn't ready for death just yet.

She resumed a measured freestyle, chanting, 'It's not far, not far at all. Another five minutes and then another five minutes and soon I'll only be five minutes away from that beacon of hope'.

No matter how much effort it took she must not let herself fall prey to the waves swirling beneath that pulsating light.

A sound, out of context, grasped her attention. She lifted her head and trod water, trying to pinpoint it. Was she beginning to hallucinate – the first stage of hypothermia? Was she only imagining the steady rhythm of an outboard motor, a boat?

She began to shake. Hope and despair fought for domination. Teeth chattering, she could barely shape words. But she had to.

'Help! Help!' Feeble.

Silence.

She listened, sure she could hear the motor again.

She took a deep breath.

'Help! Help!'

She tried to call out again, but the engine seemed to be further away.

'Help, help, over here! Over here!' A gulp of water stifled her voice.

Damn this mist. Why didn't it lift?

Then, through the haze came 'Hellooo …'

A man's voice.

'Hellooo, hellooo…'

The voice grew louder.

Caitlin swung around. 'Over here!'

A small boat emerged through the mist, an old man on board.

He cut back the engine, edged his boat closer and threw her a life buoy tied to a length of rope. Swinging the boat around, he pulled her towards the gunwale, near the stern.

Surprisingly strong hands gripped hers. With the man's help, she heaved herself out of the water and fell into the bottom of the boat and lay there, lungs and heart pumping. Never had something so hard and unyielding felt so wonderful.

Her whole body felt like a block of ice. She clasped her arms over the remnants of her shirt, shaking uncontrollably. The fisherman pulled off his waterproof jacket and pushed her arms into it. He helped her into the launch's tiny cabin, pulled a blanket off the wooden seat and wrapped it around her.

He busied himself with a tiny spirit stove. After a few minutes, he handed her an enamel mug of steaming, black liquid. 'Drink this.'

Teeth chattering behind freezing cheeks, she could only try to nod her thanks. She shivered harder, until the heat of the fisherman's strong black tea oozed down her throat.

'What happened? I saw the flash and came straight over to see if I could help.' He glanced towards the thin line of the still burning hull. 'Is there anyone else?'

She fixed her gaze on the old man's face, his steady, grey eyes under pouches of sagging skin, then shook her head. How quickly lies come when spurred by necessity.

'I fell overboard. They were trying to rescue me when, all of a sudden, the boat blew up. It was horrible.'

The less this man knew, the easier it would be to evade awkward questions. If he knew the truth, he looked as if he would want the law to know it too.

He took the wheel, opened the throttle and swung the bow towards the heads that poked above the mist. The first strong rays of the sunrise bounced off the glistening whiteness of the lighthouse.

She drew the blanket more tightly around her and slowly sipped the tea. She was meant to be dead. For all intents and purposes, she must stay dead. It was safer that way, for now.

42

Caitlin toiled up the stone steps at the northern end of the beach at Watsons Bay, in the footsteps of her rescuer, who told her his name was John McGlynn. Her legs felt wobbly, weak, and several times she grasped the handrail to steady herself.

They crossed the narrow, quiet street above the steps. The old man walked briskly, but the army blanket hampered every plodding step she took.

They stopped at a neat little cottage a few houses along, and he pushed open the small, wrought-iron gate. As she followed him up the path, she noticed a simple wooden carving of a white fish nailed to the blue front door – perhaps a good omen for a silent man who loved his life by the sea.

'In here, lass.'

At the end of the hallway, he opened another door.

'This was my daughter's room.' He waved a hand towards the wardrobe. 'You should find something in there. You're about her size.

'The bathroom's there,' he said, with another wave of his gnarled hand towards the door opposite.

He hesitated, gave her a quick nod before backing out of the room. She closed the door behind him.

Inside the wardrobe she found some jeans, sad looking tennis shoes, a polo neck jumper, some underwear and socks. When she lifted them, three ten-dollar notes, some silver coins and a moth ball fell out: a treasure trove.

'I'll pay you back later,' she said to the sepia photograph on the top of the drawers of a teenage girl with a much younger John McGlynn.

She folded the clothes and padded across to the bathroom.

She longed to revel in the shower's hot water, but washed and dressed quickly before returning to the bedroom.

The tennis shoes were too big, but three pairs of socks made them wearable. She stared at her hair and face in the mirror, then unzipped the flower-patterned vanity bag she had found in the chest of drawers. A couple of combs, a hairbrush and some hair clips tumbled out onto the bed. A plastic Alice band clung stubbornly to the bottom of the bag. She pulled it out, combed her hair, combed her fringe back, and put the headband on. Then Caitlin opened the bedroom door.

From the kitchen at the end of the short hallway, delicious cooking smells drifted towards her. Saliva filled her mouth.

She walked in and saw that the room was clean, shipshape and cosy. The table was set for one.

'I guessed you'd feel like a bit of brekky,' John McGlynn said cheerily. 'Take a seat, it'll be ready soon.'

Within minutes he'd placed bacon and eggs, mushrooms, sautéed tomatoes and a pile of toast in front of her. She looked gratefully at her saviour. He certainly knew how to look after an unexpected guest.

She was wiping up the remnants of her breakfast with the last piece of toast when John, who had been silently watching her, said, 'I took the liberty of ringing the local police. They'll need to interview you in any case, and I thought it might be easier for you to do it here.'

He frowned. The look on her face must be betraying her.

'I hope I did the right thing. Your friends have died a horrible death and boating safety is a bit of a thing with me. Anyway, I think it was my civic duty.'

She gave him a weak smile. After all, he had just saved her life.

Although she had no clear idea what her next move would be, anonymity was essential to any plan. An interview with a couple of the local plods was the last thing she needed. Somehow, she had to get away.

A knock on the front door.

'That's probably them now.'

John's footsteps on the linoleum floor sounded like a portent of doom. He left the kitchen, closing the door after him. She could hear his voice on the other side. No doubt giving them a brief rundown on the situation.

In a few steps, she crossed the kitchen, twisted the handle of a side door and opened it. No quick escape. It led to the garden.

She scurried across to what looked like a broom cupboard, praying it was deep enough to take her. She could hear John's rumbling voice floating down towards her.

'I gave her some of my daughter's clothes. You can talk to her in the kitchen.'

Caitlin climbed into the cupboard, easing a broom and mop aside. There was just enough room – thank God the old man wasn't too domestic.

Clumping footsteps crowded into the small kitchen. Ventilation slats in the door gave her a splintered view of the room.

'Nice spot you've got here,' she heard one of the policemen say.

'I didn't leave that door open. Leaves blow in. She must be in the bedroom.'

'You sure she wanted to talk to us? Constable, check the back garden. I'll do the bedroom.'

Footsteps moved off into the hall, faded, came back.

'She's not in the bedroom.'

'And she's not in the garden.'

'She can't have gone far. We'll soon pick her up. Constable, take a quick look in the street. Now, Mr McGlynn, is there anything else you can remember about this girl. Her name, any other details?'

John's slow drawl droned over to her. 'Nothing, except that she was soaked.'

'You said her hair colour seemed brown, but you're not sure because it was wet?'

'That's it.'

Caitlin heard the second policeman return. 'Nothing out the front. Perhaps she's jumped the back fence.'

'And this girl, Mr McGlynn, she's about five foot six?'

'Round about.'

'How old would you think?'

'Sixteen or thereabouts.'

Despite the circumstances Caitlin smiled, feeling a little flattered. Detail is a wonderful thing in a witness.

'All right, Mr McGlynn, we'll take another look outside, check the streets. She won't get far without any money.'

Their boots clumped down the hallway to the front door. She opened the broom cupboard a fraction. John's voice floated back from the front of the cottage. She stepped out of the cupboard, slipped through the back door and peered along the passageway that ran down the side of the house. Within seconds, Caitlin was at the front of the cottage, hiding behind a dense rhododendron bush.

She heard one of the policemen laugh. 'You're a lucky man, Mr McGlynn. It's not every day a man goes out fishing and catches a mermaid.'

John's retort was sharp. 'I hope you are treating this seriously, Constable. It was only good luck that saved her. Her friends died in the explosion.'

The embarrassed constable mumbled an apology.

She waited for the police to drive away, and then heard the door shut as John went back inside. Easing open the gate she looked up and down the street, heard voices nearby. Two girls walked along the pavement. She hurried to catch up to them.

'You are early birds,' she said blithely. 'Do you know if there's a telephone box around here?'

They looked at each other, then shook their heads.

Damn, she had to ring Martin urgently, and Quinn. But the need to put some distance between her and Watsons Bay was more imperative.

'This is the best time of the day, isn't it?' Caitlin said quickly, and laughed, as if they'd all been best friends since kindergarten.

One of the girls laughed too. 'I suppose it is, if you haven't got a hangover.'

'I said you'd regret it,' said her companion, flashing her a told-you-so smirk.

'Free champagne – irresistible. Anyway, I'm vertical, aren't I? And I can string my sentences together quite nicely, don't you think?' The girl turned a questioning gaze to Caitlin.

'You sound fine to me.'

They hurried up the street, Caitlin keeping pace with them.

'Come on,' said one friend, pulling on the other's arm, 'or we'll miss our bus.'

The girls started running. Conscious that her security lay with her being part of a group, Caitlin ran too.

At the other end of the block, the police car cruised towards them.

Caitlin tried desperately to keep the conversation going, babbling on about the sudden warm August weather; if it was like this now, it would be a hot summer.

The car was almost beside them.

'Step on it,' one of the girls said. 'The bus is there already.'

Breathless, they reached the bus and jumped on. The driver gave a cheerful, 'You just made it.' The girls paid their fares. Caitlin hesitated, until she saw the police car pull in to the kerb in front of the bus. Grateful for the money she had taken from John's cottage, she paid her fare and fell into a seat away from the girls, unable to cope any longer with their constant, high-pitched chatter – and no longer needing to.

Her heart raced as she watched one of the policemen get out of the car and walk towards the bus. Keep calm, she told herself, eyes riveted on the park that ran down to the wharf.

But the driver closed the door and pulled out from the kerb. Glancing back, Caitlin saw the constable turn in to a fish and chip shop. She felt the bus change gears to begin its journey up Military Road past The Gap, then grind its way slowly up Old South Head Road past the Macquarie Lighthouse, leaving the policemen far behind.

She huddled her shoulder into a comfortable position near the edge of the window and bunked down, trying to be as anonymous as possible. She was a ghost, with only her fears to keep her company. She wasn't even sure what day it was. Life seemed to have passed her by.

Slowly, she tried to piece together those last minutes at the studio, Martin taking her home, giving her a goodnight kiss, leaving for his chambers. Then nothing until she woke up on that boat. Those lost hours seemed an impossible mystery.

And Martin, what must he be thinking? Searching everywhere, desperate to find her.

Quinn's silence was another oddity in the puzzle. She could imagine his eyes boring into her skull when she told him of her boat adventure. Trust someone in the police force, he would say. Being a lone crusader would only get you a six by three plot. And she could just hear that detective friend of Quinn's, Scott Turner, saying it too.

She was grateful Maria was in Spain, unable to offer up prayers to the Virgin Mary for Caitlin's safety in every church she came across.

Her thoughts were rambling. Pull yourself together, she thought, you're still a long way from being safe. How does a dead person live?

She slid her eyes over the passengers around her: decent, ordinary people, leading decent, ordinary lives. Those two girls were still chattering away.

The warmth of the bus dulled her already tired senses even more. She sat up straighter, blinked her eyes. Must not fall asleep, have to work out a plan, she told herself. So tired. So mixed up.

Once she reached the city, she would ring Quinn from the GPO in Martin Place – keep ringing until he answered.

43

In the short trip from the GPO to Wollstonecraft, the garrulous taxi driver had canvassed the woes of the world, the coming election – 'Richard Brinsmead'll be the next Premier, that's what the punters say' – and, with barely a breath between, commented on the latest punch-up in the Rugby League.

Too tired to take any great interest, Caitlin had let his monologue wash over her. She was relieved she had finally managed to contact Quinn. He'd said he would be at her house in twenty minutes.

The eight o'clock news erupting from the radio caught her attention: 'An explosion on a fishing boat off The Heads … all lives lost … three professional fishermen … tragic accident.'

Fearing another discourse, she quickly paid the driver with the last of the money from John's daughter's room and closed the door of the taxi. Her spirits were uplifted by the early spring blossom as she approached her house. She retrieved the spare key from under the conch shell beside one of the pines that hedged the drive.

Before she turned it, though, she paused, flooded with doubt. *This is my home, the home my parents put so much of themselves into.*

So much love, so many wonderful memories. Yet her Celtic psyche sensed a foreboding.

After the last twelve hours – was that all it had been? – it seemed as if nowhere was safe. Once her assailants knew she was alive, they would target her until they hit their mark. She clenched her teeth and thought she must conjure up a brave face, a different voice, dampen down her fears.

Nonsense! That attitude had only ended in trouble.

Caitlin sat on the top step, the same place her dead puppy Sim had been dumped. All those weeks of pleasure that bundle of delight had given her, taken away; an animal that had hurt no one. With so much darkness filling her days she had not allowed herself to grieve for him. Now her eyes blurred with tears. She longed for his presence, to fondle his fur, but there was nothing to touch except the cold stone steps.

Her whole body began to tremble. Staying alive throughout the night had kept her nerves taut, focused, but now, so close to the sanctuary of home, they gave way. For the first time, she began to really think about what had happened. Why had the boat suddenly blown up? Was it God answering her prayers? But only a savage God could inflict such retribution. Common sense told her it was more likely a leaking fuel line, a spark from a not-so-well-maintained engine. But John McGlynn appearing out of the mist did seem like a miracle, and eluding the police had all the elements of intervention from a higher being.

And what had happened to Martin? She dreaded to think about it.

Fighting back her emotions, she stood up, opened the door and stepped inside. Daylight outside, darkness within. She quickly drew open the tall curtains in the long living room, then checked all the windows. She moved from room to room, touching pieces of furniture and objets d'art, the comfortable lounges, the bronze statue of Diana, a bust of Buddha her parents had brought back from Thailand.

At the staircase, peering up into the dim light of the 20-foot-high stairwell, the feeling of security she'd built up on the ground floor vanished. This was new territory. She gripped the banister. Take a hold of yourself, she thought, it's just nerves.

Like a child visited by frightening images, she tightened her grip and slowly, step by step, pushed her way up to the first landing. She paused again to open the curtains. Sun flooded in to warm her. Looking down onto the drive gave her goosebumps, as she recalled her would-be killer coming to clean the pool, tampering with her car.

She climbed the remaining stairs to the hallway, her feet making no sound on the thick pile carpet. One tentative step after another, each demanding every ounce of strength her muscle, sinew, bone could offer.

At the bedroom door, she paused to catch her breath. A rush of blood to her head made her dizzy. Prickling fear flushed her face. Her eyes blurred; she blinked to clear them. Dark questions spun round and round in her head. Had she and Martin even come home last night? They had left the studio together. What had happened to him? Where was he now? How had she got to the boat? She gripped the doorknob, slowly turned it and pushed it open.

The familiar sights, intimate and welcoming, had a calming effect. She started to breathe freely again. Here in this inner bastion of privacy, her fear receded.

As she opened the curtains, the light streaming in created a scene of sensuous colour, brightening the apricot wallpaper and the yellow

Louis XVI chairs she cherished. She crossed to her wardrobe. In her own clothes, she would be much more herself again.

She went into the bathroom, draping John's daughter's jeans and jumper over the cane chair, placing the sneakers beneath it. She opened the window a little to let in the crisp freshness of one of the last days of August. Among the trees, birds' small throats pulsed with energetic conversations.

She glanced at herself in the large antique mirror above the hand basin. I'm here and I'm alive, she thought. If only time would stand still, leaving me cosseted from the outside world. The muffled ring of the telephone broke the silence. She went to the open door, listened … No, nothing.

She sat down on the chair and was bending down to rub her ankles, stiff from the night's desperate swim, when she sensed something moving. Startled, she looked up.

Martin appeared in the doorway. With a cry, she ran into his arms.

For a moment, she thought he was holding her, telling her, 'Thank God you're safe.' But there was no warmth in his embrace, no kisses of loving tenderness or words of endearment.

She gazed up at him, stepped back as if hit by a gust of cold air. 'Martin?'

His silence was frighteningly mirrored in his brooding eyes. The side of his mouth twitched, the twitch that always betrayed his anger. His whole face looked as if it had been transformed into some other form of himself.

Bewildered, she said, 'Martin, what is it?'

He shook his head. 'All the trouble I went to.'

Her mouth went dry. She stepped back. 'What are you saying?'

Eyes flinty, watchful, his movements languid like a cat's, he walked towards her. 'Why do I have to do these things myself? Why couldn't you just for once do what you were supposed to do? This could have been so much easier.'

'Martin, what are you saying? What's happened?'

'I told you over and over again to stop meddling in matters that don't concern you. But no, you had to keep bumbling along until …' He heaved a sigh.

'Martin, I don't understand what you're saying. Bumbling along until what?'

'And as for Joe, that shit of a dago, bungling the monastery … And how the hell did you escape when the boat blew up?'

'Blew up?'

'I planted a bomb, timed to explode when you were offshore, destroying all the evidence. The perfect solution to a number of vexing problems.'

'You planted the bomb?'

Martin seemed amused. 'Well, I got an associate to do it. Clever fellow. I got him off a murder charge involving explosives. Fascinating stuff. He was most grateful. Does little jobs for me from time to time.'

Caitlin looked intently into the half-closed eyes of a madman, struggled to come to terms with the horror of his words. This was the mysterious mastermind, always one step ahead.

She tried to back further away from him but there was nowhere to go. His hands closed over her shoulders, twisting her around, pushing her to the edge of the bath and down onto the bathmat until she was on her knees, seeing only the brown, metallic tiles of the floor.

'Put in the plug. Turn on the taps.'

A scream died in her throat.

'What game are you playing?' she gasped, reaching over the tub and letting a dribble run into the bath.

Pulling her wet hand away, she dripped water onto the metallic tiles, and specks of gold began to glitter like minuscule fairy lights. That thought disappeared as quickly as it had come, as another uglier vision took its place. She was about to die amid a blaze of fairy lights, and almost laughed hysterically at the irony.

'Harder,' he suddenly snapped, giving her a vicious shove towards the taps.

Nausea churned in her stomach, her heart started to fibrillate. She knew Martin relished his mind games, but this was no game. She turned the taps on a fraction more and felt his hold on her relax.

'I'm in no hurry,' he muttered. 'You're going nowhere.'

She stared down into the water. How high would it have to be? She turned to face him and saw only a stranger.

'Now, a final touch,' he said with a jarring smile. 'We don't want any slip-ups, any disturbing inconsistencies, do we? The right connections fix everything.'

It all fit. The rare treat of Martin coming to the studio; it would have been easy for him to slip something in her coffee, get her onto the boat.

He cocked his head sideways, scrutinising her through narrowed eyes, then grinned. 'Get undressed. I could do it for you, but you'll leave a tidier pile than me, don't you think?'

Play him at his game and hope you don't lose.

'I'm not sure. I think I need a moment.'

'But, Caitlin, there's nothing to think through. You'll be dead, remember. When the police see the paintings in your studio, it will be easy to conclude your mind had snapped, that you had become paranoid, highly strung, in love with Brinsmead, who rejected you.

Your car is at The Gap. The classic suicide scenario.'

'You can't control everyone. Too many people would never believe I'd suicide.'

'Who knows you better than your husband? Now, off with those clothes.'

'You're a coward, Martin. That's why you've had to lean on Rushton. You didn't have the guts to try to win Hunters Hill on your own merits. People like you can only prey on the ignorant, the weak and the helpless, exploiting others as tools for your machinations. And worst of all, you take away the innocence of children to serve your perverted pleasure. You sicken me.'

His eyes, hard as polished agate, opened wide for a moment. Then a blow sent her sprawling towards the end of the bath. He grasped the front of her jumper, bunching the wool hard against her skin, twisting it tighter. She tried to push at his hand, to claw it away from the jumper. He laughed, a laugh that might have been infectious if she didn't know better.

'You're wearing out my patience,' he snarled, shoving her away.

She fell against the wall, where she crouched in the foetal position, the coldness triggering violent shivers through her body.

Pushing back a tangle of hair, she realised she had to buy time, just a few seconds to get past Martin and out of the house. But would he take more pleasure in a chase? His flickering glances and sly smile told her he was following her thoughts. She felt trapped. *Quinn, where are you?*

Martin leant over the bath to turn the taps full on. Backing away towards the vanity, he slid out the top drawer, felt around in it, then slammed it shut, slid out the next. She watched the smile return to his face.

'Never thought I'd find this thing useful,' he said, lifting out her hair dryer. Tucking it under one arm, he plugged it into the socket at the end of the vanity.

'Don't,' he barked, swinging around at her sudden lunge for the door. 'Let's make this as easy as possible.'

He pointed the dryer at the bath.

'We'll see if your affinity for water and walking through fire holds good against 240 volts of Sydney electricity.'

'You can't do this,' she whispered.

'Can't I? I admit my original suicide idea has misfired, although how you eluded those moronic fishermen is beyond me. You were all supposed to go up in smoke. But no mistakes this time. The result will be the same: suicide whilst of unsound mind. Except now you really will be dead.' He clicked the dryer on, held its whirring heat to his fingers. 'Works fine.'

In a moment of enlightenment, she saw a chance to buy more precious minutes for Quinn to arrive.

'You're not as smart as you think, Martin. You've missed something in every one of your hare-brained schemes. What makes you think this one will work? I can't have thrown myself over The Gap and then turn up dead in my bath, can I?'

'Oh, I don't agree. You couldn't face throwing yourself off such a high cliff. You were distraught, disorientated, and for some delusional reason came back to die in a place where you felt your soul belonged.'

'You're leaving too many loose ends. Okay, I might have changed my mind and come back here. But why would I leave my beloved Mercedes out there at The Gap? You know I hate travelling on public transport.'

Quinn, where are you?

She watched him run the cord through his fingers, his brown eyes now bright with the gold light of laughter as he gazed across at her. 'You thought you'd catch me out. But I'm much cleverer than you.'

'Martin, I never thought we would agree, but now you've put it so clearly, I see my life is far more important to me than what happens to those boys. Can't we talk this over? If I promise to –'

'You think I'm a fool. I can assure you I am far from that, as you have every reason to appreciate. If I agreed to let you live, you'd only break your promise and go running to that little sneak, Quinn.'

A cold shiver ran through her. What had started as a passing thought now manifested itself into full reality. He was winding himself up on a tight rope of febrile excitement. If she could only get further into his mind, reach the festering images only he could imagine.

'Connections, Caitlin. It's all about connections, the web of secrecy,' he was saying. 'The intermingling of lies and truths. Lies woven into the web by master weavers, people with the right connections. I remember your mother once telling me "It isn't what you know, it's who you know." Wise woman, your mother. Much, much wiser than mine.'

'How dare you mention my mother's name? She was worth a thousand scumbags like you.'

Martin laughed – harsh, grating. An odd, half-smiling expression came over his face.

'We're wasting time. Any blips I've left in my story, your precious Richard will erase. He's kept the ring under wraps for years. We've used the body of law, manipulating it until it was as useless as the people trying to enforce it.'

Richard? Not possible. Was his Children's Committee all a sham, a smokescreen? A naked flame of lost hope, of lost love, lit the scream that pealed around the walls.

'Would you like to test the temperature?' Martin said, running a hand through the water. 'I don't think you will find it too hot.'

He turned away, leaning back to turn off the taps.

The window of opportunity opened a fraction.

Lunging forward, her hands shot out to grab the edge of the heavy bathmat. With a strength she never knew she had, she tugged with all her might.

Martin stumbled; the dryer flew out of his hand, whirring trapeze-like through the air, for a moment, suspended. He turned his head. For a split second their eyes met.

Then he lost his balance, his long wail bounced off the walls. He hit the water. The whirring dryer dropped onto the floor to vent its deadly energy.

She rushed from the room, fled blindly down the hallway. Objects wavered, becoming watery, more unreal, as tears streamed down her face.

Her feet kept moving, across the landing, down the staircase. She wanted to shed the images of pain, yet they only grew, hot and tight inside her head; all the time, she strained to hear the sound of Martin's pursuit.

At the front door, her trembling fingers took ages to turn the key. Then she was almost falling down the steps to run from the house, heedless as to where she was going.

Police cars, doors opening, police running towards, then past her.

She felt Quinn's protective arms around her. Sobs shook her, relief tingeing her fear. She looked up into his face, bleached like a faint watercolour.

'Martin … It was Martin. He wanted to kill me.'

'It's alright, it's alright,' he said, draping his coat over her shoulders.

But it wasn't. Nothing could ever be the same again.

Minutes later, the detective, Scott Turner, came slowly down the staircase, sat on a step behind her. 'Mrs Preece …'

'I know, detective.' She turned to look up at him. 'You're going to arrest him. But he needs –'

'Mrs Preece, I'm sorry.' She saw him glance at Quinn. 'Mr Preece received a deep gash to his right temple. That gold swan tap … One of those freakish things that happen.'

'Have you called an ambulance?'

'Too late, I'm afraid.'

She gazed at the detective, at Quinn, and bowed her head.

'There's something else, Mrs Preece. At four o'clock this morning, we arrested Richard Brinsmead.'

Caitlin turned her head to the wall and silently cried.

44

Rossiter Gallery, 6 March 1974

Soft voices, the sound of a door slamming shut. Caitlin heard her friend's rapid footsteps tapping towards her from the small vestibule of the gallery.

'Thank God, that's the last of them,' she said, stopping in the doorway of the main gallery to pull off a red shoe and massage her toes.

A wry smile crossed her elfin face.

'What a surprise, all those red dots for an exhibition on child abuse. Still, you can't guess what resonates with a buyer. One fellow, an American, Victor Spiro, told me he has a connection with a New York gallery; thinks they would be interested in mounting a solo exhibition for you.'

Caitlin's eyes widened. She waved at the paintings that confronted the viewer from the white walls around her. 'A series like this?'

Lexy groaned as she pulled off her other shoe and wriggled her toes. 'Does the prestigious Charles E. Slatkin Gallery in Manhattan sound kosher enough for you?'

'Sounds too much like wiring her up for more energy,' murmured a voice from a side gallery.

Caitlin spun around. 'Where did you spring from?'

Quinn glanced over his shoulder with a quizzical expression, then shrugged. 'The front door, of course. Sorry I'm late. Got caught up with something interesting.'

His eyes tracked around the room. 'Impressive. And all those red dots. But surely now you should take a break before starting work again?'

'Precisely,' Lexy muttered. 'You've been a social outcast for months putting this exhibition together. Force yourself to do something totally outrageous, like taking a holiday. Bake yourself on a beach somewhere exotic.'

Caitlin laughed. 'No, thanks.'

She took Quinn by the elbow, pivoting him towards *The Valley*, the canvas that dominated the main gallery. 'What does it say to you?'

He studied the threatening figures hovering over Sean Tessler's still form, the steep cliff arching menacingly behind them in the darkness. A shaft of light stabbing through mist highlighted the boy's disjointed image, quiescent on a bed of twigs and glaucous gum leaves that formed the shape of a cross on the valley floor.

Quinn broke the silence. 'A call to arms?'

Caitlin gazed at him, caught the glint in his shrewd eyes, his rich voice still reverberating in her thoughts.

'Exactly,' she said.

Lexy shook her head, grimaced and, with a long, green fingernail, twitched back a curl over one ear. 'I don't know about you two, but I need to raid the office bar.'

She poured herself a stiff glass of Cointreau, poured champagne for Quinn and Caitlin, studying her for a few moments before slumping into her leather chair to inspect the bare feet she'd propped on the desk.

'I've got the perfect solution for you. Dad's holiday retreat on the Barrier Reef: work and rest.'

Caitlin sat down and took a sip of champagne. 'Maria would never forgive me. I think she's made a pact with a guardian angel to keep me always within her sight.'

Walking over to her, Quinn set a brown paper package in her lap. 'Well, this might help to fend it off.'

She looked up at him. 'What have you done?'

'Nothing. An offering from my brother, Julian.'

She frowned. 'Your brother?'

Quinn nodded. 'He passed away last week. I've been helping his family. Over these last few months, I told him about the synthesis of your exhibition. It seemed to give him a nexus of interest, a belief in the might of right, I think, at a time when he needed it.'

Quinn stared down at the parcel.

'He knew he would never finish it, but he wanted you to have it all the same. He said he thought it would appeal to your sense of honour.'

She scrutinised his features, seeing the unusual tenseness in his chiselled face. All these weeks of silence from him, a bleakness in his eyes as if hiding a burden too fragile for words.

'I'm sorry. You were so close,' she said, her voice fading to a whisper.

She untied the string, pushed back the wrapping and slowly traced her fingers over the silver box.

'It's beautiful.'

'All handcrafted. God knows how he did it.'

She opened the lid, gently folding back the black tissue paper.

'Oh, Quinn.'

She glanced up at him, before carefully lifting out the almost foot-high statuette. In silence, she studied the cinnamon-coloured wooden image of Joan of Arc. She caressed the small head, slid a hand down the partially sculpted armoured chest, onto an emergent sword hilt.

'The warrior saint,' she whispered.

'I asked him once whether it was an inspiration or a warning for you. He said you'd work it out.'

She smiled gently. 'Perhaps both. They seem to fit human nature like a well-made glove. Thank you, Quinn. It'll take pride of place near my triptych of Chinamans Beach.'

Lexy raised her eyebrows. 'You still have it?'

Caitlin nodded. 'Richard … um, I always thought it was one of my better paintings. Maybe that's why Martin always wanted to get rid of it. Even Maria won't let anyone go too close.' She tried to laugh. 'Very sentimental, the Spanish.'

She stared down at the intricately carved face. Faith and courage had been that nineteen-year-old's inner strength, answering the call of the voices of the saints, Margaret, Catherine and Michael, to drive out the English and the Burgundians in support of Charles of Ponthieu's claim to the French throne.

Caitlin sensed in herself the emergence of a fighting strength, of liberating lightness. She would banish from her mind a Martin she never knew and Richard … His name still caught in her throat. She hoped he would have the strength for what his life had become or might be. In their very different ways, both men had freed her to be true to herself, to recognise and affirm the value of doing what she had done and could do in the future to better the lives of children.

Almost twelve months ago, the path of her life had held such certitude and simplicity. She had been living in her own inner world, obsessed with truth and the integrity of her work, to the point where she had never questioned how other people lived. From Sean's death had grown the realisation that every child has the right to live in a free world, embroiling her in alien territories far from the boundaries of law, decency and truth.

Placing the statuette on Lexy's desk, Caitlin gazed at her quirky friend and then at Quinn. She had some sentience of their lives, personalities and beliefs, but deep in their inner selves, who were they?

Suddenly, she said, 'Strange, isn't it, how what we think is reality may not be reality at all.'

Quinn ran his fingers through his hair. 'Reality is what people see in the mirror of life, and from different angles, each mirror shows a different reality.'

'Perhaps,' Lexy said, 'we may see things from a different perspective, but we must try to remain true to what we believe is the truth of our existence. It's not a game.'

Caitlin nodded. 'It's indefinable, like courage. We don't understand what it means until we confront the need for it. And even when challenged, do we fully understand it?'

'Talking to some of the people here tonight,' Lexy went on, 'there's no doubt in my mind your paintings stirred a few uncomfortable truths in their lives.'

'That's what I wanted to get across. For people to start thinking about child abuse, to shake them from their lethargy. If I haven't done that, I've trivialised who I am, everything I have done.'

'Changing the subject, how about some good news?' Quinn broke in. 'I had a call from Scott Turner. The police are dropping all charges against Richard. Recognition, at long last, that the information they based their investigation on was vexatious, politically motivated and engineered.'

Caitlin stared at him, her heart beating hard. 'But why, Quinn? Why did it all have to happen? He was one of the few people really trying to make a difference. I always knew he could never have been involved in paedophilia. He and Martin were at opposite ends of the spectrum.'

Quinn nodded, 'That's why he was targeted. Richard shook the cages of the savage beasts: bigotry, selfishness, greed, perversion, lust for power. They are as entrenched in the human psyche as love, kindness and charity. Martin and Rushton wanted to get rid of Richard and his committee. He was getting too close to the truth and if he became Premier, he would've been an even greater threat. A carefully crafted web of false leads and lies, judicially leaked, was enough to force the police to act. At least he was on bail most of the time, but he had no option other than to stand down. It was enough that in the closing stages of the campaign even his party suffered. Damned by association. Coming when it did meant it had maximum impact and was enough to destroy any chance the Liberals had of winning. There's no presumption of innocence in a political dogfight.'

Quinn turned to an abstract on the wall behind Lexy's desk, a composition of colour, chaos, and question marks. After studying it for a few moments, he swung around. 'By the way, one of this afternoon's papers ran the line: "Richard Brinsmead might have been the best Premier New South Wales never had."'

He shook his head. Caitlin saw in his face his contempt for the debilitating effect of ruthless, political ambition overriding everything else.

'They used their political pawns to spread lies about him, giving the government a lifeline. Invidious and unsubstantiated rumours seized on by avaricious newspapers. It was enough to turn the tide. In politics, everything and everyone is fair game.'

Perching on the edge of Lexy's desk, Quinn grimaced. 'And not only Richard. What about you? If you hadn't miraculously survived that boat explosion, Martin would have pulled off the perfect murder. He had so much to lose.'

'If only the police could get solid evidence on others in the ring.'

Quinn turned to study the large abstract painting again.

Gently, he said, 'I think it was Euripides who first voiced the sentiment that the wheels of justice turn slowly but grind exceedingly fine.'

Caitlin suddenly became conscious of the stale cigarette smoke and alcohol fumes that tainted the air. She tried in that moment of silence to draw together what she could say but no words came, only the whisper in her brain: *Richard's free.*

But what sort of freedom would he have in his life? She looked at Quinn, and thought she saw the same question in his eyes.

'The Church has its own way of dealing with the problem. They've closed ranks. Nothing about Finbar and Loudé's complicity, only platitudes.'

'I suppose they'll be appointed to other schools, allowing them time and distance to slither away under another rock,' she said. 'The Church hierarchy is obsessed with preserving its reputation.'

'The police have asked for Interpol's help to get Rushton extradited from Switzerland. Brechtenshafft's vanished,' Quinn said. 'The investigation team have tried to rattle the conscience of the top brass in the police force, but with no luck.

'Although the scandal of paedophilia has been shown some daylight, all we've done is nip one of its tentacles. Everyone's trying to minimise the damage. It'll take a long time to change the culture of denial, if it ever happens.'

Lexy turned to Caitlin. 'What you have done required extraordinary courage. It'll keep the momentum going.'

Caitlin shook her head. 'I don't know, Lexy. I feel … I just don't know. People are …'

Without another word, she rose and left the office. Her footsteps echoed through the rooms. In contrast to her first and second exhibitions, tonight only good friends and those who appreciated her work attended. Their admiring comments came from every direction: a bizarre juxtaposition to the confrontational work that hung on every wall. She took a deep breath, struggled to hold back the tears that stung her eyes.

She paused in front of the painting she'd titled *Night Visitor*: a dark, sinister canvas. Her eyes drawn to the slit of light from a dormitory doorway that fell across a boy's bed, the silhouette of a robed figure.

She moved on to *The Valley*. Gently, she touched Sean's painted face.

Despite the ten months since his death, it seemed like yesterday. Peeling back layers of memory, she could see him again in the quadrangle of the school, almost smell the charcoal on his fingers as he sketched his tormentors.

His spirit had inspired her to fight against those with an alien concept of lust and power, which perverted the innocence of the young, used them for pleasure before discarding them like garbage.

Through her work, she had tried to break this cycle of human misery, tried to evoke courage and empower action from even the weakest adult.

Caitlin wiped the tears from her cheeks.

She drifted from one work to another: gems of images, imprints of children's pain drawn from her imagination. Most of them she would never see again, and like a mother seeing her children leave home, she dreaded their freedom, reluctant to release them into a world that might not cherish their spirit, embrace their message of justice, love and hope.

Hope. She recalled Enid Featherstone's story of the little girl who drew herself levitating in a party dress and a tiny crown. 'Yes, that's me, a princess.'

ABOUT THE AUTHOR

Carol Rozzoli was a luminary of Julian Ashton Art School, with a Catholic background and a husband who was both a politician and a lawyer. She turned her talents to writing, attending Roland Fishman's Writers Studio, completing the full novel course. From this rich background, and a passion to help children in crisis, *Cry Out in Silence* emerged from the mists of Katoomba.